Crystal and Flint

Holly Ash

Published in association with Cabin in the Woods

Editor: Lisa Howard

Cover Design: Maja Kopunovic

ISBN: 1732574006
ISBN-13: 978-1-7325740-0-7

To Mike, for not running for the door the first time you heard me rehearsing dialogue in the shower.

The five families that made up the Delta team were nervous as they boarded their space shuttle in 2176. Their mission had seemed honorable when they joined the Council for a Better Life, but now that it was their turn to leave Earth, they were starting to have second thoughts — while the Alpha and Beta teams had traveled successfully beyond the outer limits of the solar system, no communication had been received from either team since, and the Charlie team had had a fatal meeting with an asteroid while still inside the sun's orbital field. The Delta Mission was the Council's fourth attempt to search for a new planet that could sustain human life.

After seventeen years of travel, the Delta team landed on a new planet, Neophia, that had an atmosphere nearly identical to Earth's. The members of the Delta team were shocked to find that the native intelligent species mirrored them in appearance. Had they found the descendants of one of the earliest deep space missions that had left Earth in the late 2040s? For years, they looked for some evidence of a shuttle from Earth that would prove their common ancestry, but they found nothing. It was as if their God had merely given up on Earth and decided to start over on Neophia.

While their external appearances were almost identical, the Neophians possessed unique genetic traits that separated them from the Humans: among their native races, the Aquineins were capable of drawing oxygen out of liquids and could stay submerged for hours at a time, and the Sertex could — with immense concentration — blend into their surroundings, allowing them to move among the forests of Neophia unseen. The Aquineins and Sertex lived in small communities, and interaction between them was minimal, with each race preferring the ecosystem that best fit their skills.

Because of their long tradition of living in isolation, the Sertex did not acknowledge the presence of the newcomers to their planet. Shielded from sight, they simply observed the Humans to access any threat they might pose. The Aquineins, being much more curious in nature, welcomed the Humans into their communities, and it wasn't long before basic communication was established between them. As the Humans became fully assimilated into the Aquinein culture, intimate relationships began to develop between the two species. The first child of two planets was born three years after the Delta team arrived on Neophia.

Over the next ten years, the Humans taught the Aquineins everything they could about the technology that had brought them to Neophia. Given that the Aquineins had no advanced technology of their own, the Humans were shocked by how quickly they were able to understand and improve upon what the Humans showed them. Working together, they were able to engineer a portal that would provide direct passage between Earth and Neophia.

It wasn't long before new shuttles started to arrive from Earth, bringing with them plants, animals, and new technology to replace what the Human settlers had left behind on Earth.

The Human population on Neophia grew rapidly. The Sertex began to fear that Humans would soon outnumber the native Neophians and deplete the planet's natural resources.

The Sertex leaders reached out to the Aquinein leaders and pleaded with them to shut down the portal. Unwilling to cut off ties completely with Earth, the Aquineins suggested a compromise: together with the Sertex, they would create a set of citizenship laws that would greatly restrict the arrival of new Humans to the planet while allowing those who were ingrained into the Aquinein culture to remain. It was the first time the two races had worked together.

Chapter 1

The air under the subfighter tasted stale. Crystal had spent the better part of an hour lying under the machine, trying to figure out why the sub's thrusters kept shorting out at 68 percent of their maximum capacity. Her eyes stung as sweat rolled behind her safety glasses. She had had to contort her body into an awkward position so that she could reach the central wiring unit deep in the ship's underside. It was complicated and time-consuming work and Crystal was loving every second of it.

When her plans for the state-of-the-art mega submarine *Journey* had been accepted by the Lands and Waters of Neophia Military Advancement Division and she was asked to oversee the build (while receiving a promotion), she had jumped at the opportunity. She hadn't considered that she wouldn't be able to do hands on work anymore. Or how much she would miss it.

The tips of Crystal's fingers finally connected with the panel she needed to access. She grunted with satisfaction and leaned forward, weaving her other hand through the wiring to locate the release pins. She had just found them when she noticed someone standing outside of the subfighter not far from where her own feet were sticking out from under it. The shoes were far too clean and shiny to belong to anyone on her team.

"Lieutenant Commander Wolf," the owner of the shiny shoes said in a slightly trembling voice.

"Yeah?" Crystal said as she carefully removed the first of four pins holding the thruster control panel in place. She was used to people being nervous when speaking to her for the first time, especially the lower-ranked crew. It was almost like they thought of her as some kind of celebrity. It had been happening to her for most of her life.

"I have a message from Admiral Craft," Shiny Shoes said, this time without the tremble.

"I can clearly hear you so go ahead and deliver your message." Crystal removed the second pin, and the right side of the panel came lose in her hand. She shifted her body to give her left arm a little more leverage.

"I can't, ma'am, it's a secured message. You are going to have to activate it."

"All right, give me a minute." The secured message didn't concern her. These days, every message she got from headquarters had come with some unnecessary level of security. She imagined it gave the sender an elevated sense of self-importance.

Crystal removed the last two pins from the panel, freeing it. Slowly, she worked her arms out of the subfighter's guts, then slid out from beneath the machine and got her first look at Shiny Shoes. He was young. If she had to guess, she would say he had only been in the service for a few months.

"Here," Crystal said, holding the panel out to him. "Hold this for a second." It wasn't exactly an order, but

Shiny Shoes was in no position to refuse.

Gingerly, he took the panel from her. Crystal hid a grin as the thick blue gel insulating the panel dripped and pooled into the palm of his hand.

She rose gracefully to her feet. Shiny Shoes held the panel out to her, but she didn't take it, instead turning to the small portable workbench she had set up next to the subfighter. She wiped the gel off of her hands with the rag hanging from the edge of the bench before reaching for a clean plastic bag. She dropped the four pins into the bag, sealed, and labeled it.

Shiny Shoes maintained a respectful silence as she went through her procedure, but she could feel his eyes on her. She was sure she didn't look like much of an authority figure at the moment: her white tank top clung to her body, sticky with a mixture of sweat and oil; her bare arms were coated in grease; and several small red lines had appeared on her forearms, scratches she must have gotten while searching for the panel.

Crystal slid her safety glass up onto her head to hold her shoulder-length brown hair out of her face, then used another rag to wipe the sweat from her eyes and face before she grabbed her uniform top off of the workbench.

Once she had finished buttoning her shirt, Crystal turned back to Shiny Shoes, holding open another clear bag. "In here, if you don't mind," she said with a smile.

He placed the panel in the bag. Crystal quickly sealed it and handed him a clean rag to wipe his hands with. "So, how about that message?"

"Yes, ma'am! Right away, ma'am." He finished cleaning his hands before giving Crystal the small electronic tablet he was carrying.

Crystal spoke her full name and rank into the voice

identifier at the top of the tablet, prompting the screen to spring to life. She read its message quickly.

> **11:15, 5/22/2344**
> **Commander Wolf:**
> **You are to report to LAWON Headquarters at 13:45 for an emergency meeting regarding Operation Water Tiger. Be prepared to discuss status and schedule of the operation.**

A sense of dread started mounting in Crystal. Operation Water Tiger was the code name for *Journey*. What emergency could there could be regarding *Journey*'s status and schedule? She had been sending weekly progress reports to Captain Reed and Admiral Craft since they had begun construction.

Crystal read through the message once more to make sure she hadn't missed anything. Before handing the tablet back to Shiny Shoes, she pressed her thumb on the scanner to confirm receipt of the message and erase it.

"Do you have a message you would like me to return, ma'am?"

"Please inform the Admiral that I will proceed as requested."

"Yes, ma'am." Shiny Shoes turned and walked away.

Crystal leaned against the subfighter and watched him go. She had just over an hour to get to headquarters, which was enough time to either finish her work on the subfighter or get cleaned up. She decided to keep working, besides she was fairly certain she had a clean shirt in her office she could grab before she left the build site.

She returned to the workbench and started examining the panel she was holding. She saw the problem almost immediately. "Those cheap bastards," she muttered under her breath.

"Who are we talking about this time?"

Crystal whipped around to find Chief Stiner standing behind her. Her second-in-command had a curious look on her face.

"When did you learn how to sneak up on people?" she asked.

"I must be spending too much time with you," Stiner said with a smile.

"There's a scary thought," Crystal said with a smile of her own.

"Did you figure out the problem with the thruster?" Stiner motioned towards the panel on the workbench.

"Yeah, the idiots who built these used a cheap substandard filament here...and here," she said, pointing at the offending wires. "The panel can't tolerate the energy surge we need to get the thrusters to full power." She sighed. "I would be shocked if this is the only time they used this crap. I knew we should have built them in-house."

"How do you want us to fix it?"

"We'll need to upgrade the filaments on this panel. I also want to do a scan of the whole ship and replace any other substandard wiring we find. We can't have these ships shorting out during a fight. I won't put our peoples' lives at risk just to save a few cents on wires," Crystal said, her frustration clear in her voice.

"On a lighter note," Stiner said, obviously attempting to squelch Crystal's anger, "a cute guy was looking for you earlier. Did he find you?"

"Seriously, Monica, he was a kid," Crystal said, finally turning away from the workbench.

Stiner's eyebrow went up. "I'm sure I can find someone more age-appropriate for you...that is, if you want me to."

Crystal rolled her eyes. "Like I have time to go on a date."

"You would if you ever took any time off."

"I can't afford to take any time off," Crystal said with a sigh. "I can't even afford to have this argument with you. I have to finish my notes on the subfighter repair and then report to headquarters for a meeting."

"Is it another special ops mission?"

"No, I asked to be removed from the normal combat rotation once construction began on Journey. I'm sure it's nothing." Despite her words, Crystal couldn't keep the worry out of her voice. She was sure Stiner was picking up on it.

"Well, I'm sure whatever it is, you can handle it."

"Yeah, thanks. Listen," Crystal said, turning the conversation back to the subfighter, "I'll have my repair notes finished in a few minutes. Can you have someone work on these four units? I want them done by the end of the day."

"No problem. Have fun with the higher-ups." Stiner gave her a friendly nod and then headed towards the shiphands working on the other side of the bay.

Crystal arrived at LAWON headquarters exactly seven minutes before her meeting was scheduled to start, leaving her motorcycle helmet with the receptionist before heading to the military wing. After a quick retinal scan, she was granted access to proceed through the smoky-steel doors and into the main hallway. The conference room was at the end of a long corridor, she remembered, and was lined with offices occupied by some of LAWON's highest-ranking officials. Crystal walked confidently through the building, ignoring the globs of insulating gel she could feel hardening in her hair.

When she opened the door, Crystal saw Commander Dewite already sitting at the conference table. "This must be bad news if they pulled you into this emergency meeting, too," she said.

Dewite's expression went from stoic to grinning. "What happened to you?" He asked, trying and failing to contain his amusement. His dark skin and bright smile were reflected in the glossy conference table as his laugh echoed through the bare room.

"It's not really that bad." Crystal strode to the back of the room and grabbed the metal pitcher of water, holding it up to see her own reflection. Her hair was pasted to her head with gel, and her forehead was smeared with dirt and oil. She ran her fingers through her hair in an attempt to break up some of the dried clumps and used a dampened napkin to try to rub some of the grime off of her face. Unfortunately, although the fabric felt refreshingly cool against her skin, all she really managed to do was smear the dirt around more evenly. Her mirrored lips pursed in an involuntary sigh.

"That's about as good as it's going to get," she said aloud, "especially when they call a meeting on such short notice." She set down the pitcher and took a seat next to Dewite.

"They gave you an hour-and-a-half," he pointed out, still chuckling at her appearance.

"If they expect me to show up without oil in my hair, they need to give me a few days of warning, and even then, it's questionable."

"Your life must be so hard," Dewite teased.

"Finally, someone understands," Crystal said with an exaggerated wave of her hands. "And how about you? Life behind a desk seems to be agreeing with you."

Now Dewite was the one who sounded frustrated. "Don't get me started. If I have one more conference call to discuss the merits of plate A over plate B, I might actually lose it."

"Aren't you glad you took the position of *Journey*'s XO instead of captaining your own ship for the past four months?" she said with a wry grin.

"Don't remind me," Dewite said.

She had liked Dewite the moment she met him. They hadn't worked together prior to him accepting the position of *Journey*'s Executive Officer, but she had been aware of his reputation, namely that he was on the fast track—every rumor she had heard said he would make Admiral within the next five years. Accepting the position on *Journey* had derailed all of that, though. Everyone had been shocked that he had chosen to make a lateral move instead of taking one of the several promotions that had been offered to him. But within five minutes of first meeting him, Crystal had known why—he didn't care about rising to the top as fast as he could. All he wanted to do was serve where he could do the most good, and that place was *Journey*.

Crystal had been thrilled when Dewite accepted the XO position. She knew there was a lot she could learn from him. Besides, while she had been leading a combat team for the last few years, that was nothing compared to being third-in-command of a major vessel like the *Journey*. With Reed and Dewite's guidance, there was a good chance she wouldn't make a complete fool of herself.

She nodded, still half-smiling. "Do you have any idea what this meeting is about? The message I got was pretty vague, even for Craft."

"No idea." He lifted an eyebrow. "I of course assumed that you had blown your budget and were behind schedule already."

"If you had bothered to read the progress updates I've been sending, you'd know we are a few weeks ahead of schedule." Crystal tried not to sound too proud of herself, but she couldn't help emphasizing ahead. This was the first build project she had managed. Some people expected her to fail, she knew, but she refused to let that happen. The fact that she was a third of the way through construction and hadn't had any major issues was proof of her determination.

"That's what I like to hear!" Admiral Craft said as he entered the conference room with Captain Reed. Crystal and Dewite rose to their feet and stood at attention. "As you were." Craft waved them back down into their seats.

Crystal tried to decipher the expression on Reed's face as he took a seat across from her. He gave her a warm smile, but she could see the concern in his soft brown eyes. Crystal and Reed had known each other for years, ever since Reed had been one of her teachers at the Academy and had pushed for her to be allowed to take an accelerated program. He was the captain of the carrier she had been assigned to after graduation, and he was the one she had first approached with the concept drawings for *Journey*. Reed was also the one who had stood by her and pushed to get the project approved. He was one of the few constants she had in her life.

"Commander Wolf, how is the build going?" Craft

asked once everyone was seated.

"Like I was telling Commander Dewite, we are about two weeks ahead of schedule," she answered calmly, not letting her voice betray her anxiety. "Everything has been progressing smoothly."

"LAWON's Executive Board has been very impressed with the reports you have been sending," Craft said. "That's why I asked you all to come in today. The Board would like Commander Wolf to give a presentation about *Journey* at the annual Summit Meeting next month."

Dewite gave Crystal a smile that she knew was genuine. "Congratulations!"

"Thank you. I would be happy to speak at the conference," Crystal lied. The idea of speaking in front of a room full of politicians repulsed her, but she knew she didn't really have a choice in the matter. She glanced across the table at Reed. His facial expression had not changed, which made her realize there was a catch to this request.

"Fantastic! The Board has also requested that tours of the ship be given during the conference." Craft paused for a moment before continuing. "*Journey* is being ordered to report to the capital two days before the conference is scheduled to begin. I understand that this will push the completion date up nine months."

Crystal quickly did the math. There was no way Craft was serious. "With all due respect, sir," she said, "that's impossible. The ship's just a skeleton at this point. There's no way I can have her completed in five weeks."

"You'll have all of LAWON's resources at your disposal," Craft offered. That did nothing to ease her concerns.

"I'm going to need every skilled tradesperson and

craftsman in Kincaron," she said immediately. "And a hell of a lot more money." She could feel the panic beginning to set in.

"Sir, is it really that important to have the ship at the Summit Meeting?" Dewite asked. "Wouldn't it be better to wait and show her off once the build team has a chance to properly finish construction?"

The smile faded from Craft's lips as he shook his head. "It's critical that LAWON has a strong showing at the Summit Meeting. Membership is dropping, and I don't have to tell you that we've seen an increase in instability across the planet over the last several months. *Journey* can swing things back in our favor. The last thing we need is more nations joining forces with Teria."

Crystal knew that Craft was right, within the last month alone, Teria had laid claim to three unaffiliated regions. LAWON had decided not to intervene, but Crystal suspected the regions had either fallen prey to President Rank's charm or a show of force. Given the harsh laws of his country, it was unlikely they had joined him willingly. That meant it was only a matter of time before Rank went after a LAWON member nation, and once that started, Crystal feared the weaker members would fall like dominoes.

"There has to be another way to provide a sense of security to the planet without jeopardizing the integrity of *Journey*," Dewite said.

Craft removed his glasses and gently squeezed the bridge of his nose. "Just focus on making the ship look nice," Craft said firmly. "The politicians won't know the difference." He stood. "I'll leave you three to work out the details."

Crystal felt helpless as she watched him leave. "They

can't be serious," she said, breaking the grim silence. She got to her feet and leaned against the back of her chair, feeling like she would jump out of her skin if she stayed seated a moment longer.

"I'm afraid they are," Reed said. Crystal took it as a bad sign that he hadn't spoken before now. It meant there was no hope of reversing the decision.

"You got to love politicians. They would do anything to increase their membership, even if it means putting their new ship at risk," Dewite said, clearly frustrated.

"I tried to reason with them," Reed said, "but the fact of the matter is that we have orders to get *Journey* to the capital in five weeks." His voice was controlled, but Crystal could tell he wasn't happy about the order, either. "And it's up to us to figure out how to do it."

Crystal felt everything she had been working for slipping away. "*Journey*'s appearance at this conference is going to be highly publicized," she pointed out. "That's going to put us at a lot of risk."

"I agree," Reed said.

"You think someone might try to stop *Journey* from reaching the Summit Meeting?" Dewite asked.

"I'm concerned that someone might try to put *Journey* out of commission altogether," Crystal said, her hands involuntarily clenching on the chair. "If we aren't prepared to confront them…" Her voice trailed off.

Dewite's eyebrows shot up. "Who would be crazy enough to attack *Journey* on her maiden voyage? There's no way they would be able to get away with it."

"President Rank tops my list," Crystal said, her voice tense. "Followed closely by any number of anti-LAWON terrorist groups. Think of the honor and glory of bringing down the flagship of LAWON's peacekeeping mission.

The hit to LAWON's reputation would be enough motivation. There would be no coming back from that."

"So we forget what Craft said and instead we make sure the ship is combat-ready," Reed said. "I don't give a damn if the politicians have to jump over holes in the floor or if we have temporary lighting hanging everywhere. I want sonar, weapons, propulsion, communications, and life support at 100 percent. Consider everything else a luxury."

"I have to give her a hull first," Crystal said.

"Can you have her in the water by the end of next week?" Reed asked.

"I'll give it everything I've got." At least Crystal knew that Reed was on her side.

"The rest of the crew should be arriving over the next few days," Reed said, turning towards Dewite. "Focus your training on the bridge crew. I want them to function as if they have been working together for years. Send anyone not in training over to Wolf. I'm sure she can find something for them to do. And contact Dr. Emerson and have her give you a list of essential equipment she will need. Any questions?"

"No, sir," Crystal and Dewite said in unison.

"Then let's get to it," Reed said as he stood and headed to the door. "We have a couple of long weeks ahead of us."

Crystal returned to the build site with a heavy heart. The familiar buzzing and humming of tools was starting to taper off as the end of the day approached, and she knew that the team was already starting to think about going home and spending the evening with their families or going out with friends. She dreaded telling them that despite all of their hard work, now they would have to work even harder in order to meet LAWON's ridiculous new deadline. Failure wasn't an option. Considering what Craft had said, the peace and stability of the planet might depend on *Journey* being at the Summit Meeting. She wouldn't let her failure be the trigger for another war.

She wasn't surprised to find Stiner at her desk when she entered the office trailer the two of them shared. Crystal went over to her own desk, plopped down in the chair, and put her face in her hands.

"So how bad is it?" Stiner asked.

"Bad." Crystal didn't move her hands as she spoke.

"Are they shutting us down?"

"Worse." Crystal finally looked at Stiner. Her face radiated kindness and concern. Stiner had been by Crystal's side since the first day of construction, and her support and friendship gave Crystal the strength she needed to keep going each day.

Crystal tried not to let frustration creep into her voice. "I need you to gather everyone on the west lawn in the 20 minutes," she said. "Get anyone who's not here on a video call. I have an announcement to make."

"Of course." Stiner left the office without any further questions.

Crystal sat at her desk, trying to gather her thoughts. She wasn't looking forward to addressing her team even though she knew no one would argue or complain. They would take the challenge in stride, but the thought of all those eyes on her shook her to the core. She should be more comfortable with public speaking given that she had spent most of her childhood in the spotlight. It wasn't easy being the only child of two of the planet's most celebrated war heroes. Every year on the anniversary of their death — and again on Peace Day — the media would be lining up for interviews. Her grandparents had obliged most years, dragging Crystal along for the show. They thought they were honoring their fallen son and his beloved wife. What they didn't realize was that every one of those events had reopened the fissures in their granddaughter's heart. It had become easier for Crystal to avoid the press once her grandparents had passed away.

She spent a few minutes trying to organize the mess that had overtaken her desk. Anything to distract herself for a few minutes. She couldn't go up on that stage with memory of her parents still in her mind. She didn't get up until she felt she had her emotions in check.

The hum of voices reverberated across Crystal's skin as she approached the west lawn, but the sound died out almost instantly as she climbed the steps to the stage. Two hundred pairs of eyes looked back at her as she clutched the podium. Her mind instantly transported her back to the day the of her parent's funeral, when she was asked to say goodbye to them in front of the hundreds of attendees present and the millions of people whom she knew were watching the live broadcast. She had been seven years old.

Crystal took a couple of deep breaths to push away the panic. "Our orders have changed," she began, forcing herself to look at her team one person at a time. She had been working side-by-side with these people for months, so why should she have any issues talking to them now?

"*Journey* is now required to report to the LAWON annual Summit Meeting being held in Episonia five weeks from today," she continued. "I understand that this is pushing *Journey*'s completion date up by nine months. I have spent the day working with Capitan Reed and

Commander Dewite devising a new plan that we feel will best prepare *Journey* for her maiden voyage without sacrificing the quality or integrity of the ship." Crystal paused to take another deep breath, keeping her expression smooth and confident.

"I know we face a seemingly impossible challenge, but I have faith that we will not only meet expectations, we will surpass them. You have brought my dream to life with more pride and dedication than I would have thought possible. I feel honored to be a part of this team." Another pause to make sure her voice was steady.

"So go home and enjoy your night off," she said, forcing a smile onto her face. "Tomorrow we'll pass out new work assignments. Dismissed." Crystal turned and walked off the stage.

Stiner was waiting for her at the bottom step. "New work assignments?"

"Don't worry about staying late tonight, I'll get them done," Crystal assured her.

"That will take you all night."

"That's what I signed up for." This time the smile on her face was genuine. "Long hours, hard work, lousy pay…who wouldn't want to join the military?"

"Sounds like fun. Count me in." Stiner blocked Crystal's path.

Crystal knew Stiner wouldn't let her pass until she accepted her help. "There's nothing I can do to convince you to go home?"

"No, sorry."

A voice came from behind her. "Excuse me, Commander Wolf, Chief Stiner." Crystal turned to find Larry Thompson standing next to them. The hull construction supervisor had a calm expression on his face.

"Yes, Mr. Thompson," Crystal said.

"I have spoken with my team, and we would like your permission to keep working tonight."

"Are you sure?"

"Yes, ma'am."

"Permission granted." She couldn't prevent gratitude from leaking into her voice.

Thompson left to go gather his team. His place was immediately taken by the electrical supervisor, Tara Cummings.

"Commander, my team would also like permission to stay and work tonight."

Crystal noticed that all of her supervisors were waiting to talk to her. "Are all of you here to ask to keep working tonight?" she asked the group at large. Everyone nodded.

Crystal was overwhelmed by the dedication of her team. She felt a lump forming in the back of her throat and did her best to swallow it. She had to remain professional. "All right," she said, "but please stress to your teams that this is voluntary. Anyone who wants or needs to leave is encouraged to do so without any repercussions."

The supervisors nodded solemnly, and the crowd dispersed until Stiner was the only one left.

Crystal gave a short nod. "I guess I should give Marco a call, we're going to have a lot of people to feed tonight."

"What about our budget?" Stiner asked.

"Screw the budget. The brass up at headquarters is going to owe this team a lot more than dinner by the time we're done."

Chapter 2

Desi sat alone in the last row of the space shuttle. The only person on the shuttle with enough guts to talk to her had been invited up to the cockpit by the Captain. It was probably a courtesy from one pilot to another, though she knew, Justin was always able to make friends wherever he went. It was one of the few things he was better at than she was. People always seemed intimidated by her. It wasn't her looks that pushed people away — in fact, most people found her mop of long brown curls and soft brown skin attractive. What people found unnerving about her was her strength. Couple that with her tendency to speak her mind, and she understood why no one had come to talk to her. Not that it really mattered. Once the shuttle landed on Neophia, they would all be going their separate ways, anyway.

Everyone on the shuttle had volunteered to participate in the United States/Neophian soldier exchange program, an experimental program meant to build a stronger relationship between the two planets. She assumed most people had signed up in the hopes of getting away from the wars on Earth, to make a better life for themselves on a new planet that didn't require five years of mandatory military service. Hell, she figured some of them might even believe in the "strengthening ties" garbage used to promote the program.

Desi's reasons for volunteering had less to do with interplanetary relations and more to do with self-preservation. A dozen or so US officers were participating in the first round of exchanges, and as far as Desi knew, she and Justin were the only ones who would be serving on *Journey*. She was supposed to be impressed by this, but it was hard to be impressed by anything coming from this technologically inferior planet that stole everything from Earth. Neophia was the kid sister that Earth never wanted.

Finally, Desi saw Justin emerge from the cockpit. "We should be there in about an hour," he said as he plopped back down into the seat next to hers.

"Oh, boy," Desi said, failing to keep the sarcasm out of her voice.

"You could at least try to sound excited."

"I'm sorry Justin. I'll try my very best." The over-the-top smile she plastered on her face hurt her cheeks, and she was sure it did little to fool Justin.

"Come on, we have the chance to go to a planet that isn't plagued by pollution and war." he said in a tone that was almost pleading. "Where countries don't have to fight in order to ensure that their citizens have clean drinking water and food to feed their families."

The poor kid — Desi could tell that he really believed everything he was saying. "It all sounds a little too good to be true to me," she said.

"You're pathetic, you know that?"

"I'm realistic. There is no way Neophia is this dream world everyone makes it out to be."

"And how can you be so sure that it's not? You haven't ever shown even the slightest interest in learning about the planet," he said with an accusatory tone.

"Well, since you seem to know so much, why don't you give me a rundown on some of the basics?"

"What kind of basics?" Justin had a confused look on his face that made Desi suppress a sigh.

"The basics about Neophia," she said patiently. "Not everyone has spent their whole life researching it. So tell me whose side we're on, and then I'll pick up the rest as I go."

"You didn't bother to read any of the material they gave us, did you?" he asked.

"Of course not. I knew you would, so I didn't waste my time." Desi tried to lean back in her seat, but her knees bumped into the chair in front of her.

"I shouldn't tell you anything and let you make a fool of yourself."

"You wouldn't dare," she said with a snort. "Now spill, Anderson."

She sat up straight again. With all the technology on Earth, you'd think someone would have found a way to make the shuttle seats more comfortable. Then again, comfort had never been a high priority for the US military.

"We will be serving as members of Kincaron's naval forces," Justin said.

"So Kincaron is a country?"

"Yes, the largest country on Neophia. It's made up of one large land mass and hundreds of islands and underwater colonies."

"Well, I guess it's a good thing they have a navy, then."

"Which they have loaned to the Lands and Waters of Neophia."

"Which is?"

"It's kind of like the United Nations before it collapsed," Justin said, she could tell he was enjoying playing professor a little too much. "It was formed after the Great War in order to maintain peace on the planet. Every member nation supplies money, resources, and manpower to LAWON."

"And what do they get in return?"

"Protection, access to resources they wouldn't have otherwise, a chance to be part of something bigger." The longer he talked, the more animated he got. This really was a dream come true for him. She would have to try not to ruin it.

"If everyone is playing nice, why bother bringing us here at all?"

His own frown fractured Justin's utopian explanation. "Not everyone is playing nice," he admitted. "A little less than half of the planet's countries are members of LAWON, and there are a few countries that strongly oppose the organization. Of those, Teria is the most powerful and outspoken nation. They're constantly trying to undermine LAWON's authority."

"So what's our role in all of this? Are we here to enforce sanctions and embargoes? It all sounds so thrilling," Desi said. She tried not to let her skepticism show too much.

"You know that this is a voluntary position—you didn't have to sign up," Justin said in a half-admonishing way. "I know plenty of other people who would jump at the chance to go to Neophia. Serving on Neophia could be my opportunity to move my family there. My sisters wouldn't have to grow up in that wasteland we keep calling Earth."

Justin was such an idealist. Desi was amazed that the harshness of war hadn't robbed him of it. Neophia would be a good match for him, she decided. "That wasteland is our home," she said aloud.

He looked at her without saying anything for a moment. "Why are you here, Desi?" he finally asked. "Why did you sign up for this? It wasn't because of me, was it?"

Desi knew that's what Justin thought. She had been his protector for so long that it was completely feasible she would have chosen to leave Earth behind solely to look out for him. The truth of the matter was that Justin hadn't really needed her to protect him for a long time now — he had come a long way from the little kid who was constantly bullied outside of their apartment complex. "No, Justin, I didn't take this position because of you."

"Then what gives, Flint?" Justin said with wicked smile. "Is it your ego? Did you want two planets bowing down at your feet and calling you a hero?"

"Something like that." Desi turned away from him to look into the blackness outside her window. She hadn't told anyone her real reasons for volunteering, and if she had it her way, no one would ever find out.

A few weeks ago, she had been pulled out of the field and taken to D.C., where she spent the day being shuffled from one office to the next until she found herself standing in the Oval Office with the President and Secretary of Defense. They wanted to award her the Medal of Honor, they told her.

Initially, Desi was elated. After all of her hard work and sacrifice, she knew she deserved it, but then she realized she would be pulled from active duty immediately. She had already been scheduled to appear on two talk shows to talk about being a Medal of Honor recipient, they said, and the staff was in the process of lining up more appearances for her.

Desi's happiness fled. They didn't want to honor her achievements — what they wanted was a new mouthpiece. The military had gotten a lot of bad press recently, and they needed someone to boost morale and increase retention rates. She was the perfect person to turn public opinion back in their favor. Her "honor" was a double-edged sword.

When she left the White House an hour later, her head was spinning. She would never fight again, she knew — they wouldn't want to risk her getting killed while she was still useful to them. But she was a solider, not a spokesperson, dammit!

No matter which way she looked at the situation, she couldn't figure a way out. It wasn't like she could refuse. Was it even possible to turn down the Medal of Honor? And if she did, what would happen to her career? It's not like the military would ever give her a command after something like that. She was trapped.

Justin was waiting for her on the steps outside of her mom's apartment building when she returned. He had heard she was in town and had come to say goodbye, he said. He told her he had volunteered for a position on Neophia and would be leaving in two weeks. He was ecstatic.

So was Desi. She knew she had found her way out. She congratulated him quickly, then took off to find the Captain Reed he had been going on about. This was her only chance.

Luckily, she found Captain Reed just as he was getting

ready to return to Neophia and was able to convince him that she would be an excellent candidate for the exchange program. After a quick conversation and a few signatures, it was done. Going to Neophia had never crossed her mind before, but if it meant that she would still have a chance to fight, she was willing to make the sacrifice.

Five days had passed since Craft had changed the deadline for *Journey*. Her team was working around the clock pulling fifteen-hour shifts, and Crystal had taken up residence in her small office. She had tried to get the ever-increasing amounts of paperwork done back when operations were normal and had found it difficult. Now it was simply impossible. Problems caused by the increased timetables were pulling her away from the office with greater frequency than ever before. Still, despite all the setbacks, Crystal was impressed with the progress they had made. She was sure Craft would be, too, if she ever got around to writing up her daily progress reports.

Crystal was taking advantage of a rare moment of downtime to eat her lunch while reviewing the evening's work schedule. A knock at the door made her roll her eyes. She knew the respite had been too good to last.

"Enter," she said without looking up from her monitor. She glanced over the top of it to see Reed and Dewite entering her office.

She scrambled to her feet, dropping her half-eaten sandwich back onto its wrapper. "Captain, Commander. This is an unexpected visit."

Reed waved her back to her seat before sitting down in one of the chairs across from her. "I hope this isn't a bad time."

"Of course not."

"How's the ship coming along?" Dewite glanced around her office as he took the other seat. While he had been to the build site a handful of times, Crystal wasn't sure if he had ever been in her office. Had she gotten more than a few hours of sleep the past few days, she would have been bothered that his first impression was one of chaos and disorder. Under normal circumstances, the office would have been immaculate.

"We're making good progress." Crystal casually slid her unfinished lunch into the trash. Marco's fish-and-seagrass-salad sandwiches were great, but they didn't hold up well. She suspected it would be hours before she had a chance to get back to it, and by then, the sandwich would be mush.

"We've begun installing the first layer of metal plating that will make up the ship's hull," she said. "The battery units are being rushed through the manufacturer and should be here by the end of the week, and we should be able to finish installing all potable and sanitary water piping by the end of today. Overall, I'd say we're progressing on schedule." She paused to quickly scan her computer screen to make sure she hadn't missed any updates.

"I'm impressed," Reed said. "Now I won't feel so bad pulling you away for a few hours."

"Sir?" she said, confused. It was hard to think about anything aside from the ship construction right now.

"The shuttle from Earth is arriving this afternoon," Reed said, "and I'd like you to come along and greet the American officers with us."

"Oh." Crystal's eyes moved to Dewite. The two of them had often talked about having officers from Earth join their crew. They had planned to bring it up to Reed but had thought they still had time to solidify their concerns. Most of the crew wasn't supposed to report for several more months. It hadn't occurred to Crystal that the build deadline wasn't the only thing that had been moved up nine months.

"I'm sure your team can manage without you for a few hours, though from the look of it, you haven't given them the chance," Reed said, eyeing the used in cot in the back corner of the office.

"It's not that..." Crystal started to say. Her eyes bored into Dewite's, urging him to speak up. He remained silent as he returned her gaze. The coward.

She gathered herself. "It's just that—well, sir, Commander Dewite and I have some concerns regarding the placement of officers from Earth on *Journey*," she said more abruptly than she would have liked.

Her insides had twisted into knots. She hated to bring this up. She knew Reed was a strong advocate of Neophian-Human relations, and in most instances, she agreed with him wholeheartedly. But recently, tensions between Neophia and Earth had never been higher. The endless wars on Earth had escalated, and several countries had been putting pressure on Neophia to supply Earth with the resources they needed. The Humans on Earth believed that the Neophians owed them for bringing advanced technology to their planet, and they were getting tired of waiting for them to pay their debt. So far, Neophia had managed to stay out of the conflicts on Earth, but Crystal knew it was only a matter of time before either some of Neophia's nations caved to the pressure or Earth's Humans took it upon themselves to take what they felt they were owed. It really wasn't a

Human concern—she was 25% Human herself—it was a cultural concern. She didn't have any apprehensions about Humans born and raised on Neophia like her, but Humans who had spent their whole life on Earth learning to bully, fight, trick, and steal what they felt they deserved was another matter entirely. That wasn't the mentality they needed on the flagship of LAWON's peacekeeping campaign.

"What are your concerns?" Reed's voice was calm.

Crystal stared expectantly at Dewite, but he remained silent, as if to say "You started this."

"We're concerned," Crystal said, making sure to stress the first word, "that *Journey* might not be the best placement for the officers from Earth. Given Earth's history and the training they must have received, we feel they might be a...liability." Crystal took pains to choose her word carefully.

"I see," Reed said evenly.

"It really comes down to a matter of trust," Dewite said, finally rejoining the conversation. "We need people to trust us in order to be able to do our jobs, and we're concerned that the citizens we are trying to protect won't trust the officers from Earth and that distrust will then be misplaced onto the rest of the crew."

Crystal nodded. "We don't disagree with the exchange program," she said, finally feeling her guts start to untwist now that Dewite had spoken in her support. "We both feel that a lot of good can come from it, but given *Journey*'s high profile, wouldn't it be better to put them on another vessel?"

Reed shook his head. "It's exactly *Journey*'s high profile that makes it the perfect placement for them. As the flagship, we have the chance to show the rest of Neophia that we are willing to work together. To learn from one another."

He paused and looked at Crystal and Dewite in turn. "Don't you see how powerful that could be? Especially given the current public anxiety regrading Earth." His voice softened. "Believe me, I understand your concerns. I've debated them, too, but I strongly feel the benefits outweigh any potential harm their presence might cause. I need you two to trust me on this. I'm counting on you to help them get accustomed with how we do things here."

"Of course, Captain," Dewite said.

"What can you tell us about them?" Crystal asked. Her concerns hadn't lessened, but she had spoken her piece and it was time to move on. She knew when she had lost. She would do what Reed asked her to do.

"*Journey* will be playing host to two officers: Ensign Justin Anderson and Lieutenant Desiree Flint. Anderson is a very skilled pilot—I've seen him maneuver large and small vessels with expert precision. Flint is a weapons and munitions experts as well as a subfighter pilot. Both are highly respected officers with exemplary records." He paused and looked at Crystal and Dewite. They each gave a nod.

"I was a little surprised that Flint had volunteered for the program," he continued. "I was under the impression that she had been in line for a major promotion when she signed up. They almost pulled her from the program— said she was too valuable to let her leave—but for whatever reason, they relented at the last minute."

"It sounds like they will both be good additions to the crew," Dewite said. He looked down at his watch. "We should be heading to the landing pad soon if we want to get there before they arrive."

"Why don't you take a quick look at *Journey* first?" Crystal asked. "A lot has changed since the last time you were at the build site. I need to wrap up a couple of things here, and then I'll join you." Dewite nodded again, and he and Reed both stood and left, leaving Crystal amongst the piles of paperwork.

Something stirred inside of her. Was it fear? Jealousy? This Lieutenant Flint sounded like a force to be reckoned with. Crystal wasn't really worried about a little competition, although if she was honest with herself, it had been a long time since she had really felt challenged by anyone. Not since she was at the Academy. Not since Ryan.

Desi was the last one to step off the shuttle. The sight that met her was nothing close to what she had expected: instead of sleek skyscrapers and gray concrete covering the landscape, she saw tall trees and lush green and yellow vegetation. The taste of metals and bleach was gone from the air, replaced with a pureness unlike anything Desi had ever experienced. It was the silence, however, that she found the most shocking. Gone was the constant hum of air regenerators, the high-pitched beeping of electronics, and the incessant noise of audio billboards. Desi could see that the three people standing at the bottom of the platform were talking, but not a whisper of their conversation reached her ears.

Justin had already made his way down the steps. This had to be a dream come true for him. He had been talking about Neophia for as long as Desi could remember. She wondered what he was feeling now that he was actually here.

It took her a moment to notice that his gaze had shifted from the landscape to the women standing off to the side with Captain Reed. Great. They had been on the planet for all of five minutes, and Justin already had a crush. Not a surprise, though—that boy didn't know how to keep his feelings in check. He started walking towards the small group, and Desi fell into step beside him.

"Lieutenant Flint, Ensign Anderson," Reed said as he shook each of their hands, "Welcome to Neophia. It's my pleasure to introduce you to *Journey*'s senior officers: Commander Devon Dewite and Lieutenant Commander Crystal Wolf."

"Are you the Commander Wolf who designed *Journey*?" Justin asked.

She smiled. "The very same."

"It's great to meet you. I've read a lot about the ship. The helm design alone is revolutionary—for one person to be able to pilot a ship that size is incredible."

"Thank you, but even though it is possible for one person to pilot the ship using the full-body helm chairs, she'll be much easier to handle with all four helmsmen," Wolf said.

"I can't wait to try it, though." Justin said, his enthusiasm plainly showing.

Wolf couldn't help but chuckle. "Me, either," she said as she held her hand out to Justin. Desi noticed that Justin's hand lingered in Wolf's a little longer than was absolutely necessary.

Wolf turned and offered her hand to Desi. "Welcome, Lieutenant Flint. It's nice to meet you."

"I'm sure it is." Desi watched Wolf carefully for some kind of reaction. Desi had been using unconventional greetings to quickly size people up for years.

Unfortunately, it didn't work with The commander—her expression remained cool and professional. It was possible she hadn't actually heard what Desi had said, though, since a soft ringing sound had started emitting from her pocket the moment Desi finished speaking.

Desi studied Wolf as she stepped away to take the call. The Lieutenant Commander was obviously going to be her biggest competition on Neophia. Reed clearly respected her, and the fact that she was in charge of building a ship like the *Journey* showed that the top brass had a lot of confidence in her, too.

But just because Wolf had reached a higher rank than Desi didn't mean Wolf was the better soldier. If it came down to a life-or-death situation, Desi was sure she would prove herself to be superior. Desi would have to keep an eye on her possible rival until she could fully assess how big of a threat Wolf really was.

"What's wrong?" Reed asked when Wolf returned to the group a few minutes later.

Wolf didn't look happy. "The sanitation system has completely shut down, life support systems are malfunctioning, and there was a small fire in the engine room. I knew things were going too smoothly." She closed her eyes for a moment and took a deep breath. "I've suspended all related construction until we can figure out what happened."

"How far behind will this put us?" Dewite asked.

Her frown deepened. "It's hard to say. I don't even know if the issues are interrelated at this point."

Desi tried not to take pleasure in Wolf's misfortune, but she couldn't help it—the situation was giving her the perfect opportunity for her to show off her problem-solving skills even if she didn't know the first thing about building a submarine. "Life support is probably the most important," she pointed out smoothly. "Why don't you start there?"

The look Wolf gave her was decidedly less friendly than it had been during their introductions. "Life support isn't really essential while three-quarters of the ship's interior is exposed to the outside atmosphere," she said. Desi choose to ignore the anger swelling up in Wolf's voice.

"Why don't you break down the possibilities for us, Commander Wolf?" Reed said.

"Best case is that we have a bad computer chip somewhere. It's possible that could have made something in the engine room overheat and cause a fire; that same malfunction could have shut down the other systems." She paused, obviously doing some quick mental calculations. "Taking cleanup and repairs into account, we could probably be back to normal construction in a couple of hours."

"And the worst-case scenario?"

Wolf's expression went from calculating to grim. "The worse-case scenario is that the whole electrical system is fried. We'd have to strip it all out and rewire a large portion of the ship. I'd also want to have a full inspection done of all the electrical work to make sure the same thing wouldn't happen again anywhere else. In that case, it would be at least two to three days before we are back on schedule."

"Couldn't you reduce your downtime if you eliminated the redundant inspections?" Desi asked, deciding to press her luck a little. Wolf was young, at least a few years younger than Desi, and probably inexperienced. She was just being overly cautious.

"I'm sorry, Lieutenant Flint," Wolf said through clenched teeth, "but I demand absolute perfection from my team, and if that means taking a couple of extra hours to double- or even triple-check our work to ensure the safety of the ship and crew, then that's exactly what we are going to do. Unless you would prefer the ship to have a system failure while 100 meters below the surface? Not all of the crew can breathe underwater."

Wolf turned away before Desi had the chance to call her out. Of course the crew couldn't breathe underwater. That's what escape pods were for.

"Sir, with your permission, I would like to return to the build site," Wolf said to Reed.

He gave a quick nod. "Of course. Keep me apprised of the situation."

"Yes, sir." Wolf walked away without another word.

That hadn't gone nearly as well as Desi had hoped it would. She would have to do some digging, but she was sure she could find a way to get under Wolf's skin and dethrone her.

Crystal collapsed into a chair at the counter at Marco's Diner after having finished giving Craft, Reed, and Dewite an update at LAWON headquarters. Thankfully, *Journey*'s issues hadn't been too serious, and the construction would be back up and running by tomorrow afternoon. She hoped.

"You look exhausted," Marco said in greeting. He set down a large cup of kiki in front of her.

"You're my hero." Crystal took a long sip of the warm, purple liquid.

"So how many people am I feeding this time?"

"Just Monica and me."

"Did you eat any of that sandwich I sent over for lunch?"

"Some of it." She tried not to let Marco's guilt trip faze her. Crystal had known him since she was a child, when her grandparents would bring her to the diner to meet her parents in between their missions. Then, during her time at the Academy, she often joined Ryan and their friends at the diner. Now it seemed everything she ate came from Marco's. If it wasn't for him, her diet would probably consist of stale sandwiches from the cafeteria vending machine at the build site.

He gave her a friendly scowl. "Well, I expect you to eat it all this time. You have to start taking better care of yourself."

"Yes, sir." Crystal gave him a mock salute before he went back to the kitchen to start making her food. She took another big sip of her drink before pulling out her tablet to keep working.

"Excuse me, Commander Wolf, but you've got something on your lip."

Crystal looked up, startled. She hadn't noticed the officer from Earth sitting a few seats away from her. Quickly, she wiped the purple foam off her lip. "It's Anderson, right?"

"Yes, ma'am." He ran his hand through his coffee-colored hair, his soft brown eyes not quite making contact with hers. A light pink crept across his cheeks as he smiled.

She picked up her drink and slid over so that there was only one empty seat between them. "We're off-duty, you can call me Crystal."

"Justin." He waved a hand towards the kiki. "I've

never seen a drink that color before."

She held it up. "We call it kiki. It's the Neophain version of coffee, but it's about five times stronger than what you have on Earth. I live on it." She took another sip and set it back down. "How did you end up here?"

"After Captain Reed dropped us off at the dorms, I decided to go for a walk. This seemed like a good place to stop."

"It is. Everyone from LAWON eats at Marco's. It's the best place to hang out if you want to find out the latest gossip." She lowered her voice conspiratorially. "You see over there?" she asked, nodding her head towards a table in the corner. "That's Commander Penland. He teaches military history and strategy at the Academy. The woman with him is Sargent Staley, the toughest drill Sargent at the Academy. And over there are Admirals McCraw and Alexandar. Marco has pretty much fed the entire LAWON military at one point or another."

"I feed some of them more than others," Marco said, reappearing with a plate for Justin.

Crystal's eyebrows went up when she saw what was on the plate. "Did you order that on purpose?" she asked Justin.

"He asked me to make him a traditional Neophian dish," Marco said before Justin could answer. He grinned.

Crystal shook her head and snorted. "So you made him sinsari?"

"What's sinsari?" Justin asked.

"Searoach larva," Crystal said, making no attempt to hide her amusement.

"Covered in a wonderful root cream sauce," Marco added.

Crystal rolled her eyes. "Why do you even have that on

the menu?"

"I like it," Marco said.

"Well, here goes." Justin cut off a small piece and put it in his mouth. Amused, Crystal watched his lips pucker and a tear roll down his cheek. "How can it be so spicy and sour at the same time?" he managed to gasp out.

"I promise I won't judge you if you spit it out," she said, trying not to laugh at his anguish. "Hey, Marco, make him a burger, would you? My treat."

Justin quickly swallowed the sinsari. "You don't have to do that."

"After eating that, you deserve it." She barely restrained herself from patting him on the back in sympathy. "You must be pretty excited to be on Neophia—that's the only reasonable explanation I can think of for actually eating that."

Justin grabbed a nearby napkin and dabbed at his sinsari-caused tears. "I've been dreaming about coming to Neophia for as long as I can remember."

Crystal studied him thoughtfully. "Earth can't really be that bad…"

"You've never been there, have you?" he asked.

"No, I haven't."

"It's dirty and loud and the people range from being rude to downright cruel. Every kid grows up learning how to be a soldier, whether they want to or not. It's no place to raise a family."

"Is that what you want? The whole wife-and-kids thing?" asked Crystal.

"Well, yeah…I mean, I enjoy being in the Navy, but I never saw it as lifelong commitment." He shrugged. "I always saw myself married and raising kids, maybe working as a commercial submarine pilot giving sightseeing tours or something. How about you?"

"Oh, I'm career military."

"You never thought about settling down, having kids?" Justin pressed.

Fortunately, Marco returned before Crystal had to answer. "Here's your food," he said, setting down a bulging bag and a drink carrier with four large cups in it.

Crystal had never been more grateful for an interruption in her entire life. Justin's question had been an innocent one, but there was no way she could answer it. She wasn't sure why she had asked him such a personal question in the first place. She was usually so careful when talking to people. What was it about Justin that made her let her guard slip? She would have to be careful to avoid that in the future.

"This is way too much food," Crystal said, changing the subject.

"I threw in some fruit and pastries for tomorrow morning. You can't survive on kiki alone."

"What would I do without you?" she said with a smile as she stood up and grabbed her food.

"You aren't eating here?" Justin asked.

"No, sorry, I have to get back to the build site. I'm sure I'll see you around."

Crystal quickly left the restaurant but then paused and glanced back through the window. Justin appeared to be deep in conversation with Marco, who was laughing at something Justin must have said. She could almost feel the chef's belly laugh rumbling through the walls of the diner.

She would have to be careful around Justin, Crystal decided. He seemed to have a way of getting people to open up to him. Not that Marco was really closed off with anyone, but still... She needed to do a better job of keeping her guard up the next time she saw him.

Chapter 3

Crystal arrived at the training center before the sun had risen, feeling the early morning dew soaking through her shoes as she walked across the open field. She loved this facility. She had used it several times in the past to train her counterterrorism strike team. The large field and adjoining woods were the perfect place to train. At least a few members of the team were coming straight from basic training or the Academy, but the majority were coming from other assignments, and she doubted they had maintained the level of physical fitness she required from her combat team.

The obstacle course loomed in the distance, still shrouded in morning fog, it beaconed to Crystal like a lighthouse. It wasn't exactly like the one she had gone through at the Academy, but it was similar, and it brought back memories of her Academy days. Its slick metal bars, splintering wood, and frayed ropes had been the backdrop to one of the most significant events of her life. That was where she had met Ryan.

A few weeks after Crystal had started at the Academy,

she had decided to do some extra runs through the course. She had asked a few of her classmates to go with her, but they all declined, saying they preferred to spend their free time hanging out at the rec hall, so she headed out on her own. She was used to doing things on her own. She couldn't afford to lose focus given the expectations people had of her, expectations based on her parents' reputations. She had just finished her second run through the course when she saw Ryan leaning against a tree at the end of it.

"Not bad," he said as he started to walk towards her.

"Not great, though." She could have turned around and started another run, but she didn't. In retrospect, part of her wished she had—that would have made her life much simpler. But instead of walking away, she walked towards him. Maybe it was the fact that she hadn't really connected with anyone at the Academy yet, or maybe it was the way his smile shone in the orange hue of the setting sun.

"You know, I'm pretty great at this," he said with a confident smile.

"Oh, really," she replied with her own sarcastic grin.

"I just made it on the leaderboard. It's pretty unheard of for someone in their second year." He was just cocky enough to be charming without coming across as conceited. Crystal fed off his confidence, something she had been lacking for a long time.

"What place are you?" She was impressed. It had been years since anyone had made it onto the leaderboard, let alone a second-year recruit. She certainly wasn't on it, although her mother had had held the sixth-place spot ever since her final year at the Academy.

"Tenth, but I'll be at the top of the list before I graduate.

I could help you if you want."

"Really? That would be great. I'm Crystal...Crystal Wolf." She hesitated a moment before telling him her last name, dreading the inevitable reaction. The same thing always happened once people realized who she was: the conversation would quickly turn into an interrogation about her parents' sacrifices and what it was like growing up as their child.

Ryan won instant favor by not mentioning her parents. Instead, he simply smiled and held out his hand. "Ryan Craft."

Crystal recognized the name immediately—his father was a well-decorated war hero and was currently serving as one of Neophia's most celebrated naval captains. She accepted Ryan's hand and returned the favor by not asking about his father.

He didn't let go of her hand as he led her to the start of the course. Once they were there, he took a step back and looked at her. "Ready?"

She grinned in response. He raised his hand, signaling their start, then dropped it. They ran through one obstacle after another until it was too dark to see. Finally, they stopped, both of them breathing hard.

"We should do this again sometime," Crystal ventured once she had caught her breath.

"I'd like that," he said, sounding equally exhausted and satisfied. "How about tomorrow? Same time and place?"

"Sounds great." Unsure of what to do with her hands now that there wasn't a wall climb, she awkwardly folded them behind her back. Then turned and headed back to her dorm, feeling happier than she had in a long time.

They met up the next night at the course and every

night after that for the next several days. By the end of the fifth evening, they were spending more time talking than exercising. That was the night he walked her back to her dorm instead of parting ways at the course. The night after that, he kissed her. From then on, they were a couple, a team no one could break.

Desi surveyed the firing range. It wasn't nearly as advanced as what she was used to. For one thing, the targets were stationary, which baffled her. How was she supposed to teach her team to shoot with precision when the targets didn't move? She would have to talk to Reed to see what her other options were—this wasn't going to cut it.

"Here a little early for training, aren't you, Lieutenant?"

Desi whipped around to see Wolf walking towards her, which was a surprise. Desi had studied her team list at length last night, and Wolf's name wasn't on it.

"I think it's important to be familiar with the training facilities," Desi said, keeping her voice flat. As much as she might hate it, Wolf outranked her. And while she might not like the person, she had enough respect for the rank to behave accordingly.

"I can appreciate that, although I don't think you have much to worry about. From what I've heard, you're a good combat officer."

Desi made note of the false friendliness in Wolf's voice. "I'm the best—that's why they asked me to head up *Journey*'s combat division." Desi turned away. She knew if she didn't end the conversation now, she would say something she'd regret.

"Wait a minute," Wolf said as she stepped in front of Desi. "I think you're confused. I'm the head of *Journey*'s combat division. But you're more than welcome to join my team, if you think you're up to the challenge."

Why couldn't Wolf have let Desi walk away? That would have been better for both of them. "Obviously, your information is out of date," Desi snapped. "Why don't you run back to your ship and fix another toilet?"

Wolf's eyes hardened. "I'd be careful, Lieutenant—that almost sounds like insubordination. I could have you thrown off of this assignment. You could be spending the rest of your time on Neophia pushing papers in an office."

There was no backing down now. Desi's big mouth had already gotten her in trouble, so she decided to go with it. "I'd like to see you try." She took a step closer to Wolf, putting herself inches away from the other woman's face.

To Wolf's credit, she didn't back away. She seemed as ready for a fight as Desi was.

"That's enough!" a voice rang out across the field.

Desi quickly stood at attention the moment she realized the voice belonged to Captain Reed. She silently cursed herself while she waited for him to reach them. On Earth, she wouldn't have been concerned—her reputation allowed her to push the limits with little to no backlash— but she wasn't sure that would be the case on Neophia.

"At ease," Reed said once he had reached them. "I had hoped to get here first to prevent whatever misunderstanding that was about to play out here. As I'm sure you have figured out, you have both been told that you are to lead *Journey*'s combat division. Technically, this is correct: *Journey* will have two combat teams, and you will each command one."

"So there will be a primary and secondary team?" Desi

asked.

"No, both teams will be considered equal," Reed said, giving each of them a hard stare in turn. "The lead will be given to whomever is best suited for that particular mission. However, I would like both teams to work together whenever possible. Is that understood?"

"Yes, sir," Desi and Wolf said in unison.

"Good. Then I will leave you two to work out how you want to handle training."

Desi didn't move or speak until Reed was out of sight. The last thing she wanted to do was work with Wolf. She would only slow Desi's team down. There had to be a way to prove that her team would be the best choice, no matter what they came up against.

"How do you want to handle this?" Wolf asked.

"You train your team and I'll train mine. After two weeks, we'll see who the better combat leader is," Desi challenged her.

"You're on." Wolf walked away without another word.

Two hours later, Crystal found herself standing in the middle of the training field. The sun had risen and the ground was now dry beneath her feet. Thirty pairs of eyes followed her as she paced in front of her team. They were evenly spaced, standing in three rows of ten, and they looked good: fit, energetic, and overall in high spirits. She hadn't bothered to assess them any more than that. Given her past training experiences, she expected most of them to quit before the week was over. She would be happy if she ended the four weeks of training with a solid team of twelve she could depend on in any situation.

Crystal's gaze lingered across the field, where Flint had

brought her team straight to the firing range. The other woman's team was standing around her in a semi-circle. No structure or discipline there.

Crystal quickly averted her eyes. She couldn't spend the week comparing herself to Flint. Crystal knew how to train a combat team—she had done it before. She wouldn't let Flint get in her head and make her second-guess herself.

"Let me be the first to welcome you to *Journey*." She stopped pacing and turned to address her team. Her eyes immediately met Justin's. She hadn't realized he had volunteered to be on the combat team. She really should have found some time last night to review the team roster she assumed was buried in her inbox somewhere.

She forced herself to look away from him. "For those of you who don't know me, I'm Lieutenant Commander Wolf, and I have been leading combat missions for LAWON for the past three years. All of you are here because you have proven that you can handle the added responsibility that comes with being a member of this team. I want to stress that this position is voluntary and will remain voluntary. My expectations are high. If at any time you feel you are not up to the challenge and want to be removed from the team, please do not hesitate to tell me."

Crystal paused for a moment, thinking she had heard someone trying to stifle a laugh. Now, though, everyone was stone-faced and silent. "My training methods may differ from what you have experienced in the past," she continued. "I have my reasons for that. Each of you must maintain a high level of physical fitness at all times."

She stopped again—this time, she was certain she had heard someone trying to cover up a laugh. When she scanned the team with a sharper gaze, it didn't take her long to find the soldier who had been laughing.

She walked over and stood in front of him. He was biting the inside of his cheek in a desperate attempt to regain his composure, she saw. The wind had blown his blond hair into his bright green eyes, but he made no attempt to brush it away.

"Is there something wrong, Lieutenant?" she said sternly.

"No, ma'am," he said in a voice that was forced and halting. Crystal knew he was still trying to suppress a laugh. Despite that, he never broke his stance: he kept staring over her shoulder with his eyes locked on the horizon.

"We are going to start today with a run." Crystal was addressing the whole team, even though she hadn't moved. "The path in front of you is approximately three miles. You have twenty-two minutes to complete it and return to this same spot. In the meantime, I need to have a word with Lieutenant Grady." As she said his name, she stared again at the man in front of her.

Neither Grady nor Crystal moved as the rest of the team took off. Then, after thirty long seconds, Grady broke out into a huge grin. The laughter he had been suppressing bubbled to the surface as he scooped Crystal up in huge hug and spun her around.

"Jim, put me down!" Crystal said with a laugh. She was thrilled to see her closest friend again. They had known each other for years, ever since she had graduated and then been stationed on the *Expedition* under Captain Reed's command. She had volunteered for the combat team, and Grady had taken her under his wing. They became fast friends that year. Then, after that, their friendship had turned into an unbreakable bond during the years they had worked counterterrorism together. Crystal knew the grin on her own face was as big as his.

"What are you doing here? I thought you were working a special ops mission." Aside from a few coded messages he had sent to let her know he was still alive, Crystal hadn't seen Grady in over a year.

"Yeah, I was," he answered, still smiling. "I just got back yesterday. That's when I found out Reed had offered me a position on your boat. How could I pass that up?"

Crystal laughed and shook her head. "Funny — Reed never mentioned he was considering you. I thought he was only considering the best officers in LAWON for a position on *Journey*."

Grady adopted a dramatic expression. "I'm sure he knew how heartbroken you'd be if I turned it down. You probably would have quit the service, locked yourself in a room somewhere, and just cried and cried and cried."

"You sure do think highly of yourself," Crystal said.

"And you don't?" He raised his eyebrows at her and spoke in a high-pitched voice. "'I'm Crystal Wolf, and I have been leading combat missions for LAWON for the past three years.'"

"First of all, I don't sound like that." Grady started to protest, but Crystal shot him a look. "Second, I was doing fine until you started laughing."

"No, you weren't. I was trying to keep you from embarrassing yourself. We couldn't have the team lose respect for you the first day out." Now he was waggling his eyebrows.

"I'd watch it if I were you — remember, I outrank you now."

"Only because you built the higher-ups a fancy new

ship to parade around."

"And what have you done to warrant a promotion in the last two years?" she said, mostly teasing.

For once, Grady was at a loss for words.

She gave a satisfied nod. "That's what I thought." She turned and starting running toward the woods. After a few hundred yards, she turned around. "Oh, and Jim," she called to him while running backwards. "Now you only have nineteen minutes left to complete the run."

Crystal took off at full speed. After a few seconds, she heard Grady's pounding footsteps and labored breathing behind her as he tried to catch up. Crystal couldn't help but smile. After everything that had happened with Flint that morning, it was good to know she had at least one unwavering ally by her side.

An unexpected perk of coming to Neophia was that no one knew who Desi was—with the aid of a plain black jacket, she was able to blend in with the rest of her team. They had gathered near the firing range and formed themselves into small groups while they waited for their leader.

She moved anonymously from one group to another, wanting to get an idea of what her team was truly like. What better way to do that than to eavesdrop on their conversations? Most of what she heard was pretty standard: "How long have you been in the service?" "Where did you serve before?" But one conversation in particular did catch her attention.

She was standing behind a group of three men. From what she had heard, Desi assumed they were all fairly new to the service, though one of them appeared to be a few years older than the others. Desi examined him out of the corner of her eye. His name tag said "T. Price," she saw, and he had ensign stripes on his uniform.

"We're still serving with Wolf even if we aren't on her team," Price was saying. That was what Desi had been afraid of. She had spent the majority of her time yesterday asking anyone she could about Wolf, and no one had had a bad thing to say. In fact, most people viewed her with an awe-inspiring reverence that Desi didn't understand. Sure, Wolf's resume was impressive, but it was no more impressive than her own.

"Yeah, but I expected to actually be on her team. Didn't you? I mean, it's the whole reason I volunteered for the combat division in the first place," said one of the guys standing near Price.

"Of course I expected to be serving under Wolf," Price said. "Who knew there would end up being two combat teams? It's never been done before, as far as I'm aware, but I got to believe that Lieutenant Flint has to be just as good as Wolf, or she wouldn't have been given her own team." This Price guy was starting to grow on Desi — at least he had the right attitude.

"So what do you know about Flint?"

"I was given the same information as you," Price said with a sly smile.

"Come on, Ty, we know you hacked the system."

Price quickly looked around to see who else was listening. He caught Desi's eye and gave her a mischievous smile. Desi wondered if he knew who she was. How easy was it to find information about her here? She knew it wouldn't be too hard if they were on Earth — her image had been on the news on several occasions — but she had no idea if the same newscasts were shown on

Neophia.

"Well," Price said, lowering his voice…although not lowering it enough to keep his words from reaching Desi's ears. "I didn't have a lot of time, but I do know she's from Earth and that she has a lot of combat experience. She's been serving in war zones since she was nineteen."

"Do you know what she looks like?" the other man asked. "Is she here?"

Price didn't say a word—instead, he simply locked eyes with Desi again. So he did know who she was.

Desi wondered why he hadn't said anything sooner. Maybe he was trying to prove his loyalty to her? Calling her out would not have won him any brownie points, that's for sure. Either way, Desi took it as her cue to start the training. She walked to the front of the group, taking her jacket off as she went. She tossed it aside then turned to face her team.

"I am Lieutenant Desiree Flint." She glanced across the field to see Wolf's team taking off for a run. What a waste of time. They only had a couple of weeks to train their teams. Desi considered it critical that her team learned how to shoot properly. After all, there was no reason to run if you've already shot everyone who's chasing you.

"I don't know what training you have received in the past," she started, "and to be honest, I don't care. I have spent my entire career serving in war zones, and I am here to teach you the advanced combat strategies we've developed on Earth.

"This," Desi pulled her gun out of its holster and held it high for her team to see, "is the new standard combat weapon for all of *Journey*'s combat forces. It has five settings instead of the two your traditional combat gun has. I want you get familiar with it. Get comfortable with it. By the end of the week, it should feel like an extension of your arm."

She lowered the gun but still held it out in front of her. "The first setting is most often used for training purposes. It gives off a small electrical pulse that feels similar to static electricity, and it causes no visible or lasting damage to most advanced lifeforms. The second setting is slightly stronger, although while it may slow your enemy down, it will do little to stop them. Bruising and swelling may occur at the location of the hit. The third setting is most commonly used during combat missions. It emits a pulse that will render those hit unconscious for upwards of twenty minutes. Minimal permanent damage is possible, depending on the location of the hit. The first three settings do not have any effect on inanimate objects."

She paused to survey the team to make sure they were paying attention. "The fourth setting most closely resembles the effects of traditional metal bullets," she continued. "Depending on the location of the hit, it can be fatal. Significant and potentially long-lasting damage often results from using the fourth setting. In addition, it can be used against inanimate objects like plastic, wood, or plaster.

"The final setting is the most powerful and should only be used in the most dire of circumstances." Desi powered her gun to the fifth setting, turned towards the firing range, and fired. Her shot hit the target dead center. The small explosion that followed elicited gasps that assured Desi she had gotten her point across.

"Any questions?"

No one spoke.

"Then line up, and let's see how well you shoot."

Desi spent the rest of the day correcting grips and

adjusting sights. Overall, she was impressed with her team, they eagerly listened to her and applied everything she suggested. She could see the benefits of having a voluntary military compared to having mandatory service the way it was on Earth.

The person who surprised her the most was Price, who was easily the best shot of them all. After a few hours of observing him shoot, she was so impressed that she asked him to work with the members of the team who needed some extra help.

Desi was thrilled with the progress they had made. She felt confident that they would destroy Wolf's team.

Exhausted, Crystal gathered her team outside of the locker rooms. She had worked them hard all day — several runs through the obstacle course had followed their three-mile run, and then she had led them through a series of intense team-building exercises. Crystal was impressed that she hadn't heard a whisper of anyone wanting to quit. In fact, by the end of the day, her team was functioning as if they had been working together for years.

"Great job today, everyone," she told them. "I truly believe that this is the best combat team in LAWON. We'll meet back here tomorrow at 0600 hours." Crystal's team was quiet as they dispersed, but their heads were held high.

Crystal was about to head into the locker room to get cleaned up herself when one of Flint's team members caught her eye. He slowly made his way over to her. Crystal's heart tightened, and ice ran through veins. She felt anger grow inside of her with every step he took towards her.

"Hi," he said cautiously.

"What are you doing here, Tyler?" Crystal was surprised by the coldness in her own voice.

"I joined the military."

"I can see that, but you haven't answered my question."

"I wasn't happy with the jobs I was getting with my programming degree, so I decided to change careers. I actually just graduated from the Academy. I guess you could say it was in my blood." The words tumbled out of his mouth.

Crystal could tell he was nervous, but she felt no sympathy for him. She didn't like to mix her personal and professional lives. Tyler? Standing in front of her, and as a soldier? "Of all the ships in the fleet, why *Journey*?"

"Turning down a position on the flagship would have been career suicide," he said flatly. "And I knew you would be here. I thought maybe it would give us chance to reconnect." He paused. "Your ship is amazing, by the way. I've been following its construction."

"No," Crystal said through gritted teeth. She couldn't believe this was happening. She desperately wanted to stay calm and maintain some semblance of professionalism, especially since she was aware that everyone was watching them. She feared she was losing her internal battle, though.

"'No' what?" Tyler asked, confused.

"It's been ten years, Tyler. Ten years, and I haven't heard a word from you. And now you show up with no warning and want to make small talk." She managed to keep her voice calm and quiet, but she was sure anyone within a five-mile radius could feel her anger. This was not how she wanted her team to see her.

"I thought this could be good for both of us," Tyler pleaded.

"I've gotten along just fine without you for all these years. What makes you think I need you now?"

"But Crys..."

"I don't have time for this." Crystal turned and walked away. She was halfway to the parking lot when she heard footsteps behind her. It was Grady, she knew. She was sure he had heard her exchange with Tyler, and while he wouldn't have understood what it was about, he would have sensed instantly that something was wrong. He was always there when she needed support, whether she asked for it or not.

Crystal didn't acknowledge him—she couldn't think of anything useful to say, anyway. Instead, she grabbed her helmet, quickly put it on, and revved her bike. She waited a few seconds for Grady to jump on behind her and then pulled out of the parking lot.

Chapter 4

Crystal weaved her motorcycle in and out of traffic. She knew she should probably slow down, especially with Grady on the back, but her reckless driving was feeding the flame that was burning inside of her. Besides, Grady was probably enjoying the speed and the near misses they were having with the other cars on the road.

They pulled up to the gate at the Academy, showed their identification, and were let in. Crystal finally pulled to a stop outside of the administration building. Grady wordlessly kept up with her as she marched towards Reed's office. Crystal didn't break stride until she was standing outside of his door. Before she knocked, she took a deep breath in a feeble attempt to calm her anger.

Reed opened the door with a huge smile, making Crystal's resolve waver. For a moment, she was at a loss for words, but was saved when Reed spoke first.

"Jim," Reed extended his hand to Grady. "I'm so glad to see you. I was afraid you weren't going to make it back in time."

"Thank you, sir," Grady said as he shook Reed's hand.

"I'm thrilled to be able to serve with you and Crystal again."

"Sir, I need to talk to you," Crystal said, finally finding her voice.

"Of course." He stepped aside to let them in, motioning towards the chairs in front of his desk.

Grady took a seat. Crystal did not.

"So, what do you need to talk to me about?" Reed leaned against his desk while Crystal slowly paced in a small circle in the back of his office, too much on edge to sit down.

Reed looked at Grady, who just raised his eyebrows in Crystal's direction.

"Tyler Price," Crystal said. She stopped and turned to look at Reed.

"Ah, I had a feeling this might be about him. I take it you saw him today."

"Why didn't you tell me?" Crystal was painfully aware of the whine in her voice.

Reed looked at her with a steady gaze. "When I first began crew selections, I decided not to burden you or Dewite with that process. You had enough to worry about—after all, you've been building the ship. It's true that when Price's file was brought to my attention, I thought about telling you, but I didn't want you to dwell on things. The truth of the matter is, we need him. The decision to offer him a position was made with the best interests of the ship in mind."

"I'm sorry to interrupt," Grady said, "but who is this Price guy, anyway?"

"He's my brother." Crystal's anger was finally starting to dissipate. It was never easy for her to stay angry at Reed, and she certainly couldn't be angry now, when he was treating her like a respected colleague even though her behavior was reminiscent of a petulant teenager.

"I didn't know you had a brother," Grady said. Crystal tried to ignore the tone of betrayal in his voice. Of all the people in her life, Grady should have known she had a brother—it was the role he had been filling in her life for the past five years. Crystal hadn't intentionally kept it from him, though. It had just never come up before now.

"He's my half-brother on my father's side," she said slowly. "I haven't spoken to him in ten years. I just don't understand why we need him. He can't really be that good, can he?"

Reed nodded. "We do. There's no one else who even comes close. Here, take a look at his file." Reed sat down at his desk and pulled out an electronic tablet.

Crystal took the tablet from him and sat down in the chair next to Grady to look through it. Tyler's scores were impressive, she had to admit. He had scored above average in just about every area, and his combat scores were extremely high...although not quite as high as hers, she noted with a twinge of sibling rivalry. But his technical skills were off the charts, especially in computer programming.

"See what I mean?" Reed said once Crystal had handed him back the tablet.

She stifled a sigh. "From a purely professional standpoint, I do. We're lucky to have someone with his skillset on *Journey*"

"And from a personal standpoint," prodded Grady.

"What I don't understand is that if it was so important to him that we reconnect, why did he wait until today?" Crystal said, still frustrated. "Why didn't he reach out to me privately? He had every opportunity. I've spent the last four months just a couple of miles away from the Academy, building *Journey*. There had to be a better way for him to go about contacting me than just show up like this."

"There's only one person who can give you those answers," Reed said sympathetically, "and he's not in this room. For what it's worth, I am sorry I didn't tell you. I guess I take it for granted that you can handle anything thrown at you—you're one of the strongest people I know."

"Thank you, sir." That said, Crystal didn't feel very strong at the moment. She should have handled seeing Tyler differently. She had let her emotions take over and had ended up making a fool of herself. She wouldn't let that happen again.

"And can I say one more thing?" Reed asked.

"Of course."

"Think about giving Price a chance. He's the only family you have."

"I will." Crystal gave Reed a small smile as she and Grady stood to leave. Reed gave them another nod as they exited his office.

"Are you all right?" Grady asked once they were outside of the building.

Crystal shrugged. "You know me—I'm always all right." She hoped he hadn't noticed her voice catching at the back of her throat.

"Be straight with me." Grady stood in front of her, blocking her way. He searched her eyes for some hidden emotion that wasn't there—she felt completely drained.

"It's been a crazy day, but I promise I'm fine."

"OK," Grady said after a short pause. "Then why don't we jump back on that bike of yours and you take me back to the dorms? You did kind of kidnap me."

"You were a willing hostage," Crystal said, attempting a smile. "Thanks, by the way."

"It was nothing. Now, come on kid! I'm starving." He tousled her hair and threw his arm around her shoulder. Together, they walked back to the parking lot.

"Just give me something," Desi said for the hundredth time since leaving the training field. She was slowly making her way through the buffet line at the dorm mess hall trying to find food she recognized.

"No," Justin said in an offhand way that was starting to be annoying. He moved along in front of her, scooping small portions of several Neophian foods onto his plate.

"At least tell me how Wolf's training compares to what you received on Earth."

"Sorry, Desi, I'm not going to tell you anything."

"But we're friends."

"What does that have to do with anything?" Justin was already at the end of the buffet line. "Everyone already knows about this competition you have going on with Wolf. I'm not going to risk putting my team at a disadvantage by telling you about our training program." He gave her a hard look. "You've got to respect that."

Desi was having a difficult time deciding what was safe to drink among the pitchers of multicolored liquids. She poured herself a glass of what she hoped was water before turning to face Justin. "I don't have to respect that."

"Yes, you do. Come on, let's find somewhere to sit." He started leading them into the main room.

The mess hall was crowded, with new members of *Journey*'s crew constantly trickling in. Desi did a quick scan of the room before honing in on a table: there Price was, sitting in a back corner. She was surprised he was alone—he had seemed to have at least a few friends during training that afternoon. Maybe no one wanted to be seen with him after the little spectacle he had had with Wolf after training?

She should probably leave him alone to deal with his embarrassment, but Desi's curiosity got the better of her, and she made a beeline for his table. Justin followed closely in her wake. "These seats taken?"

Price looked up, distracted. He waved towards the empty chairs. "Help yourselves."

She sat down and waited while Price and Justin exchanged quick hellos. Desi hadn't realized they were bunkmates. She would have thought Justin would have mentioned that, especially after the argument with Wolf. He'd been rambling on and on about her for most of the day. He hadn't given up anything useful, though—he just kept talking about how smart she was and how much everyone respected her. There had even been some mention of how beautiful she was, but Desi blocked out the memory of those words to keep from gagging.

"I was really impressed with your performance in the field today," Desi said to Price.

"Thanks," Price said without looking up from his plate.

"How long have you been in the service?" Desi needed to get the conversation rolling before she could ask the question she was really interested in, and one-word answers weren't going to cut it.

"I actually only graduated from the Academy last week."

"You're kidding!"

"Nope," Price said. They were back to one-word

answers, but at least this time he was maintaining eye contact.

"Aren't you a little old to just be graduating?" Desi asked. Based on his appearance, Price was in his late twenties, same as she was. The rest of the recent graduates were more like twenty-one.

"I took a detour on my way to the military."

"A detour?"

"Yeah, though IT."

"That's one hell of a career change," Desi said.

"It wasn't easy, especially being twenty-two in a class of sixteen years-old."

"Sixteen years-olds? Did you go all the way back to high school?" Desi asked.

"No, on Neophia we complete our general education at fifteen and start specialized career education at sixteen. Most people graduate from the Academy at twenty-one."

"How do people even know what they want to do with their lives at sixteen?" Desi said

Out of the corner of her eye, she noticed that Justin was no longer paying attention to their conversation. What was distracting him?

Then she saw Wolf and Grady on the other side of the room. They had both jumped up from their seats, and it looked like they were squaring off for a fight. Desi watched in eager anticipation. It would be nice to watch Wolf be put in her place.

Unfortunately, Wolf and Grady suddenly collapsed back into their chairs, laughing. Desi guessed that she would have to be the one to bring Wolf down a few notches the next time the opportunity presented itself. She gave a mental shrug. Back to why she was sitting with Price.

"So, what was with you and *Journey*'s princess this afternoon?" Desi asked, trying to pose the question in an offhand way.

"Excuse me?" Price asked.

Desi gritted her teeth. She really needed to work on being more subtle, apparently. But that was a challenge for another day. "You and Wolf. That was a pretty heated argument you two had at the end of training. It's all everyone has been talking about."

"Oh, I'm sure she'll love that," Price muttered.

Desi could tell he was putting his defenses up. She would have to strike fast if she wanted any answers. "Did the two of you used to date or something?"

"Or something." Price pushed his food around his plate, obviously not wanting to talk about it. Desi was not deterred.

"Something like what?" Desi could feel Justin watching her intently. She was sure he was appalled by her behavior—he usually was when she did something like this. Normally, he would have stepped in by now to apologize for her bluntness, but this time he was keeping his mouth shut. Desi suspected he wanted to hear Price's answer even more than she did.

"Crystal is my sister." Price dropped his fork onto his plate in frustration.

"Your sister?" Justin asked.

"My half-sister, actually."

"You guys didn't meet for the first time today, did you?" This was better than anything Desi had hoped to hear.

"Of course not. We were teenagers when we first met. It's just been a while since we've seen each other."

"How long?" Desi asked.

"Ten years, give or take."

"What did you expect would happen?" Desi was trying not to laugh—he was clearly upset. "That you'd show up and the two of you would go skipping off as best friends?"

"I don't know what I expected. We used to be close..." Price's voice trailed off as he looked back down at his mashed potatoes.

Crystal's spirits had risen considerably during the brief ride from the Academy to the dorms where *Journey*'s crew was being housed. Unfortunately, the moment she walked into the mess hall, her eyes locked with Tyler's. Her spirits took a nosedive as he gave her a small smile that she couldn't manage to return. For the second time that day, she had to physically turn away from him.

Reed was right, she knew—she should give him a chance. But that was easier said than done when she couldn't seem to get over the betrayal she felt every time she saw Tyler. After they had met, they had become close; she had been thrilled to have a sibling in her life. Growing up as an only child had been lonely. Ever since she joined the military, though, she had no longer felt that loneliness. She didn't need Tyler now the way she had needed him when she was fourteen. She wasn't even sure if there was a place for him in her life anymore.

Distracted, Crystal sat down at a table with Dewite, quickly introducing him to Grady as they both sat down. "How was training this morning?" Dewite asked.

"Fine," Crystal responded absent-mindedly. She kept glancing up from her food to look across the mess hall at Tyler. He was chatting with Anderson and Flint, looking at ease. He seemed to be handling the aftermath of their reunion much better than she was.

"How does the team look?"

"Good. Strong."

"All right, what happened to the ship?" Dewite asked with concern in his voice.

"Wait, what?" Crystal finally gave Dewite her full attention. "Nothing! The ship's fine. Unless you know something I don't?"

"Then what's going on with you? You never give one-word answers, especially when it comes to work. You love to talk about work," Dewite said.

Grady nodded in agreement. "It's a bit pathetic, really," he said. "You should try to find a hobby or something. It would make you more interesting."

"Contrary to popular belief, I do have a life outside of *Journey*," Crystal said indignantly.

"Could have fooled me. When was the last time you took a day off?" Grady challenged her.

Crystal folded her arms across her chest. "I took a day off last month."

Grady looked at Dewite for conformation. "She did," he acknowledged, "but she used it to attend a submersible design conference." His gaze tracked back to Crystal. "Where I believe you gave the keynote address?"

"Yeah...that doesn't really count as 'not working,'" Grady said.

"Sure it does," Crystal protested. "It wasn't even a LAWON-sponsored conference—it was put on by a group of independent researchers."

"What was your speech about?" Grady asked.

"The pros and cons of regenerative hulls on commercial and private submersible vehicles."

"Like the one you designed for *Journey*," Dewite said.

"Well, yeah."

"So, in other words: work," Grady concluded.

"Like you two are so much better," said Crystal, her arms still folded.

"I take a week off every year to go see my family," Dewite said.

"I know, but when you get back, you're more stressed than when you left, and we all have to hear you complain about the visit for weeks. Besides, you are aware that given your rank, you are entitled to ten weeks of leave per year?" Crystal said, raising her eyebrows at Dewite.

"And you—" Crystal faced Grady, who had been snickering. "Didn't you cut your last vacation short after only one day to take a voluntary undercover assignment that lasted for over a year?"

Grady stopped snickering. "What's your point?"

"My point is that we're all happiest when we're working, and I really don't see anything wrong with that."

"Of course you don't. You're no fun," Grady said.

"You don't know what you're talking about, I'm loads of fun."

"No, you're a workaholic," Grady said, getting to his feet so that he could tower over Crystal.

"And you're nothing more than an adrenaline junkie." Crystal rose to her feet and squared off with him.

"Do you really want to do this, little girl?"

"Bring it on, old man." Crystal took a step closer to Grady and attempted to puff out her chest.

"Knock it off, you two," Dewite said.

Crystal and Grady collapsed back into their chairs, laughing. Dewite just shook his head and sighed. "So, Crys, what does have you so distracted today?"

"Ensign Price." Crystal nodded her head in Tyler's direction.

"I'm going to need a little bit more than that," Dewite said.

"He's her long-lost brother," Grady offered in between bites of timbu chips. He offered some to Crystal and Dewite, but they both waved them away. Crystal couldn't understand how Grady could eat them—they were basically chewy tree bark, albeit roasted and seasoned tree bark. Most of the Sertex she knew loved them, maybe the taste helped them get in touch their ancestors.

"That raises more questions than it answers," Dewite said.

"My father had an affair during the war, and Tyler Price is the result," Crystal explained. "Now he's joined the military and wants to reconnect."

Dewite looked surprised. "Then why aren't you over there reconnecting?"

"He hasn't made any effort to contact me for ten years, and now he shows up and wants to behave like my brother again. Am I supposed to pretend he didn't vanish?"

"Of course not, but it's a two-way street," Grady said.

Crystal didn't like where he was going with this.

"You and I are close, right?" he continued.

"Yeah," Crystal said.

"And we've known each other a long time, right?"

"Right."

"And I probably know you better than just about anyone."

Crystal pursed her lips. "What's your point, Jim?"

"My point is that until an hour ago, I would have gone to my grave swearing you were an only child."

"You know I don't like to talk about my past."

"I know, but it makes me wonder how much effort you've put in. Can you honestly say he's the only one at fault?"

Grady was right: she hadn't made any effort to find Tyler. If she remembered correctly, she was the one who had sent the last email to him and not the other way around, but that did little to ease the guilt she was starting to feel. She wanted to tell herself she hadn't tried to reconnect with him because she had been busy and too focused on her career, yet she knew that was an excuse. It was easier to blame Tyler for everything. She was just as much at fault, though...maybe even more so. At least Tyler had known where to find her. She had no idea where he had been during the last ten years.

She sighed. "I hate it when you're the voice of reason."

"Me, too," Grady said with a gentle smile. "Now go over there."

With a resigned sigh, Crystal got up and started the long walk across the mess hall. It felt like it would have been easier to break out of an enemy's prison than to make that hundred-yard trek. It didn't help that Tyler was sitting with Flint, either. Halfway across the room, she glanced back at her table. The encouraging smiles from Grady and Dewite gave her the courage she needed.

She stopped by Tyler's table. "Hi," she said meekly, ignoring Flint and Anderson and focusing all of her attention on Tyler.

"Hi," he said cautiously.

"About this afternoon—"

Tyler interrupted her before she could finish. "Don't worry about it—it's forgotten."

"Can we talk?"

"I'd love that. Why don't you join us?" To Crystal's dismay, Tyler pulled out the chair next to him. The last thing she wanted to do was bare her soul in front of Flint and Anderson. On the other hand, what would Tyler think if she turned him down again? It was possible that he didn't want to be alone with her. Still, she couldn't talk in front of all three of them.

"I...um...I thought maybe we could go for a walk or something."

"All right," he said with a smile.

"Hey, Crys, I hate to interrupt, but..." Dewite was suddenly standing next to her.

"No problem," Crystal said gratefully. She felt her confidence return as she looked at Dewite. He had a serious expression—something had happened. Still, whatever he had to tell her would be easier to deal with than trying to fix things with Tyler.

"I received a message from Captain Reed," Dewite said. "He needs to see us at headquarters right away."

Crystal turned back to Tyler. "Another time," she said, feeling a mixture of relief and disappointment.

"Another time," he repeated.

Crystal and Dewite started walking towards the mess hall exit. "Do you want me to drive?" Crystal asked him.

He snorted. "There's no way I'm getting on that death machine of yours."

Crystal shook her head, not breaking stride. "Where's your sense of adventure, Commander?"

Chapter 5

Crystal and Dewite were shown to the War Room as soon as they arrived at headquarters. Monitors showing satellite images, news reports, and maps covered every inch of wall space. Several people were seated around the table at the center of the round room, and technicians were seated at computers running around the perimeter of the room. Their whispers hung in Crystal's ears as she quickly took the seat next to Captain Reed.

She was amazed to find a black glass placeholder with her name and rank engraved on it. Did LAWON make one for every officer on the off chance they were summoned to a meeting in the War Room? That seemed like an inefficient use of resources.

"Thank you all for coming on such short notice," Craft said. He was standing at the head of the table in front of a large screen.

"As the command teams of the three LAWON ships in the area, it is my responsibility to inform you of the Terian military's recent activity," Craft began.

Crystal glanced at the captains of the two other ships

who were also seated at the table. Captain Pollard, the current captain of *Expedition*, was there with her command team. Crystal had started her career on that carrier, back when Reed was still the commanding officer. Pollard had taken over from him two years ago, Crystal remembered, when he had been asked to return to the Academy to teach some advanced classes.

Crystal recognized Captain Russo and his chief engineer, but not anyone else on his team. Russo had been captain of *Legacy* for almost seven years. The submarine was currently in dry dock for some much-needed upgrades, upgrades that were about to be cut short since *Legacy* was currently occupying the holding bay that *Journey* was going to be moved to in just four more days. Crystal avoided looking the *Legacy*'s chief engineer in the eye.

"What kind of activity?" Pollard asked.

Craft looked grim. "They have set up camp on a LAWON island, although they have not yet made any claim on it. The island is uninhabited—it's classified as a wildlife preserve. It's owned by the country of Vectero and managed by the Ravenwood Science Institute. Scientists from the Institute are using the island for research purposes."

Craft hit a button, and an image filled the main screen as well as the smaller built-in table screens. "Right now, we are just working off of what our satellites have picked up."

Crystal studied the image carefully. The time stamp showed it had been taken less than ten minutes ago. The picture was so clear that Crystal could read the manufacturer's label on the tents in the center of the frame. Still, despite the high quality of the image, it told her nothing useful. She touched the table screen in front of her, zooming out so that the island was nothing more than a green speck on a blue backdrop. There was nothing around the island for hundreds of miles.

Why had President Rank positioned troops there? Crystal knew he wasn't interested in any scientific merits the island might possess — the only thing Rank cared about was power. There had to be something else about the island that he needed. Considering that it was a huge risk to go after LAWON controlled-land, the payoff had to be just as huge.

"Do we have an underwater map of this area?" Crystal asked a bit hesitantly. Seeing as she was the most junior office at the table, she wasn't exactly sure if she was allowed to speak up at this kind of briefing.

Apparently, her comment was welcome — Craft nodded and tapped another button, and a new map appeared on her screen. This time, as she zoomed out, several underwater colonies appeared. The island was close to six of them.

"Take a look at this." Crystal swiped her hand across the screen, sending the image to Reed and Dewite. The other teams were involved in their own side conversations.

"You think Rank is using the island as a means to stage an attack on one of these colonies?" Reed asked.

Crystal nodded. "I'm afraid so — it's the only scenario that makes sense. Mainland Teria is over 2,000 miles away, and their nearest occupied land is 500 miles away. They don't have any territory in this area. If he can gain control of one of these colonies, he'll be perfectly positioned to lead an attack on Oceananica or Kincaron's southern region, and without the support of those two countries, LAWON would crumble. The smaller nations would never stand a chance against Rank—Neophia would be thrown into a state of chaos."

Reed looked just as troubled as she felt. "The only question is, what colony is he going to go after?" he mused aloud.

Dewite had been scrutinizing his own screen. "This one." He swiped his image over to Crystal and Reed.

Crystal read through the colony's profile quickly. Rexing was an underwater mining colony with a stable population of 1,500. The population breakdown was 42% pure Sertex, 36% Sertex-dominant, 15% Aquinein-dominant, 6 % Sertex and Aquienein mixed, and only 1% Human-dominant. Gaining control over it would supply Teria with rare mineral resources and also increase the number of Sertex pureblood elite inhabitants that Rank prized. Most importantly, it wasn't a LAWON nation.

"Attention, everyone! We are receiving a transmission you'll all want to see," said one of the technicians.

"We're too late," Crystal said under her breath as she looked at the main screen.

She could almost feel Rank's tangible presence in the room the moment his face appeared on the main screen. Acid started to churn in her stomach as he began to speak. "My fellow citizens of Neophia, greetings from Teria!" he began. "As President, it is my honor to inform you of the peaceful merger that has taken place between Teria and the Rexing mining community. As a sign of good will, Teria has placed a military unit at the colony to help protect them from those who might wish to stop this merger from occurring. I implore the rest of the nations of Neophia to allow Teria and Rexing to work through this transition in peace." He gave a single nod and a smile that seemed more calculating than genuine. The screen went black as soon as the message ended. Rank has been taking over colonies so frequently in the last few months Crystal had his speech memorized.

Crystal waited for someone to say something. LAWON had to have some kind of response. They couldn't let another colony fall to Teria, not even if that colony wasn't a member of LAWON.

No one spoke, so finally she did. "What are we going to do?" she asked the room at large. She couldn't stand the silence any longer.

Craft frowned and tapped a finger against the edge of the table before responding. "Captain Pollard, I want you to take the *Expedition* to the island. Maybe an increased LAWON presence in the area will encourage the Terian military to vacate our land."

"And what about the colony?" Crystal pressed.

Craft looked unhappy but determined. "There's nothing we can do for them now." He stepped away from the table. "You're all dismissed."

"You can't be serious! You're going to send a carrier to defend an uninhabited island, but when it comes to the lives of 1,500 people, you're going to look the other way?" Crystal knew she was crossing a line, but she hoped her history with Craft would protect her from any serious ramifications.

"Dismissed," Craft repeated. Crystal didn't hear any anger in his voice, though she knew he was good at maintaining a calm demeanor no matter how he felt.

Everyone except Crystal stood. Craft gave her a curt nod. "Reed, Dewite, Wolf—please stay."

Once the room was empty, Craft sat down across from the three of them. "I understand your frustration, Crystal,

I really do, but there is nothing we can do."

"Sir, there has to be something," she pleaded.

Craft let a hint of frustration show on his face. "Without a distress call, we can't interfere with a non-member nation," he said. "For all we know, Rank's message could be genuine—maybe this is what both sides want. If we go barging in there, we could start another war."

"We all know that Rank was lying," Reed broke in. "If Rexing had really been considering joining sides with Teria, our intelligence teams would have picked up on it." Crystal was grateful to have him on her side.

"Has anyone else noticed that Rexing is only about 25 miles away from the route *Journey* will be making to the capital?" Dewite said.

Crystal glanced back down at her screen. How had she missed that detail? Not only had Rank gained a colony rich in resources, now he was perfectly positioned to mount an attack during *Journey*'s maiden voyage.

Craft didn't look happy. "You're right," he admitted. "Well, *Journey*'s sail date is still four weeks away—we have plenty of time to chart a new course. It will be easy to avoid coming into range of the colony. Rank has to know this. I doubt very much that he is after the ship."

"With all due respect sir, what if you're wrong?" Crystal asked.

Craft shook his head. "Crystal, I have no doubt that one day you will be standing in my place. When that day comes, you can make the call, but until then, you're just going to have to trust me," he said, standing. "Dismissed."

They filed out behind him.

Desi was done relying on word-of-mouth techniques: if she wanted to learn about her opponent, she needed to do her own research. She went to the rec room with her computer in hand and got to work at the small table in the back corner of the room. A surprising number of articles came up when she searched for Wolf, so she focused on the most recent ones. She skimmed through one headline after another: "Daughter of War Heroes Graduates Top of her Class," "Only Child of War Heroes Receives One of LAWON's Highest Honors," "Commander Wolf, Daughter of National Heroes, Designs State-of-the-Art Submarine"…

A familiar voice interrupted her. "What are you working on?" Justin asked.

"I'm researching Wolf." Desi didn't look up from her screen.

"Did you find anything?" Justin sat down next to her. Desi wondered what he was hoping to see. She was pretty sure Wolf wouldn't have her relationship status, or that she had a soft spot for idealistic humans who enjoyed star gazing and day dreaming posted online.

"Nothing useful, although everything I'm finding mentions that her parents were war heroes."

"I wonder what they did that made them heroes," Justin said.

She shrugged. "They died. Although so did a lot of other people."

Justin looked like he was about to say something, but just then Price came walking into the rec room with a computer of his own tucked under his arm. He noticed Justin and Desi sitting together and came over to join them.

Desi didn't care if Price overheard their conversation. "It was a war," she said bluntly. "I don't understand why their deaths were any different."

It was obvious Price could tell what they had been talking about. "What happened to them was different," he said.

"What do you mean?" Justin asked.

"It would be easier if I showed you." Price tapped a few keys on his computer and then turned his screen toward Justin and Desi. A video showing two people standing on top of a platform over two clear glass tanks of water. Their hands were bound behind their backs. The man's face was covered with a black sack, but the woman's was not: she stared down at the camera lens, her face bruised and bloody. Even Desi found the determination in the woman's eyes intimidating.

"Are they Crystal's parents?" Justin asked.

"Yes. Their names were Kendra and Jedidiah Wolf," Price said.

A man wearing a black uniform stepped onto the platform and spoke in a langue Desi didn't understand. Not that that mattered—Desi couldn't take her eyes off of the woman. As soon as the man finished speaking, he placed a bag over Kendra's head, too.

The platforms beneath their feet opened, then quickly closed. Kendra and Jedidiah were plunged into the tanks. After about a minute, Jedidiah stopped struggling, and the camera zoomed in on Kendra. Almost five more minutes went by before she finally stopped moving.

"That was broadcast live on every screen on the planet," Price said.

"So you watched your father die?" Desi asked.

"I didn't know he was my father at the time."

"And Crystal?" Justin asked.

Price's eyes were dark. "She saw it. She probably didn't realize what was happening at first—she was only seven years old when they were killed—but she saw it."

What must it have been like for Wolf to watch her parents killed on live TV? Desi wondered. Sure, images of war were easy to find on Earth, but you had to go looking for them. If you wanted to hide from them, you could. Wolf hadn't had that same luxury.

"What happened to the man who killed them?" she said aloud. If Desi's mother had been on that platform, Desi would have dedicated her life to making him pay.

"That's Nathan Rank, and he's now the president of Teria," Price said. "The Wolfs were highly decorated soldiers: Kendra was the captain of the most successful subfighter division our side had, and Jedidiah was in charge of the ground troops stationed in Teria. About six months before they were captured, they went on an undercover mission together."

"Why did Rank drown them?" Justin asked.

Price's eyes narrowed. "He wanted to humiliate them, and the best way to humiliate an Aquinein is to drown them."

"How do you know all of this? Weren't you just a kid when it happened?" Desi asked.

"They spend a whole year at the Academy teaching us the details of The Great War," Price answered. "They don't want it to be repeated."

"I still don't get what the big deal is," Desi said, frowning. "Yes, their death was tragic, and broadcasting it live was horrific, but what did it change? Why is it mentioned in every press release about Wolf?"

"At that point, Rank was losing ground and resources

quickly," Price explained. "He needed something to motivate his troops, and he thought their deaths would be that motivation."

"Was it?" Justin asked.

Price shook his head. "No. In fact, it backfired. The Kincaron government praised the Wolfs, saying they were martyrs. The media took that and ran with it — they made Crystal the face of her parents' sacrifice. It gave our side the motivation they needed to make the final push. Three months later, the war was over."

"And what about Crystal?" Justin had taken Desi's computer and was looking through all of the news articles she had pulled up.

"She's been in and out of the public eye her whole life — the media likes to pull out old footage or try to get an interview with her every year for Peace Day. For the last couple of years, though, she's managed to avoid it. Most people don't recognize her anymore. Still, everyone knows about the orphan daughter of the heroes who ended the war," Price said.

Desi couldn't imagine what it would have been like to grow up with that kind of pressure hanging over her head. It didn't change the way Desi felt about Wolf, but at least it explained her annoying need for perfection. And now Desi had better insight into her opponent's mind, which just meant it would be easier for Desi to find a way to prove she was the better officer.

Chapter 6

Crystal gathered her team in the middle of the training field after lunch. She had been working with them for four days now, with every morning dedicated to physical fitness and afternoons set aside for the more interesting training sessions.

"This afternoon, we're going to focus on hand-to-hand combat," Crystal announced to her team. "It's important to know how to defend yourself without the aid of a weapon. Lieutenant Grady has graciously volunteered to help demonstrate what we'll be doing."

"No, I didn't," Grady called from the back of the group.

Crystal ignored his protest. "Lieutenant Grady, would you please join me?"

With a resigned sigh, Grady made his way to Crystal's side, just like she knew he would. Despite Grady having a good six inches on her, they both knew they were evenly matched sparring partners. "We're going to show you a few basic moves I want you to work on this afternoon, and then everyone will pair off to practice."

All of her team members were nodding their heads.

"All right," she turned to face Grady, "try to punch me."

"I'm not going to hit you," Grady said softly.

"Come on, Jim, this is a demonstration," she said, her voice soft but determined. "I can't show them anything unless you try to punch me."

"Fine."

"And don't hold back, either."

"I got it." Grady pulled back his arm and swung it towards Crystal's face.

Crystal dodged the punch and grabbed his arm as it moved past her. In one swift movement, she flipped Grady to the ground. He landed roughly on his back.

"See, this is why I didn't want to be your volunteer," he said as he laid on the ground at Crystal's feet.

She grinned at him but directed her words to the team. "Sometimes defensive moves can be more effective than offensive ones. When someone is coming at you, it's important to use their weight and momentum to your advantage." She couldn't keep the devilish grin off of her face. It had been too long since she had sparred with Grady.

Crystal offered Grady her hand to help him back to his feet. He accepted her hand, but then instead of helping her up, he flipped her over his head onto the ground behind him.

"It's also important to remember to never let your guard down." Grady rose to his feet, leaving Crystal in the grass. "When you think you have beaten your opponent, that's when they'll strike."

"Thank you, Lieutenant." Crystal was on her feet again. She should have expected him to do something like that, but she had felt a little off her game all day. What was making her so distracted?

Her eyes involuntarily wandered to Anderson. Their conversation at Marco's had stayed with her, and neither the chaos of the build site nor the repetitive structure of training had driven him from her mind. She found herself spending what little free time she had seeking out his company. If his presence was starting to make her work slip, though, that was all the more reason to be careful about how she thought about him.

She suddenly heard Flint's voice from behind her. "Hand-to-hand combat? That's cute."

Crystal turned to see Flint leading her team across the field to the obstacle course on the other side. "It's a little old-fashioned," Flint continued, "but cute nonetheless." Her smile struck Crystal as predatory.

It took all of Crystal's willpower not to say anything. She just hoped Flint would keep walking so that she could get back to teaching her team the skills she knew they would need.

Unfortunately, she didn't. "See this here?" Flint removed her side arm from her hip and showed it to Crystal in a mocking fashion. "It's called a gun. It makes what you're teaching impractical."

Crystal took a deep breath. Her mind was screaming for her to let the taunt slide by unnoticed, but she couldn't do it. It was time to put Flint in her place. "Fine. But how would you defend yourself if you didn't have your gun?" Crystal gritted out.

"A good soldier—hell, even a semi-decent soldier—will always have their gun when they need it," Flint said as she faced Crystal and planted herself in a firm stance.

"And if someone takes your gun away from you?" Crystal took a step closer to Flint.

"No one can take my gun away from me."

"Oh, I see." Crystal slowly turned and took a few steps away from Flint. Before Flint could register what was happening, Crystal kicked the gun out of her hand, sending it flying.

Crystal didn't even try to suppress her smile at the shocked look on Flint's face. "I guess you're not as good as you thought you were." She knew that was a cheap shot, but Flint had no clue what they would be dealing with once they set sail. What else could she do?

She didn't see Flint's nostrils flare in rage, nor did she see Flint's fist coming toward her face. She did, however, feel it connect with her jaw. Crystal was surprised by the force of the punch: it caused her to stumble back a few steps and end up on one knee. Had Flint's aim been a little more accurate, she probably would have been knocked out.

Without pausing to consider her actions, Crystal shifted her weight, swung her leg around, and swept Flint's legs out from under her, jumping to her feet as the other woman fell to the ground.

Flint was back on her feet in an instant. She attempted to punch Crystal again, but she no longer had the element of surprise, and Crystal was easily able to deflect it and then deliver two punches of her own.

Flint dodged the first punch, but the second one connected with her right eye. Still, she managed to remain on her feet, then surprised everyone by kicking Crystal in the chest, making her stagger back. She started to throw another punch to deliver the final blow while Crystal was struggling for breath, but Crystal saw it coming, and she grabbed Flint's arm and threw her to the ground using the move she had just demonstrated on Grady. Flint hit the ground hard and was slow to get back up.

They squared off again. Crystal still hadn't managed to fully recover her breath, and Flint was moving with a slight limp. All of Crystal's attention was focused on her opponent—she was only vaguely aware that both teams had encircled them in hopes of having a better view of the fight.

"What's going on here?" Reed's voice rang through the crowd. Everyone quickly stood at attention.

Crystal had been so focused on Flint that she hadn't seen Reed approaching, but she couldn't miss hearing the anger woven into his words.

"A training exercise, sir," Flint responded quickly.

"Is that true, Commander Wolf?"

"Yes, sir," Crystal said. It wasn't really a lie—after all, she had been doing a hand-to-hand demonstration before Flint had gotten involved.

"Go to medical and get yourselves checked out, then report to my office," Reed said.

"Yes, sir," the two women said in unison.

Without another word, Reed turned and left.

The stiff plastic chair in the medical center waiting room provided little comfort. Desi had just finished with the doctor and had been told that aside from a sprained ankle, there was nothing wrong with her. That knowledge didn't do much to stop every muscle in her body from aching, though. It had been a long time since Desi had been in a fistfight, and Wolf was good. She assumed Wolf could have caused a lot more damage if she had really wanted to. Maybe Desi should reconsider brushing up on her hand-to-hand combat skills, she thought, if only to prevent being upstaged by Wolf again.

"Two bruised ribs, nice work," Wolf said as she came back into the waiting room. Desi was surprised that there wasn't a hint of malice in Wolf's voice. If someone had given Desi two bruised ribs, she would have been pissed.

"You didn't do so bad yourself." Desi lifted up her pant leg, exposing her bandaged ankle. She attempted to mimic Wolf's friendly tone, but she kept her guard up.

"Is it broken?"

"No, just sprained."

"Good. I'd hate to put you out of commission already. I've watched you shoot, you're really good," Wolf said.

"Thanks." Desi was taken aback by the compliment. Had Wolf hit her head during their fight? This wasn't the same stuck-up know-it-all she had been putting up with all week. "How about that?" Desi said, motioning towards Wolf's ribs. "Will it slow you down any?"

"No, I've survived worse. Besides, you're not the first person to kick me in the chest, and I doubt you'll be the last."

"So this is a common occurrence with you?" Desi joked.

"Unfortunately," Wolf said with a self-deprecating laugh. "That's the thing about combat here—it's subtle, intimate."

"War is war no matter what planet you're on," Desi said.

"But we're not at war. This is peacetime."

"Call it what you want, it's all the same."

"Just when I was starting to like you," Wolf said with a sigh.

"What's that supposed to mean?" Desi asked defensively.

"You're arrogant, Lieutenant, just like the rest of your planet, and that arrogance is going to get someone killed one day." Wolf's matter-of-fact tone made Desi angrier than her words did.

"You're saying Earth is the arrogant planet?" Desi said in disbelief. She rose to feet, taking care not to put her full weight on her injured ankle. If Wolf wanted to go for round two, she was ready.

"Yes, that's exactly what I'm saying," Wolf said calmly. "Humans always seem to forget that you were the ones who sent out a spacecraft to find a new place to live. You were the ones who came to Neophia seeking help and sanctuary. Your planet has been ripping itself apart for centuries. You can't even breathe on Earth any more without the air regenerators, and you've killed nearly everything that once grew there. Still, though, you think you are so much better than us, that you're so superior with all of your technology that just winds up disconnecting you from the person next to you and your advanced weaponry that causes more wars than it solves. If that's the way of the future, you can keep it. We don't want it here."

Wolf's voice held no hatred or malice, just a deep frustration. That didn't do much to squelch Desi's anger, though — Wolf had insulted her home, and she felt honor-bound to defend it.

"If Earth is so far beneath you, then why is your planet constantly trying to mimic ours?" Desi challenged her. "You use our technology whenever you can, your military structure is modeled after ours, and your government is based on ours, too. Hell, you even speak our language." Checkmate, Desi thought.

"You don't get it, do you?" Wolf said, rolling her eyes.

"The only reason we speak English is because it was easier for my ancestors to learn your language than for Humans to learn the common Neophian tongue, let alone either one of the ancient languages. When Humans arrived on Neophia, the Aquineins bent over backwards to welcome them, to make them feel like they were part of the people. They modified their government structure to make it easier for Humans to participate in community life. They were a gentle race, and Humans took full advantage of that. As for the military, we had no need for one until Humans arrived and established one. Of course it's structured after Earth's military. It just one of the countless imports Humans have forced on Neophia."

Desi was at a loss for words, and that infuriated her. Wolf had to be exaggerating to make her point, she thought, racking her mind for any tidbit of information about the early settlements that she could throw in Wolf's face. She came up empty. If only Justin were here. He would know what to say. Though at this point, Desi was pretty sure he would side with Wolf. The traitor.

"We shouldn't keep the captain waiting." Wolf turned and left without another word. Defeated, Desi hobbled after her.

Captain Reed didn't say a word as he let Crystal and Flint into his office. Crystal avoided Reed's eyes, embarrassed by what had happened. She never should have let Flint get to her—their spat had been unprofessional. For a moment, Crystal had thought the fight had helped build a little camaraderie between them, but now Crystal deemed it a lost cause. She doubted they would ever be able to have anything more than a professional relationship, and even that seemed unlikely.

Reed took a seat behind his desk and silently surveyed them. Finally, Crystal raised her eyes to meet his. What had happened was wrong, she knew, and she would take responsibility for her part in it.

"I was extremely disappointed by what I witnessed at the training facility today." Reed's voice was calm and even. It would have been better if he had yelled. "Despite what you told me, I know very well that was not a training exercise. I had hoped that you two would put your differences aside and work together to train our combat division. I expected much more out of both of you."

Reed's words sliced through Crystal. She hadn't thought it was possible for her to feel any more ashamed. She was wrong. After everything Reed had done for her, she had let him down. Crystal knew how important this exchange program was to him.

"I am aware of the informal competition you have going on between you," Reed continued. "After today, I should abandon the idea of having two combat teams. However, most of them have little to no field experience, and if you could both approach this matter purely as a training exercise, your competition could be valuable. I will give you both one more chance to behave as the officers your rank suggests you are, but if I hear of any more childish fighting between the two of you, I'll pull you both out of the combat division. Any questions?"

"No, sir," Crystal and Flint said together.

"Dismissed," Reed said.

Crystal and Flint left the office together and headed towards the parking lot. Flint's sprained ankle was making it hard for her to keep up, but Crystal didn't slow down for her. Crystal was already on her bike by the time

Flint finally caught up.

"Where are you going?" Flint asked.

"Where do you think?" Crystal said, irritated. "I'm going back to work."

"Probably a good idea. Your team is going to need all the training they can get if you expect to have any chance of winning."

Crystal was flabbergasted. Flint really hadn't listened to a word Reed had said to them. "Unlike you, combat isn't my only responsibility." There was so much more Crystal wanted to say, but she refrained. Instead, she put on her helmet and started up her bike.

"Wait!"

Crystal raised the visor on her helmet, annoyed. Flint had already put her hours behind schedule. "What is it now?"

"I came here with you," Flint said

"Your point?"

"How do you expect me to get back?"

"You're a big girl—you figure it out." Crystal lowered her visor and pulled out of the parking lot, leaving Flint stranded.

Chapter 7

The build site was a scene of organized chaos, with Crystal standing in the middle of it checking and rechecking her tablet and trying to direct traffic. There were so many jobs going on simultaneously that it was getting hard to keep the teams out of each other's way. Two weeks ago, she had known the name of every person working on *Journey*, but now almost every face she saw belonged to a stranger.

"You know, you're going to have to patch these holes if you expect this thing to move through the water," she heard someone say.

Crystal turned to see Grady and Justin walking towards her. "You're real funny, you know that?" she said to Grady. "What are you guys doing here?"

"Since we don't have combat training this morning, we figured we'd see if you could use any help around here," Justin said.

Crystal felt her tension recede ever so slightly. "I could really use a few more safety spotters."

"Isn't there anything more exciting I could do?" Grady

said.

"Oh, I'm sorry, were you posing as an electrician on your last undercover assignment, or maybe a forklift driver?" It was hard to keep sarcasm out of her voice. "Did you develop a passion for laser welding that I'm not aware of?"

"Well, no…"

"Then go over there and make sure nobody walks under those cranes."

He nodded, reluctant but obedient.

She watched Grady walk away, thinking how strange it was to see him on a construction site. He looked so out of place that it was comical. But at the same time, she was really touched that he had given up his morning off to help her.

"Is it always this crazy around here?" Justin asked, drawing her attention back to him.

"It's always pretty hectic, but today is especially crazy," Crystal said with a sigh. "The ship's four battery units were delivered this morning, and I have two days to get them installed and finish building the ship's hull so she can be moved into the water."

"The ship runs on batteries? How do they get recharged?" Justin asked.

"The outer layer of the hull is made of a bioregenerative skin material," she explained. "It pulls energy from the water that passes over it to kinetically charge the batteries. *Journey* will be the first ship of its size to function completely on clean energy."

"What about backups?"

"We do have a few backup generators, but hopefully we'll never need to use them. The ship can run at full power for about 100 hours on one fully charged battery, so with four batteries constantly being charged, we have a lot of built-in redundancies."

One of Justin's eyebrows went up. "It sounds pretty incredible. Why doesn't everyone use this kind of design?"

Crystal shrugged. "It's extremely expensive to manufacture, plus the installation is complicated and time-consuming. I just finished running all of the tests on it last year." Crystal could feel her cheeks growing warm. She really wasn't bragging, but a small part of her hoped that Justin was impressed. She wasn't sure why, but his opinion mattered to her.

"So you invented the ship's bioskin?"

She shrugged again, this time with modesty. "It was actually Captain Reed's idea—I just helped him develop it."

"Wow—" Justin started to say.

"Behind you!" Crystal called, interrupting him. She reached out, grabbed his shirt, and pulled him against her. A second later, a forklift flew by, just inches from where Justin had been standing.

"Thanks," Justin said softly.

"Don't mention it." Crystal didn't release her grasp on his shirt, and Justin didn't pull away. The noise of the construction site faded away as Crystal's eyes held Justin's. Her breathing slowed to match his so that their chests were rising and falling in unison. They were barely touching, but in that moment, Crystal felt like they were locked together.

"Are you two going to stand around all day, or are you going to do some work?" a rough-sounding voice broke in.

Crystal finally let go of Justin's shirt, turning to see who had called out to them. Under normal circumstances, she wouldn't have put up with one of the workers speaking to her like that, but this time, she felt like she needed to thank him. She and Justin were colleagues—she had to keep things professional, not swoon over him in public.

"I'm sorry, Commander," the man said quickly. "I didn't realize it was you."

"Don't worry about it." Crystal walked over to him. The more distance she put between herself and Justin, the easier it was to regain her composure. "Is there something I can help you with?"

"The last load of hull skin just arrived, and I could use someone to help unwrap and stage it. I don't really want to pull anyone away from the installation."

"Of course not. I have just the man for the job." Crystal waved Justin over. "Here—tell Ensign Anderson what you need him to do." Crystal gave Justin a quick nod before walking away.

She was distracted for the rest of the morning, catching herself spending more time watching Justin than coordinating the build teams. More than once, a team member had to repeat her name several times to get her attention. What was it about Justin that drew her to him? He was a nice guy, sure, but it had to be more than that. She had met plenty of nice guys over the years, and none of them affected her the way Justin did. This had to stop— her work was too important for her to be distracted.

She took a deep breath and tried to focus on the tablet she was holding. Her team was depending on her to give everything she had to the build, she knew. She was just starting to be able to concentrate again, but then she glanced up and caught Justin smiling at her as he stacked several panels of bioskin on a pallet. Crystal was about to return his smile when she heard Grady yelling from behind her. She hadn't heard what he said, but she had heard the panic in his voice. She spun to face him...

...and was horrified to see that one of the straps on the hoist had snapped, and the load of sheet metal dangling from the crane was swinging violently back and forth. The load came within inches of crashing through *Journey* before swinging away again. She was so relieved that it missed her ship that she didn't notice that the load was now swinging directly at her. Vaguely, she heard the snapping sound of one of the other straps breaking, but she didn't register what it meant.

The next thing she knew, she was laying on her back. The ground was still vibrating with the force of the load crashing to the ground just inches away from where she had been standing. A heavy warmth enveloped her: Justin. He had pushed her out of the way and shielded her with his own body. He had saved her.

For the second time that day, they were pressed tightly against one another. This time, though, Crystal refused to look him in the eye. "I'm all right. You can get off of me now."

Justin quickly got up and offered her his hand. She let him help her to her feet, but she made sure to pull her hand from his the second she had both feet on the ground. "Are you sure you're not hurt?" he asked.

"I'm sure." Crystal quickly scanned the build site to make sure no one else had been injured. The only casualties seemed to be several sheets of metal that had become twisted and bent in the fall.

"Crys!" Grady was running over to her. He looked her over quickly, then let out a deep breath. "Thank god Justin has quick reflexes! Why didn't you get out of the way when I yelled?"

She fidgeted, unwilling to tell him the real reason. "I guess I was distracted."

"You're working yourself to death," Grady said. His relief had clearly turned to frustration. "When was the last time you slept?"

Crystal was grateful that Grady was blaming her absentmindedness on her work and not Justin— otherwise, Grady might try to have Justin transferred. "That depends…what day is it again?" she said with a small smile.

"Look, we have bridge drills in a little while. Why don't you come with us? It'll take your mind off the construction, maybe give you a chance to recharge," Justin offered.

"I agree with Anderson." Grady stood next to Justin and crossed his arms.

Crystal shrugged. "Sure, why not? Maybe getting away from here for a few hours will help."

"It's nice of you to join us for once," Desi said to Wolf as she entered the training-turned-simulation room at the Academy that had been rebuilt to loosely resemble *Journey*'s bridge. Under normal circumstances, Desi had been told, they would have had at least a week to run drills on the ship before they launched, but given their accelerated timeline, the drills had been crunched into just a few days.

This was their third round of simulations, but it was the first time Wolf had shown up. Whenever Desi had asked why Wolf wasn't there, she was fed some line about the other woman having more important things to do.

That was a load of garbage, Desi thought. Her service record was longer than Wolf's, so if anyone should be excused, it was her. Granted, it had been several years since she had served on a ship—she had been serving as a Navy Seal for the past five years—but that was beside the point.

Wolf shot Desi a look, but she took a seat at the engineering station without saying anything. She hadn't spoken to Desi at all since they had left Reed's office. Desi took her silence as a sign that she was getting under Wolf's skin. She was excited for the opportunity to dig in a little deeper, and showing Wolf up during the simulation would be a great way to do it.

"Things must be going well at the build site if you're here," Dewite said to Wolf as he entered the bridge.

"Well enough. It was suggested to me that I take a break," Wolf said. Desi noticed that Wolf's eyes lingered on the back of Justin's head. She knew that Justin had a crush on Wolf, but was it possible that Wolf shared his feelings?

"All right, people, let's get started," Dewite said to the room at large. "Just like before, a random scenario has been loaded into the system. Even I don't know what it is. The scenario will only end once we have restored the ship to normal operating conditions or it's been destroyed." Dewite sat down in the captain's chair and started the program.

Desi looked down at her screen and waited. The first simulation, a head-on attack from an enemy ship, had happened right away. The second, a computer virus, had taken longer to start showing up. Desi hoped today's simulation wouldn't be some kind of mechanical breakdown that would give Wolf a chance to excel and leave Desi with nothing to do.

"Sir, I have several small objects I can't identify showing up on the sonar," Miguel Santiago said. He was the ship's communication officer and was covering sonar duties for Stiner, who was still at the build site.

"Put it on the main screen," Dewite said.

The screen in the front of the room came to life. Desi recognized the shadowy objects immediately. She almost wished she didn't.

"We're heading directly into a mine field," Desi said, making sure to keep her voice steady.

"Anderson, change course," Dewite ordered.

"No time, sir," Justin said.

The sudden vibration in Desi's chair when the first mine went off surprised her. The lengths they went to to make these simulations feel real was impressive. A second wave of vibrations followed the first—they must have hit another mine. Several screens around the room flashed red, indicating that their operators had been injured or killed.

"Damn it!" she heard Grady say next to her. His screen was flashing "Fatal Injury." He threw his headset down and stepped away from his station.

"Full stop! Now!" Wolf yelled as a third explosion shook the room. She had taken over the captain's chair. Dewite was now standing in the back of the room with his arms folded. Desi didn't know what kind of injury he had sustained, but apparently it was enough to take him out of the game. Now Desi was next in the chain of command—if Wolf went down, the ship was all hers.

"Price, damage report," Wolf ordered.

"Hull integrity is at 40%, and we are taking on water in sections 9, 15, and 32," Tyler said crisply.

"Evacuate those areas and shut them down."

"Yes, ma'am."

Desi looked around the bridge and saw that only a third of the crew was left at their stations: only one helmsmen and Justin remained at navigation stations, and Wolf was alone at the command stations. Now that Wolf was in charge, it was going to be a lot harder for Desi to surpass her performance, especially if Wolf managed to get them through the exercise without killing off the rest of the crew. Desi would have to figure a way out of this before Wolf did.

"Santiago, give me a scan of the minefield on the main screen," Wolf ordered.

A complicated web of mines appeared on the screen. They appeared to be random, but Desi knew better—there had to be some kind of pattern. She just had to find it.

"Anderson, can you get us out the way we came in?" Wolf asked.

"No, ma'am—the mines have filled in behind us. There's no way I can retrace our trajectory," Justin said.

"Not acceptable," Wolf said with a brief shake of her head. "Price, find us a path out."

"Shockwaves from the three explosions have pushed the mines outward, leaving a gap," said Price. "It's big enough for us to possibly pass through, but the path narrows again before we'd be out of the minefield."

"So we make the hole bigger," Desi said.

"What's your plan, Flint?" Wolf asked.

"If we blow up the mines ahead of us, they'll push the other mines out of the way, giving us a path out of here," Desi explained.

"The ship's hull can't handle another explosion," Wolf warned her. "We'll have to choose which mines we set off very carefully. Are you sure you can do it?"

"Of course I am."

Wolf didn't hesitate. "I'm transferring laser control from Grady's station to you. A 20% charge should be enough to detonate the mines," she said.

Desi swelled with pride. This was the moment she had been waiting for. "Price, tell us which mines we need to hit."

Price gave a quick nod. "I'm sending you the firing coordinates now. We need to be at least 150 meters away from the explosion—if we're not, we risk breaching our hull."

"With lasers at only a 20% charge, I'm going to need to be within 275 meters of the target to ensure detonation," Desi said. "That's cutting it pretty close."

"So we'll be careful. Anderson, can you and Gleason handle it on your own?" Wolf said to Justin and his one remaining helmsman.

"Yes, ma'am," Justin assured her.

"All right, Flint, fire lasers," Wolf ordered.

Desi held her breath as she fired. If she was off by even a few centimeters, she could hit the wrong mine and destroy the ship. She would be solely responsible for their failure.

She wasn't: the laser hit exactly where Desi had intended.

"Nice aim!" Wolf said. "Take us forward." Desi finally let herself breathe again.

They slowly moved through the minefield. The path was narrow, but Desi trusted Justin to get them through it. She was a little surprised to see that he was cutting it so close to the bottom of the opening, though, instead of taking the ship through the center of it.

"Anderson, your pitch is too steep. Don't forget to compensate for the decreased salinity on Neophia compared to Earth," Wolf said.

"Right... Purging ballasts slowly," Justin said. A few seconds later, they were centered within the gap and could easily move through it. It took them another ten minutes to get out of the minefield altogether.

A round of cheers erupted in the room when all of the screens turned green and flashed "Mission Success." Desi graciously accepted the congratulations she knew she deserved. The one person who should be thanking her the most, she thought, was Wolf. But even though Desi's plan had gotten them through the simulation, Wolf hadn't said anything to her. Instead, she was standing at the back of the room next to Dewite. Neither looked ready to join in the celebration.

"All right, everyone settle down," Dewite said. Desi instantly quieted, sure she was about to be publicly commended for her quick thinking and on-point targeting.

"Despite what those screens say, we lost today," Dewite said grimly. "If you were killed during the simulation, raise your hand."

Desi looked around the room and saw that more people had been killed than she had realized.

"Count them," Dewite said. "That's twenty-seven team members we lost during one mission. Twenty-seven families will be told their loved one isn't coming home. Does anyone know what the acceptable loss is for a mission?"

No one answered. Even Desi knew enough to keep her mouth shut.

Finally, Wolf spoke. "Zero. Any mission where we lose

someone is a failure," she said. "We only celebrate missions where everyone makes it home."

Crystal had no idea why she had accepted Justin's offer. She had had every intention of returning to the build site once the simulation was over, but here she was at Marco's diner, pretending to read a menu she knew by heart. She couldn't remember the last time she had actually sat at one of the tables rather than at the counter.

"You guys got pretty serious at the end of training today." Justin put down his menu, apparently preferring to focus on her.

"It is serious. It's too easy to forget what those red screens really mean." Crystal was relieved to be talking about work and not anything personal—she had feared Justin might have had other things on his mind when he asked her to dinner. Now her fears seemed silly, though. He was always so interested in learning about Neophia, and she was happy to tell him more about her homeworld. "I'm sure you've heard that sentiment before on Earth."

"Not really," he said, shaking his head. "As long as you accomplish the mission, they don't really care how many people they lose—there's always another team waiting to take your place."

Crystal hoped her face didn't betray her disgust. "That's awful! It must be hard to stay motivated with a mindset like that."

Justin looked more thoughtful than dismayed. "I honestly never really thought about it before today. That's just the way it is," he said.

Marco ambled out from behind the counter and came

over to their table. "What can I get you two?" he asked. He was giving Crystal an amused smile as he looked from her to Justin.

She knew he must think they were on a date. Would be rude to correct his misassumption? She didn't want to hurt Justin's feelings.

"Surprise me," she said, handing over her menu.

"I'll take whatever she's having," Justin said. They sat in awkward silence for a few minutes after Marco left. Crystal was trying to come up with a safe topic of conversation when Justin said, "You said your grandparents used to bring you here as a kid, right? Did you grow up around here?"

Crystal had wished he had asked her something less personal, something more related to her work or Neophia in general. She didn't want to talk about her past. Then again, at least he hadn't come right out and asked about her parents. "Kind of, I guess. I grew up in the Homestead colony."

"What's that?"

"It's an underwater colony a couple of miles off shore from here. A lot of military families live there—it gives them a sense of separation from the daily life of the military, but they're still close enough to report to base if there's an emergency," she explained.

Justin looked intrigued by the concept. "What's it like there? We don't have a lot of underwater colonies on Earth. The US goverment started to build a couple, but then they had to pull resources away from the construction to help with the war efforts," he said.

Good—Crystal could steer the conversation away from her childhood and talk about life in an underwater colony instead. That was a much safer topic. "Homestead is a bubble colony: it's mainly just homes, a small downtown area with some stores, one restaurant, and a couple of public parks. Nothing special."

"A 'bubble colony'?" he repeated.

"Imagine someone put a big glass dome over five or six city blocks and then put it on the bottom of the ocean." She shrugged. "Pretty simple, really."

"Are all underwater colonies like that?"

"No, there are also modular colonies that are pre-constructed on land before they're installed. They tend to be sturdier than bubble colonies, and they have more of an industrial feel — no outside spaces or anything like that. Then there are the built-in colonies. Those are usually associated with mining operations, and they're constructed directly into the side of a cliff or a mountain."

Marco interrupted her explanation with their food. "Here you go," he said as he set two identical plates down in front of Crystal and Justin. They each smiled in thanks.

"Do you have any family back on Earth?" Crystal asked as Marco headed back to the kitchen. She picked up her sandwich and took a bite. Juices exploded in her mouth, and a rich smokiness flooded over her taste buds.

Justin was looking at her cautiously. She guessed he hadn't recovered from the sinsari incident, and she didn't blame him. "It's chicken," she said, her mouth full.

Justin nodded, looking relieved. He happily took a bite of his own sandwich. "Yes, to answer your question, my parents and three younger sisters live on Earth."

"What made you leave?" Crystal asked as she nibbled at the orange and red kelp chips on her plate.

"I don't know… I've wanted to come here for as long as I can remember, I guess. I'd ultimately like to move my whole family here. Stop my sisters from having to fight in the wars, get them away from all the pollution so they can have an easier life."

"That's really sweet, Justin." Crystal made the mistake of meeting his eyes and felt herself being pulled in. She couldn't let Justin distract her, but she couldn't look away, either. A part of her wanted this dinner to never end.

Her thoughts were rudely interrupted with the arrival of Grady. "Why didn't you guys tell me you were coming here?" Grady said. He gave them both wide grins and plopped down at their table, grabbing a few of Crystal's kelp chips as he sat.

Crystal couldn't tell if she was happy or annoyed at the interruption. She stifled a sigh. At least Grady would keep her from getting lost again.

"It was a last-minute kind of thing...please, help yourself," Crystal said, rolling her eyes at Grady.

"You two have known each other a long time, huh?" Justin asked.

"About five years," Crystal said. "My first assignment was on the *Expedition*, where Grady was already serving."

"And then we did two years of counterterrorism work as a team," Grady chimed in. "You should see her lead a strike team into a terrorist stronghold. It's terrifying."

Crystal threw him an amused look. "It wasn't that big of a deal. Grady was the one in real danger. He would go undercover and try to get close to the organizational leaders to gather information. I was always afraid he would make some smartass remark and end up getting himself shot before he could get the intel back to me," she said as she pulled her plate out of Grady's reach.

"Did you ever do any undercover work?" Justin asked her.

"Are you kidding?" Grady threw his head back and let

out a laugh that filled the small diner.

"No, I never went undercover," Crystal said, ignoring Grady's outburst.

"Why not?" Justin asked.

Grady answered before she could. "Because Crystal is the worst liar on the planet—they would have seen through her cover in minutes. Whenever we had to meet in person during a mission, I was convinced she'd get me killed."

"So what made you get out of counterterrorism work?" Justin asked.

"I got hurt," Crystal said, silencing the last remnants of Grady's laughter. She knew he still felt incredibly guilty about what had happened on their last mission together. They had been assigned to dismantle the Church of Devine Clarity, the deadliest terrorist organization they had taken on. Grady had only been undercover with them about a month when his cover was blown. Crystal should have called off the mission, but instead, she had decided to strike before the Church had a chance to retaliate, in part because Grady had gotten them a detailed blueprint of the building they were using as their headquarters. Having that inside intel had made Crystal feel confident her team could bring down the organization.

It seemed that they had—everything had gone perfectly until they were leading the Church's founder out in handcuffs. They had thought they had won, and their guard was down. But she and her team should have known better. They hadn't gotten everyone out of the building, after all: a sniper had still been in hiding, and he had taken a shot at Grady. Luckily, Crystal had seen the flash of sunlight on the sniper's scope and had pushed Grady out of the way just in time. She was the one who was hit, and she had spent the next six months recovering in the hospital.

She told Justin an abbreviated version of the story, ending with, "Maybe it was a blessing in disguise, though."

"What do you mean?" Justin asked.

"*Journey* was just a dream at that point—nothing but doodles on scrap paper drawn in between missions. All that time in rehab made me focus on what the *Journey* could be, how I could take her from concept to reality. It's not like I had anything else to work on."

She smiled, remembering the excitement of coming up with the initial ship designs. "If it wasn't for that bullet, *Journey* wouldn't be here."

Chapter 8

The sun was just starting to set as Crystal left the smaller office she kept at the edge of the training field. Her team had long since gone home, but she had stayed behind to make a few calls to suppliers. She needed to rush already-rushed orders if she was going to have any chance of completing the construction of *Journey* on time.

The lights were on at the firing range, she was surprised to see. She had assumed she was the last person there. She headed towards the range, curious, and found Justin there. "What are you doing here so late?" she asked him.

He looked happy to see her. "I thought I'd get in some extra practice in while I can. It's been a while since I was on a ground combat unit, and I'm a little rusty."

"You're still one of the best shots on the team," Crystal said.

"I used to be better." Justin lined up his sights again and took a few shots. They all hit within an two centimeters of the target's center.

"Do you want some help?" Crystal asked. She set her

bag down, pulled out her gun, and positioned herself beside him. There were about a hundred different things she needed to get done before the end of the day, but she was happy to spend some time helping him.

"Sure." Justin stepped aside and let Crystal take his place in front of the target.

"Try holding it like this..." She held up her gun and fired a single shot, hitting the dead center of the target.

Justin whistled. "Impressive!"

"Thanks, I was lucky—had one of the best snipers in the LAWON military as my mentor," Crystal said, re-holstering her gun. "Why don't you try it again?"

This time, Justin made sure to mimic Crystal's stance, with Crystal giving him a few more tips before he fired. His shot landed closer to the center of the target.

"Much better," she said with a smile.

"You know, you're pretty good at this military stuff," Justin said.

"I should be, I've devoted every second of my life to it." Crystal leaned against the safety rail at the back of the firing range and looked at Justin. She really needed to get back to the build site, but she couldn't tear herself away— she felt herself come alive when she was with him, and she wanted to feed off of his positive energy for as long as she could. She would need it if she was going to make it through the evening's workload, she knew. They were putting *Journey* in the water tomorrow morning.

"How do you find time for anything else?" Justin asked.

"Like what?"

"Like friends, family, hobbies. You have to have something in life besides work." Justin holstered his gun, too.

"I hate to disappoint you, but my life isn't that complicated," she said.

"What do you mean?" Justin leaned on the railing next to her. His arm brushed lightly against hers. Had it been anyone else, she would have immediately adjusted her stance to break the contact.

"Work is my life—there isn't anything else." Crystal shifted to face him. She wondered how much she should/could tell him. It wasn't easy for her to open up to people, but the look in Justin's eyes made her feel like she could trust him. After all, she had been more open with him in the past week than she had with most people she had worked with for years. It was a strange feeling.

"I don't have any family," she finally said. "My parents were killed when I was young, but even when they were alive, they were never a constant in my life, they would only come home for a few days here and there in-between missions. They were rarely both home at the same time. My grandparents raised me, really, and they passed away when I was at the Academy."

She paused, briefly struggling not to react to the sympathy she saw on Justin's face. If she was going to tell him her life story, she was going to tell him in a dispassionate way. "Everyone I know is involved with the military in some capacity," she continued. "It's the only constant I have in my life. I don't have any friends outside of the service. If I have free time—and that's hardly ever— I work on ship designs or review combat missions."

Justin frowned. "You must get lonely," he said. There was a sadness in his voice that Crystal didn't understand. She knew her way of life wasn't for everyone, but it worked for her. She didn't need anyone feeling sorry for her. Especially not Justin.

"Not really," Crystal said, giving him a genuine smile. "I chose this life, and I'm happy with it."

"What about love?" Justin asked.

"Love's a fairytale, it only exists in stories," Crystal said, shrugging.

"You don't honestly believe that, do you?"

"I didn't always," she admitted.

"What changed?"

Crystal felt a twinge in her chest. Now they had entered dangerous territory. She knew she should end the conversation now, walk away before she said something she'd regret, but she didn't.

"I fell in love and learned what that word actually means," she said, again being careful to keep her voice even. "What it costs to be in love with someone. How it can destroy you if you're not careful." She stared across the firing range as she spoke, subconsciously noting the way the setting sun was casting long shadows across the field. Memories threatened to overwhelm her, but she pushed them back down.

"Maybe it wouldn't if you found the right person," Justin said.

She turned back to him. "I've never seen any evidence to support that theory. There's only one thing that comes with love and that's pain," she said stubbornly.

"Not always." Justin leaned towards her, and Crystal found herself mirroring his movements. By the time she realized what was happening, it was too late to stop it.

Justin gently pressed his lips against hers, and Crystal felt electricity building inside of her. For the briefest of moments, she kissed him back, but then her rational side kicked in, and she stepped away from him.

"I can't... I'm sorry. I have to go," she said quickly. She

tried not to run as she left the training field, not daring to look back.

tried not to run as she left the training field, not daring to look back.

"This is bad, Justin, really bad." Desi paced back and forth in front of Justin. She had known something was wrong the second he walked into the rec room with that stupid grin on his face. It hadn't taken much coaxing for him to tell her what had happened.

"What the hell were you thinking?" she said even though he hadn't responded to her last statement. He actually seemed proud that he'd kissed Wolf. He was clearly only half-listening to what she was telling him. How infuriating! She was just trying to help him. They had only been on this planet for a week, and he had already ruined things for himself.

Finally, he said something. "It's not like I planned to kiss her… We've been spending a lot of time together, and it just felt right." He shrugged.

"Why are you throwing away everything you've dreamed of for some girl you just met?" Desi fumed.

"She's not just 'some girl.' She's smart, talented, funny —"

"And she's your commanding officer!" Desi interrupted. It was driving her crazy that Justin couldn't see the bigger picture. "You're lucky she didn't report you to her commanding officer!" That was harsh, but Desi needed to get her point across. You couldn't just go around kissing your CO no matter how much time the two of you had been spending together.

"You make it sound like I assaulted her." Now Justin was the one who sounded defensive.

Desi took his tone as a good sign — at least he was

finally listening to her. "Did you?" she asked, keeping her voice low. Desi didn't care what the story would do to Wolf's reputation, but she didn't want it to destroy Justin's.

Fortunately, there were only a handful of people in the room, and for the most part no one was paying attention to them. Still, she saw Grady sitting in the corner concentrating a little too hard on the tablet in his hand. He wasn't looking in their direction, but she was sure he had heard everything, and she knew Wolf and Grady were friends. Would he be upset that Justin had kissed her?

"Come on, Desi, you know me better than that. It was an innocent kiss. Besides, she kissed me back."

Justin picked the worst time to say that—Price was just walking by. "Who kissed you back?" he asked.

Desi swallowed a sigh. Great, another involved party. This whole mess was spiraling out of control.

"Commander Wolf. He kissed Commander Wolf," she said, letting her anger get the better of her. He was going to find out, anyway—Justin wasn't exactly trying to keep it quiet.

"How many times do I have to tell you that it wasn't a big deal?" Justin said. "We were talking, we kissed, and then she left." He still had that goofy smile on his face.

Price's eyebrows had climbed nearly to the top of his forehead, but Desi couldn't tell if he was happily surprised or angry about the news. "I'm going to find her," he said, turning to leave.

"No, you're not," Desi said.

He turned back, a hard expression on his face. "But I'm her brother!"

"And you haven't spoken to her in years. I'm sure you're the last person she wants to see. Now sit down."

Reluctantly, Price took a seat next to Justin. "Both of you need to stop acting like you're back in high school," Desi said sternly, looking from one to the other. "You're military officers! Behave like it. Don't you think Commander Wolf has better things to do than deal with the two of you?"

"Why are you defending her? You don't even like her," Justin said.

"My personal feelings don't matter: she is our commanding officer, and you should treat her with the respect her rank demands," Desi said forcefully.

The lovesick smirk on Justin's face slipped away. She had finally gotten through to him.

Out of the corner of her eye, Desi saw Grady leaving the room.

Crystal moved briskly through the crowded corridors of *Journey* without any particular destination in mind — her only goal was to keep moving, to put as much distance between herself and Justin as possible. She wasn't even sure how she had ended up back at the build site. All she remembered was jumping on her bike and leaving the training center. Everything between then and now was a blank.

After wandering aimlessly for a while, she found herself alone in the crew mess. She sat down at one of the tables, but quickly rose to her feet again. There were too many thoughts running through her mind for her to be still.

How had things escalated so quickly? One moment they were talking, and the next... How had that happened? The worst part was that she had kissed him back, even if only for a moment. An intense moment. A moment that had awakened something inside of her that she thought had died a long time ago. This was exactly why she never let her guard down—it was safer to keep everyone at an arm's length. She stared up at the ceiling, lost in thought.

Eventually, she shook herself out of her reverie and dragged a ladder to the middle of the room. Before she climbed the ladder, she rummaged around in the building material that had been left in the room for a bundle of wire, her mind and body still on autopilot. She was on the ladder and halfway through removing a ceiling panel before she realized what she was doing: fixing the lighting circuits. This was good. Normal. This is what she was good at. Electrical work would require her full attention, and she would be forced to stop thinking about Justin.

Or so she had thought—she heard boots on the paneled floor and looked down to see Grady standing at the foot of the ladder. "So what happened?"

She sighed. How did he always know when something was going on with her? She appreciated his concern, but was glad he couldn't see the flush on her face. How could she tell him what happened, when she wasn't even sure herself?

"I don't know what you're talking about." Crystal tried to sound calm, but she was sure he could hear the panic in her voice. She was glad her head was buried in the ceiling. She wasn't sure she was ready to face anyone.

"Come on, Crys..."

"He kissed me, OK?" The words fell out of her mouth.

"I know," Grady said gently.

She reluctantly climbed down the ladder. "You do?"

"Yeah. I overheard Anderson telling Flint about it in

the rec room."

"Oh, that's just great." Crystal sat down on the bottom step of the ladder and put her face in her hands. This couldn't be happening. Everyone would know within an hour. Her reputation would be ruined. She had worked so hard to get where she was, and she had thrown it all away in a second.

"What are you doing here, anyway?" Grady pulled over a chair and sat down in front of her.

"Installing emergency lighting."

"That's not what I meant."

"I know." Crystal looked up at him. "I had to do something to stop thinking about what happened."

"The kiss was that bad?" Grady asked. Crystal thought she detected a slight laugh in Grady's voice even though his face remained calm and serious.

She hesitated before answering. "It wasn't bad, no…"

"Then what was it?"

"It was unexpected." Crystal choose her words carefully. It wasn't that she hadn't enjoyed the kiss. She had, more than she was willing to admit. It just never should have happened.

"That's for sure," Grady said. This time, he did laugh aloud.

"You're not helping," Crystal said.

"I'm sorry." Grady took a second to compose himself. "Why don't you walk me through what happened?"

Crystal got up and started to pace. She had to think rationally if she was going to make sense out of things. What had triggered the kiss? If she knew that, she could make sure it would never happen again.

"Justin had stayed after the training session to get some practice time in at the firing range," she began. "I offered to help him. We ended up talking."

"What were you talking about?"

"Just work, hobbies, life outside of the military. That kind of thing."

"You don't have a life outside of the military," Grady said.

"I'm aware of that." Crystal stopped pacing and turned to face him.

"There had to be something else," Grady probed. "Something to give him an indication that he could kiss you."

Crystal pursed her lips, thinking. "I might have brought up my parents and grandparents…"

Grady looked surprised. "You never talk about your family. Not even with me."

Crystal tried to ignore the hurt look that flashed across his face. She had been hurting him a lot recently. Her throat felt thick, so she coughed to clear it. "Well, um…then we started talking about love…"

"He told you he loved you?" Grady nearly choked on the words.

"Don't be ridiculous. We were talking more about the existence of love."

A long pause. "And then he kissed you?" Grady asked.

Crystal didn't like the disappointed way he was looking at her, as if her kissing Justin had somehow personally offended him.

"Yes." She didn't tell him that she had kissed Justin back. "I don't know what it is about Justin—he makes me feel."

"Feel what?"

"Just feel."

"Are you going to explore this? See if there's something

between you two?"

"Absolutely not!" she said more loudly than she had meant to. She forced calm into her voice. "I mean, I can't. I'm his commanding officer." She had to approach this logically: find the root cause of the problem, then put a fix in place that would prevent it from happening again. This was no different than troubleshooting a mechanical issue on a ship. Justin had kissed her because she had opened up to him. She had let him in. That could never happen again. She would maintain a sense of friendly professionalism when she was with him, of course—as she would with anyone—but there wouldn't be any more dinners at Marco's or late nights at the firing range. From now on, it would just be about work. She had plenty of practice at pushing her feelings down, after all.

"It's not against regulations for officers to date, you know," Grady pointed out. "You would just have to disclose it. I know Reed wouldn't have a problem with it as long as it didn't affect your work. You probably don't remember, but on the *Expedition*, Reed had a running log of who was dating who."

Crystal wondered how many times Grady's name appeared on that list. She sighed and pulled a chair over to him. "That's not the point." Now that she had figured out how to prevent another kiss from happening, she felt much calmer. "We both know military relationships never work."

"Yes, they can—look at your parents," Grady offered.

She nodded. "Exactly. Look at my parents. We spent very little time together as a family, my father cheated on my mom at least once—that I know of—and they ended up being murdered together."

Grady looked doubtful. "That's not what I was talking

about..."

"But it's true. My parents are the perfect example of why military relationships don't work." She felt focused again. It didn't matter that Justin kissed her or that she kissed him back—the simple truth was that love and the military didn't go together, and the military was her life. What she felt when she kissed Justin was irrelevant.

Grady threw up his hands in a gesture of surrender. "So what are you going to do about Justin, then? Have him transferred? Maybe sent back to Earth?"

Crystal frowned. "Of course not. We can just pretend like it never happened. I think that would be best for everyone."

"Right—that's the mature way to handle it."

She rolled her eyes at him. "I'm going to tell him that the kiss was a one-time thing, a mistake. I'm sure he'll understand. He probably feels the same way I do."

Chapter 9

Crystal had been at the build site for the past thirty-six hours. In the two days since she had kissed Justin, she had thrown herself into her work. That wasn't that hard to do—the workload had increased substantially now that *Journey* had been moved to the holding bay.

Crystal was only slightly surprised to see Justin standing in the corner of the launch bay when she walked in. She had done a good job of avoiding him during training yesterday, but she knew that eventually they would have to talk about the kiss. A quick glance at her watch told her combat training had ended three hours ago. Had Justin been waiting for her all that time? He didn't make a move towards her even though she was sure he had seen her. No sense in delaying the inevitable... She steeled herself and walked towards him.

"Ensign Anderson, is there something I can help you with?" The formal greeting felt strange, but Crystal knew it was necessary—she had to maintain her distance.

"We missed you at training today," Justin said. Crystal had asked Grady to lead combat training for the last few days. They were focusing on identifying Sertex soldiers when they were camouflaged, and no one could teach that better than Grady. He had the strongest Sertex blood of anyone she had ever worked with.

"Yeah, sorry. I've had a lot of things going on here that needed my attention." Crystal couldn't quite meet Justin's eyes. Could he tell she was lying? She hoped not. "How did it go? Were you able to ID the Sertex?"

He nodded. "By the end of the day, almost everyone had mastered it."

She felt a half-smile come to her lips. "Grady's a good teacher when he wants to be."

"We need to talk," Justin said.

"About what?" She could only hope that he would adopt her pretend-like-it-never-happened strategy.

He was keeping his expression neutral. "You know what about. But I can see that you're working."

"I'm always working," she said, finally meeting his gaze.

"So maybe later tonight, after you've finished here? I could meet you somewhere."

"I'm probably going to be here all night." At least this time she wasn't lying to him.

"Could you take a break? I think it's important that we talk."

He was right, of course. She couldn't avoid him forever. The sooner they figured this out, the easier things would be for both of them.

"OK, but not here." The bustling launch bay wasn't the best place to have a private conversation. Crystal was certain that the whole crew had heard about the kiss — she didn't need them to know all the details of the fallout as well.

She headed out of the launch bay with Justin following her. They walked in silence until she found an empty room. "In here," Crystal said as she held the door open for him. They entered the dimly lit room, and she made sure that the door was shut behind them.

She turned to look at him expectantly, not willing to be the first to speak.

"When we kissed," he began awkwardly, "well, I've...I've never felt anything like that before. It was like I didn't know what being alive meant until that moment." He hesitated, clearly uncomfortable. "Did you feel any of that?"

She had to admire his straightforward approach—it obviously wasn't easy for him to talk about what had happened, either, yet he had taken the plunge anyway. Still, she couldn't let herself start talking about her own feelings.

"What I felt doesn't matter," she said.

"Of course your feelings matter," he protested. Crystal turned away. She didn't want to come across as cold, but she knew her emotions would get the best of her if she looked at him for too long.

"Look, I'm not trying to push you into saying anything. I'm just trying to understand what happened." Justin reached out and touched her shoulder, gently turning her back towards him. "I think there's something real between us," he said. "But if it's all in my head tell me and I'll back off."

Crystal cursed the kind eyes that met hers. She had made her decision—she couldn't allow herself to waver. "It's more complicated than that. This job makes everything more complicated."

"It doesn't have to." Justin reached out his hand to her.

It was a sweet gesture, but she didn't reciprocate.

"Yes, it does," she insisted. "We're military officers — it's not like we get to punch out at the end of the day and leave our work at the office. Too many people are depending on us. If we lose focus even for just a second, people could die. I'm not willing to risk having our relationship wind up compromising our work."

She could tell that Justin was trying to hide his feelings, but he wasn't as well-practiced at it as she was. The carefree smile he usually wore when he was with her wavered, and when it returned, much of its previous warmth was gone.

"What I told you before we kissed hasn't changed," she went on. "I'm sorry, but I know that relationships and military life can't coexist. You can only have one, and I chose the military a long time ago. It's nothing personal. It's just the way things have to be."

Justin pressed his lips together and nodded. "I guess I should go, then." He didn't look at her as he made his way to the door.

"Justin!" Crystal wasn't sure why she called after him. The least she could do was to let him leave on his own terms.

He paused, his hand hovering over the door knob. "I am sorry it has to be this way," she told him. "I really do enjoy spending time with you. Maybe we can find a way to be friends. Eventually."

His shrug wasn't convincing. "Maybe one day." The door clicked shut behind him.

Crystal was exhausted, physically and mentally. She couldn't remember a more trying day in her entire career.

Right after her uncomfortable conversation with Justin, she was needed in the ship's engine room, and from there, she went from one team leader to another — it seemed as if everyone had issues they couldn't solve without her help. Still, she was grateful for the unending stream of tasks that kept her from thinking about her conversation with Justin and the way she had hurt him.

It was close to midnight by the time she made her way to the small cafeteria on the build site. She hadn't eaten anything since lunch and was hoping to find something in the vending machines to sustain her.

Tyler was sitting alone at a table in the corner, so absorbed in his computer that he didn't notice her enter. She could have left without him knowing she was there, but she found something comforting about his presence. Besides, she had promised Reed she would give Tyler a chance, and she had yet to live up to that promise.

"Working a little late tonight?" Crystal said as she walked past him, heading to the wall of vending machines.

Tyler looked up and smiled. "You're one to talk."

"This is a normal night for me." Crystal made her selection: ham sandwich rather than tuna salad. Too bad the vending machines weren't as well-stocked as Marco's diner.

She took her food to Tyler's table and collapsed into the chair across from him.

"Long day?" he asked with a small laugh.

"You have no idea." She took a bite of her sandwich. As she had feared, it was dry and tasteless.

"You want to talk about it?"

"Not really. What are you working on?"

"I'm programming your bridge." Tyler entered a few

more commands before closing his laptop and setting it aside.

"Don't stop on my account," Crystal said between bites. Her hunger made the sandwich marginally acceptable.

"I could use a break, actually. It's some of the most complicated coding I've ever done." He gave her an aggrieved look.

She tried to look innocent. "Sorry."

"You do realize it's not generally necessary to recode every standard program LAWON uses on its ships" he trailed off delicately.

"*Journey* needs to have more flexibility than what standard programs offer." She put down her sandwich, suddenly concerned. "You will be able to get it done, won't you?" If Tyler couldn't get the bridge programmed before the launch date, they were done. She wouldn't put *Journey* out in open water without the extra defenses he was building into the system.

He patted his laptop. "Yes," he assured her, "I'll get it done."

"Good." Crystal shifted in her seat and accidentally sent a jolt of pain through her side. Her ribs still hadn't fully healed from her encounter with Flint earlier in the week. Dr. Emerson had said it could take weeks for them to fully heal and had recommended rest to help them heal faster. Crystal had tried not to laugh when the doctor had told her that, although she had accepted pain medication. Unfortunately, though, she'd forgotten to take any since the morning. She tried to hide her wincing and hoped that Tyler didn't notice—she hated showing any sign of weakness.

"How are you feeling after the fight with Flint?" Tyler

asked. So much for masking her pain.

"I'll be fine—it's really not a big deal. I've been through worse."

"I know."

"Have you been checking up on me or something?" Crystal found that comment a little disturbing. Having an older brother she didn't talk to was one thing, but having a brother she didn't talk to but who had been following her life from afar was kind of creepy.

"No, not really, but they teach us some of your counterterrorism missions at the Academy. Including your last one."

"Well, that's just great." Crystal hated the idea of her past work being dissected in a classroom. Especially her last mission, when she had been shot. She could almost hear smug voices discussing what they would have done differently to avoid ending up in the hospital. As if it had been that simple.

"How did you end up at the Academy, anyway?" she asked, changing the subject. "The last time I saw you, you were on your way to some computer college or something like that."

"You mean the University of Lacordon? The most prestigious computer science school on Neophia," Tyler said.

"Yeah, that. What happened with that?" she asked, then took another bite of her sandwich.

"I graduated at top of my class, was headhunted by several of the biggest tech companies in Kincaron and started working with one of them right after graduation," he said modestly.

"It sounds like you got everything you wanted. What changed, then?" Crystal asked. She was feeling a lot more relaxed now that they were no longer talking about her.

Tyler sighed. "The realization of what my life had become. I was spending all of my time behind a desk, surrounded by stark walls, and the only personal interaction I had was when someone called with a computer problem. I was basically an overpaid computer repair guy. One day I just couldn't take it anymore, so I quit and applied to the Academy. I wanted to do something that would actually make a difference, you know?"

She nodded. "I do. It couldn't have been easy, though, leaving everything behind to join the military."

Tyler smiled. "I've never been big on easy."

"What about friends and family? Do you have a partner?" She leaned towards him slightly. "Do I have any nieces or nephews running around out there?" Crystal had forgotten how easy it was to talk to Tyler. The very first time they had met, their connection had been strong and instantaneous. She was surprised by how quickly they were recapturing that.

"No, I haven't made you an aunt," he said with a small laugh. "But there was a girl in college…we were together for years. I really loved her."

"What happened?"

Tyler's expression went from wistful to grim. "She started to develop radical ideologies. As you can imagine, that put a strain on our relationship, so eventually, I left. Later, I heard that she joined an organization that was responsible for a string of consulate bombings."

"The Neophian Liberation Army?" Crystal asked. She noticed that he didn't use the word "terrorist." It must be easier to deal with losing someone to an "organization" instead of a "terrorist group." Too bad she hadn't thought of that when she lost Ryan.

"How did you know that?" Tyler asked.

She nudged him. "Didn't you pay attention in class? I worked counterterrorism—I led the raid that took out their home base."

Tyler looked surprised. "Well, I guess they didn't teach every single one of your missions at the Academy."

"Do you still have feelings for her?" Crystal asked. That was something she had struggled with for a long time after she lost Ryan, until it became easier to just feel nothing at all. Maybe Tyler would be able to explain it to her in a way she hadn't been able to figure out herself.

"A part of me will always have feelings for her," he said, sadness shading over his words. She knew exactly how he felt. "I mean, I loved her, and nothing can change the time we had together. That doesn't mean I want her back, of course—breaking up was the right choice."

"How do you move on?" Crystal pressed. "After everything she must have put you through, how do you get past it?"

Tyler paused a moment, then shrugged. "I don't know, honestly. Time helps. I think the biggest thing for me was realizing that her decision to join the NLA didn't have anything to do with me. It was completely separate from our relationship. I didn't force her to join or push her towards it—in fact, she kept it from me for a long time. Looking back, the fact that she didn't trust me enough to share that part of her life with me was probably the biggest indicator that we weren't meant to last. Does that make any sense?"

"More than you know." Crystal said slowly, thinking. The similarities between Tyler's past relationship and her own was shocking. Maybe their father's DNA carried more than strong Aquinien traits and an urge to join the military: maybe their shared DNA was what made them fall for the wrong person.

A comfortable silence settled on them until Tyler finally broke it. "Enough about me—what else have you done during the last ten years? It was like you disappeared once you went to the Academy."

"After grandma and grandpa died..." Crystal's voice trailed off. Did Tyler know they had died? He hadn't made an appearance at either of their funerals. She hadn't told him the news—she'd become so withdrawn after losing them both in such a short period of time that she honestly couldn't remember much of the months that had followed.

"I know," Tyler said softly. He didn't offer any explanation for his absence, and Crystal didn't ask for one. Nothing either of them said could change the past.

Crystal cleared her throat. "Anyway, I got permission to do an advanced program at the Academy. I took classes year-round and graduated a year early. After graduation, I was placed on the *Expedition* under Captain Reed, which is where I met Grady. I served there for about a year and then was assigned to lead a counterterrorism strike team...and that's what I did pretty much up to the start of *Journey*'s construction."

He raised his eyebrows at her. "And you? Do you have anyone special in your life?"

Crystal made sure her voice was flat and calm. "There was someone once, yes, but it didn't work out." For a brief moment she thought about elaborating, but then quickly came to her senses. She wasn't ready to talk about Ryan, not even with Tyler.

"I heard Flint made you her second," she said before

Tyler could ask any follow-up questions.

"She did, although I'm not sure what she's thinking. I don't have any field experience." A blush formed on Tyler's cheeks.

"I'm sure you'll do great. Leadership is about more than practical experience." Crystal gave Tyler an encouraging smile that prompted his face to return to its natural color. "Hey, I meant to ask you earlier: what's your submersion time?"

"Huh," Tyler said, clearly caught offguard by the change of topic. He paused. "I can easily go six hours, eight if I push it. Why?"

"I could use your help after training tomorrow. If you're up for it, that is."

"What kind of 'help'?" he asked cautiously.

"It's nothing dangerous, I promise," she said with a small laugh. "We're flooding *Journey*'s holding bay tonight. I want to conduct a visual inspection of the outer hull once she's wet, and I could use an extra set of eyes. It shouldn't take more than four or five hours."

Now he looked eager. "Count me in."

"Great," Crystal said, rising to her feet. "I'm going to head back to my apartment and try to get a few hours of decent sleep. I'll see you tomorrow." She grabbed her now-empty plate and headed towards the nearest disposal receptacle.

"Hey, Crys!" Tyler called after her.

She turned. "Yeah?"

"What's your submersion time?"

"Fourteen to sixteen hours," she said with a smile. She tucked the plate into the receptacle and walked out.

Chapter 10

Crystal heard a noise at her office door and looked up to see Tyler standing there. "So, who's ready for a swim?" Tyler said as he stepped into the office.

She burst out laughing at the sight of his neon-yellow swim trunks. "What are you wearing?" she asked, trying to catch her breath.

Tyler glanced down at his outfit. "What's wrong with it?"

"Besides the fact that you look like you're ready for a rousing game of beach volleyball?"

"It's all I had," he said defensively.

"Then it's a good thing I picked this up for you." Crystal tossed him a bag.

He pulled out a thin black wetsuit and looked at her, confused. His confusion was understandable — normally, Aquiniens tried to have as much skin exposed to the water as possible, because that made it easier for their skin to pull oxygen out of the water and increased the amount of time they could stay underwater.

"It's made of a special material that lets the water pass

through easily," she said with a wide grin. "Trust me, you'll feel like you aren't wearing anything."

"Hmm..." He was moving the material through his fingers, examining it carefully. "Where did you get it?"

"I have some connections in the purchasing group from my days on the strike team. That's a classified military grade material designed specifically for Aquinien fighters. It will also dampen shock waves from an explosion and reduce the effects of a gunshot. I ordered one for every Aquinien on the combat teams."

"Flint's team, too?"

She nodded. "Yes, Flint's team, too. Now go get changed and meet me down at the dock in ten minutes."

He nodded back, then disappeared. She finished a few things in the office before heading down to the dock to gather the things they would need.

A thrill of excitement ran through Crystal as she got their equipment ready. Recently, she hadn't had much time to spend in the water, and she missed it. Although to her surprise, what she was really anticipating was spending the afternoon with Tyler. Swimming was one of the first things they had bonded over—it would be nice to do it again.

She spotted Tyler heading towards her with a big smile on his face. "Better?" he asked. He stopped in front of her and turned to show off his new outfit.

"Much better. Now, how about some accessories?" she said as she attached a small computer to his forearm. "This will automatically detect temperature and pressure anomalies around the ship."

"What exactly are we looking for?" he asked as he studied the computer attached to his arm. Crystal should have known that would be his favorite part of the process.

"Anything that might indicate a weakness in the ship's integrity." She attached an identical computer to her own arm.

"Thanks for clearing that up," he said wryly.

She made a face at him and then walked to the edge of the bay. "Let's just get in the water and start looking."

They dove into the water in unison. Crystal closed her eyes and focused on the water passing over her skin, feeling the usual second of protest from her lungs before her Aquinien skin took over her respiration functions.

She opened her eyes and smiled. She had forgotten the way water could wash away all of her stresses and frustrations. At that moment, she was simply one with the water around her.

Tyler was swimming in large circles in front of her, reminding her of the time they had spent swimming as teenagers. It was nice to see that some things hadn't changed.

She shot forward, cutting him off, and they raced across the ocean floor as they pushed each other to go faster and deeper. Tyler caught up with her after a few minutes and motioned to *Journey*'s looming outline. She smiled at the sight of the ship. To her, its curved edges and the steel-blue color of its skin make it look alive.

They started their inspection at the nose and slowly worked their way back to the stern, noting minor imperfections and small pinhole leaks on the seams as they went. Fortunately, nothing Crystal saw was overly concerning. A repair team would be able to take care of it all.

They had completed about half of their inspection when Crystal's wrist computer started to vibrate. Glancing down at it, she saw they had been under for four hours. She decided they should head to the surface—no sense in pushing Tyler's submersion limit when they could finish the inspection tomorrow.

She swam over to him and tapped his arm, drawing his attention away from the external piping he was examining. The look he gave her made her feeling of satisfaction immediately dissipate: his eyes communicated alarm. He held up his computer to show her that the pressure readings coming from the pipe were climbing rapidly.

She took a closer look at the pipe. As one of the main air supply lines for the ship, it shouldn't be generating any pressure whatsoever. Her own internal alarm bells started clanging as she exchanged worried looks with Tyler.

A sudden explosion burst the pipe, sending out a steady jet of pressurized air and violently pushing Crystal and Tyler away from *Journey*. Luckily, Crystal was able to quickly get her somersaulting under control and reorient herself. She began frantically scanning the area for Tyler.

When she saw him, her shock intensified: he was lying unmoving on the ocean floor. She had to fight the urge to hyperventilate—if she panicked, she would be of no use to anyone. Things were bad enough already without her drowning. She had to pull herself together.

During her Academy training, she had learned how to handle situations like this, and she had to trust in that training now: take one thing at a time and block everything out except the most critical task. The first thing she needed to do was get Tyler to the surface. If he regained consciousness while still underwater, she knew, his body would try to take in air through his lungs rather than his skin and he would drown.

She swam to him as fast as she could, careful to avoid

the jet of pressurized air coming from the broken pipe. He was alive, she saw with relief. A large gash had appeared on his forehead, and although it looked bad, she didn't think it was life-threatening. She wrapped an arm around him and pulled him to the surface.

She laid his limp body on the dock's hard surface and pulled out her communicator. Were his lungs going to take over his breathing now that he was out of the water? She wasn't sure. "I need an emergency medical team sent to the dock immediately!" she half-gasped, half-yelled.

Crystal glanced back down at him. He wasn't breathing, but his skin was damp. Good — so his body was getting at least a little oxygen. Her own panicked breathing started to even out. But what about the teams working on *Journey*'s interior? They had been having issues with the alarm system for days. They might not have realized that their air supply was quickly draining into the ocean.

She activated her communicator again. "Stiner! Section 17 of the air supply is compromised. Evacuate the ship."

Her gaze fell back on Tyler. How long would it take the medical team to arrive? She had to get his lungs working, she decided. She began to perform CPR, schooling her mind into stillness so that she could focus on compressions and breaths. If she let herself think about whose life she was trying to save, she wouldn't be able to do it. She had just gotten Tyler back in her life. Losing him now would destroy her.

Crystal didn't realize the medical team had arrived until they were pulling her off of her brother to take over doing CPR. She collapsed onto the dock, her hands shaking and her heart racing. Was he going to make it? The entire team was clustered around him, blocking her view.

It seemed like an hour passed before she heard him coughing. She crawled over to him.

"I thought you said this wouldn't be dangerous," Tyler croaked when he saw her. Her fear was instantly replaced by overwhelming relief. She couldn't stop a laugh from escaping her lips. He was going to be all right.

Crystal stayed with him until he was placed on a stretcher and taken to medical for additional testing. That was just a standard precaution, the paramedic assured her.

She nodded reluctantly as she watched them leave with Tyler. She had to trust them — she had other things to take care of now. Given that she had ordered an evacuation of *Journey*, some people were going to be looking for answers.

Crystal headed directly to the mustering area, not even bothering to change out of her swim gear. Team leaders were standing among the groups of people taking roll call, she noticed. At least the emergency procedures appeared to be working.

She set her sights on the white pop up tent that had been set up to act as the incident command center, standard practice for all emergencies. All voices ceased as soon as she stepped inside. Clearly, they had all been waiting for her arrival.

"Are you all right?" Reed asked her.

"Yes, sir, I'm fine. Did everyone make if off the ship OK?" Crystal asked.

Stiner nodded. "We got everyone out in time. A few people are complaining of shortness of breath and headaches, so the medical team is checking them out now."

"Good."

"Can you tell us what happened?" Reed asked.

"Ensign Price and I were performing a visual inspection of *Journey*'s hull," she began. "We were about to resurface when Price noticed some irregular pressure readings coming from one of the air supply pipes. A few seconds later, the pipe ruptured."

"Where is Price?" Flint asked.

"He was knocked unconscious by the blast, but the paramedics were able to revive him. They're taking him to medical for tests, but they believe he will be fine." Crystal was only vaguely aware of the robotic tone of her voice.

"That's convenient. Now he might not be able to participate in the competition tomorrow. That will give your team an edge," Flint said.

"You think I did this on purpose!" Crystal exclaimed. She felt a rage rising in her that she hadn't felt in a long time. "Tyler could have died, and you're concerned about some stupid training exercise? What is wrong with you?" Crystal was losing control. Her hands were starting to shake and she could feel her throat contracting. She couldn't tell if she wanted to cry, scream, or punch Flint in the face.

"Why was he even there in the first place?" Flint asked.

"I asked him to help me." Crystal was having a hard time getting her eyes to focus on her surroundings. She could feel herself slipping away, and there was nothing she could do to stop it.

"So you are responsible," Flint said flatly.

"Anderson, get her out of here! Now!" Reed cut in.

Crystal hadn't noticed Justin standing on the other side of the tent, but now she watched him grab Flint's arm and pull her out of the tent. It seemed like she was viewing the entire scene through tinted glass.

Crystal felt frozen. Flint was right: she was responsible. Tyler had had no reason to be there. He wasn't even on the build team. Her reasons for asking him to inspect the ship with her had been completely personal—she had wanted to bond with him again, to relive something they had loved to do together as teenagers. He was the only family she had left, and her selfishness had almost cost him his life. It was her fault.

Crystal felt someone's hands clenching her shoulders, but she was having a hard time focusing on the face that was now inches from her own.

"Hey, kid, look at me."

She knew that voice. Grady. Crystal's eyes darted back and forth until she was finally able to lock her gaze on his.

"This was not your fault," he said slowly and clearly. "Do you understand me?"

She made herself focus on his calming eyes, putting all of her faith in his bright green gaze. He could get her through this. They had brought each other back from the edge before.

"This was not your fault," he repeated. "It was an accident. You did not cause this."

The pressure he was putting on her shoulders was helping her recenter herself. Crystal felt her heart rate starting to slow.

"Come back," Grady said patiently. "You got this, all right? You can handle this."

She nodded and reached up to place her hands on his shoulders, mirroring him. "Thanks," she whispered. She only released him after she was sure she was back in control.

Taking a deep breath, she turned towards the rest of the command staff. "Let's figure out how to patch that hole in my ship." Her hands were steady again. The others nodded, their expressions calm.

Crystal walked over to the table, where Stiner had already pulled up a 3D schematic of *Journey*'s exterior. "This whole section of piping will need to be replaced," she said, pointing at the affected area. "As soon as that's done, we can start pumping in breathable air again and then try to figure out what caused that section to become pressurized in the first place."

Reed nodded. "Sinter will oversee the repair team," he said.

"I can do it, sir," Crystal said.

"I know you can, but you've been through enough today."

Crystal started to protest, but Reed cut her off. "I want you go get checked out by Dr. Emerson, and then I want you to go home and rest."

Crystal simply nodded and left the tent. She didn't have it in her to argue.

"What the hell was that?" Justin demanded. He released Desi's arm once they were out of earshot of the others.

"What's the big deal?" Desi said, rubbing her arm. Justin had a surprisingly strong grip.

"Here we are in the middle of an emergency, and you're picking fights with a senior officer in front of the entire command team! Do you want to get yourself court-martialed?" Justin snapped.

Desi hadn't really given much thought to the consequences of her words. On Earth, her reputation would have protected her from any kind of punishment. All she had been trying to do was capitalize on Wolf's moment of weakness. To give her team an edge over their competition. That's what a good leader did, after all: guarantee their team's success.

She waved a hand dismissively. "That wasn't really an emergency." she scoffed. "The evacuation was successful—no one was hurt, and once they patch that pipe, the ship will be as good as new."

"You don't even care that Price was hurt, do you?" Justin was glaring at her with his arms folded across his chest.

"Of course I do!" Desi said indignantly. "He's an important member of my combat team, and I need him at his full strength. But you heard Wolf—the medics said he'll be fine."

"That doesn't make it OK for you to go after Wolf," he said, his voice still edged with anger.

Desi tried not to roll her eyes. "You make it sound like I attacked her. I just called her out. It's not my fault she couldn't handle it."

"You used to stand up to bullies, not be one," Justin said.

"You're just mad that I proved how incompetent Wolf is! A few harsh words thrown in her direction, and she has a full-on panic attack. That's not who I would want leading me into combat," Desi said. She hated that Justin wasn't on her side. He should be thanking her for showing Wolf's true colors, not haranguing her for it. Desi's actions might have saved his life—at least now he would be prepared if Wolf lost her self-control on the battlefield.

"You have no idea what's she's been through." Justin was still glaring.

"Oh, and you do?" She raised her eyebrows and crossed her own arms. "Come on, Justin, we've all had teammates who were killed in action. It's part of the job. I don't see you breaking down into a hyperventilating mess because I brought it up."

"Captain Reed wouldn't have given her a combat team if she couldn't handle it." Now Justin didn't seem to know what to do with his hands—he kept alternating between running them through his hair, waving them in the air, and clenching them into fists at his side. Desi had never seen him this angry before. She should probably back down a little, she knew, but backing down wasn't in her nature.

"You're only standing up for her because of your childish crush. I'll let you in on a little secret: she doesn't have feelings for you," she said. It felt good to finally tell him that. "You can stop protecting her."

"This isn't about Wolf," Justin said, almost biting off his words. "This is about you making a fool of yourself in front of your commanding officers. You aren't untouchable here, you know."

"I never said I was."

He shook his head, his angry expression shading into disappointment. "You've changed since we've come to Neophia. I don't know what you're trying to prove, but I don't like the person you are anymore."

Justin turned and walked away. Desi tried to think of a witty remark to say to his back, but she came up blank. She just stood, watching him, then started walking back to the dorms on her own.

Crystal had been staring at her reflection in the glass door of the medical facility for at least five minutes. Dr. Emerson had given her a quick checkup and cleared her, saying she just needed some rest. She knew she should go back to her apartment, but first, she had to make sure Tyler would be all right.

Grady's voice jarred her away from her reflection. "I figured I'd find you here," he said as he walked over to her.

"I know I should go in there and see how he's doing — I need to make sure he's all right — but I can't get myself to go in." She didn't turn away from the doors as she spoke. "When I look at those doors, I don't see a place to heal, a place where people walk out whole again." Her voice lowered. "I see Grayson and Pruitt who went in and never came back out. I see Dax who was gone before we even got him over the threshold. I see the eight factory workers the NLA sniper gunned down before McKenna got a clean shot at him. I see the twenty-seven primary school kids that didn't make it home because it never occurred to me that the Church of Divine Clarity would target school buses."

When Grady spoke, his voice was equally soft. "I get it. The world on the other side of those doors is a cruel and unpredictable place, a place where you can be laughing with a friend one second and then in the next be surrounded by doctors who are trying to get your friend's heart beating again."

He paused before continuing, obviously just as sunk in his memories as she was sunk in hers. "Trust me, I know. I've spent far too much time at the bedside of a friend who was fighting for her life after she took a bullet that was meant for me," he said.

Crystal finally turned to look at him. "Jim, when are you going to let that go? It wasn't your fault."

"And what happened to Price wasn't yours, but that doesn't take away the guilt, does it?"

"No. No, it doesn't." Crystal left the entrance and walked over to the stone half-wall to lean against it.

Grady joined her, putting his arm around her. She gently rested her head on his shoulder, once again grateful for his presence. "We've been through some crazy stuff together, haven't we?"

"Yes, we have," Grady said.

"Do you think it ever gets easier?"

"I doubt it, but we keep doing it anyway."

"Why do you think that is?" Crystal asked, lifting her head to look at him. "Why do we keep putting ourselves through this?"

He ventured a smile. "Because it's worth it. We volunteered to bear the burden of making the planet a safer place. I think we handle it better than most people can."

She sighed. "I didn't handle things very well back there—I can't believe I lost control in front of the entire command team. Maybe I'm not cut out for combat missions anymore."

"The doctors wouldn't have given you a passing score on your psych exam if they didn't think you could handle it," Grady said, trying to reassure her.

She appreciated his words, but she didn't agree. "Doctors can be wrong," she said.

"We all have demons that we deal with on a daily basis," he insisted. "You probably have more than most, but you keep fighting anyway. Any one of us would have struggled in that situation. Plus, Flint was egging you on. You should have seen Reed after you left—he was pissed."

She felt her face harden. "That's no excuse. I should have been able to keep it together long enough to get the job done. I could have fallen apart once I was alone." Crystal slightly shifted herself against the wall. The stones were digging into her thighs, but she didn't mind—the pain was keeping her grounded.

"You think you can hide behind that tough exterior you show the world," Grady said gently. "You wear it everywhere you go, like it will protect you, but I know the truth." His arm around her tightened.

"Oh, yeah? What's the truth," she asked with a small smile.

"That you feel things more profoundly and deeply than anyone I've ever met, even if you hate to show that side of yourself."

"That's because it's my greatest weakness."

He shook his head. "That's where you're wrong. It's one of your greatest strengths."

Crystal let Grady's words settle in. He might be right—he did know her better than anyone else did, after all. What harm could come from being a little more open with her emotions? Not with everyone, of course, but with the few people who were close to her.

"I don't know what I would do if I had lost him…. I mean, it's hard every time we lose a teammate, but it's different with Tyler." Crystal rested her head on Grady's shoulder again.

"He's your brother," Grady agreed.

"I don't think I could have survived it."

She felt him half-turn as he nudged her head off of his shoulder. "Thankfully, we don't have to worry about that." His voice had gone from serious to joyful.

Curious, she looked up to see that Tyler had just walked out of the hospital looking annoyed but otherwise perfectly healthy. "Tyler," she cried, running to him and throwing her arms around his neck. "I'm so relieved," she said into his chest.

"Hey, it's OK—I'm fine," Tyler said. If he was surprised by her outward display of affection, he didn't say so. He simply returned the pressure of her hug as he held her.

"What did the doctors say?" Grady asked.

"They couldn't find anything wrong, and believe me, they tried. I'm clear to return to active duty in the morning."

"Flint will be thrilled," Crystal said under her breath, finally releasing him.

"Why?" Tyler asked.

"Never mind—doesn't matter. I'm just glad you aren't hurt. I couldn't live without myself if something had happened to you."

"You know it was an accident, right? It wasn't your fault that the pipe exploded," Grady said for what had to be the hundredth time.

"He's right, Crys, there was nothing you could have done to stop it," said Tyler.

"I could have gotten you out of there sooner. I could have pushed you out of the way the second I realized the pipe was going to blow. I could have—"

Tyler interrupted her. "No, you couldn't have. There wasn't any time to do any of that."

She took a deep breath. "You're right," she said,

shaking her head slightly. She wouldn't let herself go down that dark path again. Opening herself up a little bit was one thing, but she didn't want to risk losing control again. Grady was partly wrong—letting your emotions take over wasn't a sign of strength. She was a military officer, and she would act like one.

"How about we get you back to your apartment?" Grady said.

Crystal chose to ignore the worry in his voice as she worked to shut down the feelings that were threatening to overtake her. She allowed Grady and Tyler to walk her home without protest.

Chapter 11

"You're the one administering the exercise?" Crystal asked as she approached Dewite. She and her team had just arrived at the Academy for the competition against Flint. Dewite was standing outside of an old building at the very back of campus, one of the few buildings she had never been in. She was under the impression that it had been condemned a long time ago.

Dewite arched an eyebrow. "Reed wanted to make sure you and Flint played nice," he said.

"That's just fantastic," she muttered. But between their earlier fight and their argument last night, it was no wonder Reed had assigned them a chaperone. "Where is Flint, anyway?" Crystal glanced at her watch. Flint had seven minutes to show up.

"I haven't seen her yet."

Crystal resisted the urge to mutter again and instead pointed at the building. "What is this place?" she asked.

"One of the Academy's original combat training buildings. The last time it was used was before the war."

"So why are we using it?" Crystal took a step back to

survey the building. It was two stories tall and looked to be about 400 meters wide. Several of the first-floor windows were boarded up, and the whole building was covered in a blanket of grime.

"Do you know how hard it is to find a facility you haven't used before? We couldn't give your team an unfair advantage," Dewite said.

"Maybe you should have—she's probably going to need it," Flint said from behind them. Crystal and Dewite turned to see her approaching the site with her team.

"So nice of you to join us," Crystal said through clenched teeth. She had promised herself she wasn't going to let Flint get to her again no matter how hard Flint pushed her.

"That's enough, you two," Dewite warned them. "This is supposed to be a friendly competition—at the end of the day, we're all on the same team."

He raised his voice to address everyone. "The object of today's exercise is simple: you will each be given a flag and an area of the building to use as your home base, and whichever team can secure the opponent's flag and return it to their base first wins. Your area of the building is designated on these blueprints."

Dewite handed each of them a document tube. Crystal opened hers and pulled out a roll of paper. "Be careful with those—we don't have electronic copies."

"How old is this place?" Crystal said under her breath as she carefully returned the documents to the tube.

"You will have one hour to strategize and get your team in place," Dewite continued. "All weapons are to be locked in at level 1. One hit and you're out, no matter where on the body the hit is. I'll be monitoring the whole exercise, so don't try to pull anything."

At that point, Dewite glanced over at Flint, which Crystal found highly amusing. "Any questions?"

No one spoke or raised a hand.

Dewite gave them a curt nod. "Good. Your hour starts now."

"Good luck." Crystal extended her hand to Flint.

"You're going to need it." Flint walked away without acknowledging Crystal's hand.

"So much for a friendly competition," Crystal said to Dewite. Before he could reply, she left him and rejoined her team.

"Gather up," she said, looking over her shoulder to make sure that Flint's team wasn't within earshot. She pulled out the blueprints and unrolled them on the ground.

"All right...it looks like we have to defend the eastern section of the building," she said, pointing. "The north side appears to have an observation room—that's probably where Dewite will be. The south side is the main entrance, and it looks like there's a large open atrium here."

She shifted and indicated another area of the blueprints. "I doubt this area was assigned to Flint. So that leaves the western portion of the building. Anderson, what do you think Flint is going to do?"

Justin didn't say anything—in fact, he looked startled. It was the first time Crystal had addressed him directly since she had told him there was no future for them. He had been cold towards her over the past few days, which hadn't surprised her. She was sure he had to protect himself, too. But they needed to have a decent working relationship if he was going to stay on her team.

"Come on, Anderson." Reed had asked them to make

this a training exercise, and she was determined to carry out her orders. She had to know that her team could function without her. "You know Flint better than anyone here—you know how she likes to work, what her strengths and weakness are. Use that knowledge to your advantage."

"All right," Justin said, sounding determined. He crouched down next to Crystal to get a closer look at the blueprints. "She'll probably dedicate most of her resources to her offense."

"Why?"

"Her ego is her biggest weakness. She wants the win, badly."

"So she'll be leading the charge?" Crystal prodded.

"Absolutely."

"And where do you think she'll put her flag?"

Justin considered the drawing carefully before he spoke. "There." He pointed to a small closet in the back corner of the building. "It's small, easy to secure. She wouldn't have to devote a lot of men to guard it."

Crystal gave him an approving nod. "I completely agree. Get a team of six together—I want you to lead the offense."

"Yes, ma'am," Justin said. His smile was so big that Crystal wondered if this was his first time taking point on a mission. He stood and went to gather his team.

"And Grady, you are going to lead our defense," she went on. Grady was by her side in an instant. "We'll put our flag here." She pointed to a large room in the center of their side of the building. With three entry points from three separate hallways, it wasn't an easily defensible location. It was, however, the perfect way to test her team. "I don't want anyone to get through to me before

Anderson is back with their flag."

"Any suggestions on how you want me to accomplish that?" Grady was looking at her like she had lost her mind.

"Do you remember the raid we led on the Church's outpost on Delphton Island?" Crystal said with a huge grin. "That should take Flint down a few pegs, don't you think?"

"I love the way your mind works," Grady said with an equally big smile.

Desi's confidence was overflowing as she led her team through the deserted hallways of the building, certain she had made the first move. She and her team had stepped out of her area the moment the hour was up. Four men were guarding their flag, which she thought was a bit of overkill. It would be impossible for Wolf's team to pass her without being seen, let alone find the small closet she had put the flag in. There was no way they were going to lose.

She hadn't filled her team in on what her master plan was since all they needed to do was follow her orders anyway. She had spent most of their training time yesterday teaching them the hand signals she would use to give orders after having found out — to her shock — that no such system was taught at the Academy. The element of surprise must not be that important on Neophia.

Desi moved through the building, hugging the wall as she went. Her team followed faithfully behind her. At the first split in the hallway, she sent a two-man team to scout the other path while the rest of them pressed forward on the main path. Desi had studied the building's blueprint thoroughly and was sure she was leading them in the right direction, even if they hadn't come across a single member of Wolf's team yet.

Still, as she and her team continued through the hallways without seeing a trace of anyone else, a sense of unease began to grow inside of Desi. After everything she had heard about Wolf, she knew things couldn't possibly be this easy—she must be missing something. She decided to double back and see if Wolf was trying to sneak up behind them, but the path behind them was just as empty as the one in front.

"Status report," Desi whispered into her headpiece. She had expected to hear from her scout team by now.

Silence. "Status report," she repeated a little louder.

"Do you think they've been taken out?" Price asked.

"No, they knew to report back at the first sign of Wolf's team. Even if they were killed, we should have heard something by now. I wonder what Wolf's plan is?"

"At the Academy, they taught one of her missions where she had the Sertex members of her team follow behind the enemy and capture them. Maybe she's trying that tactic again. It would explain why we're missing so many people."

Desi shook her head. "We would have seen something if they were trying to pick us off from behind. Trust me, I'd know if we were being followed."

"We wouldn't have seen anything if they're Sertex," Price said.

"Quiet," she said. Had she heard faint snickering coming from behind them?

She signaled for her team to get down as she scanned the hallway, her finger hovering over her trigger. There was nothing to fire at.

Finally, she stood. "Let's keep moving."

Crystal paced the room, impatient. She was used to being in the middle of the action, not standing on the sidelines. It was important to see how the team functioned without her, yes, but the waiting was killing her. The large open room where she had stationed herself held six desks and a wall of computers. Although it looked like the ideal setup for a command center, it was obviously a useless place to secure her flag...which she had stuck in a pencil holder on the desk in the middle of the room in the hopes that the vulnerability of the flag would act as a motivator for her team.

For the thirtieth time, she pulled out her communicator to check that it was turned on. She hadn't heard anything from her team since the exercise started twelve minutes ago. Then again, she hadn't really expected to—she had told them to only contact her if they ran into trouble.

A desperate need to do something, anything, drove Crystal to one of the computers. She punched a few buttons on it. Nothing happened. Not a surprise considering how ancient it looked. She folded her hands on top of her head and turned away, starting to pace again. How was she going to make it to the end of the exercise without losing her mind? Inaction drove her crazy.

She was on the opposite side of the room when the soft hum of the computer's fan reached her ears. She spun on her heel, facing it, and watched in amazement as the wall of screens sprang to life. It only took her a minute to get back in front of the computer she had accidentally turned on.

This would have been the perfect time to have Tyler with her. He would have no problem figuring out how the old machine worked. All she could do was aimlessly click through icons until she found what she was looking for. Suddenly, the screens on the wall filled with live images from the security cameras around the complex.

Finally, she could see what was happening. It didn't take her long to spot several small groups of Flint's team tied and gagged in rooms throughout the complex. Her team's plan was working: Grady's unit was slowly thinning out their competitors. She didn't bother to try to find Grady on the screen — given that Sertexs were almost impossible to see in real life when they were camouflaged, there was no way she would be able to see them through a camera lens.

She turned her attention to trying to find Justin's team. It had been a huge leap of faith to put him in charge of the capturing the flag without any kind of direction, but then again, he had shown a lot of natural leadership skills during training. She hoped her trust in him wasn't misplaced.

When she finally spotted his team on the security feed, they were running full-out in the perimeter corridors of the building. The security cameras didn't pick up sound, but Crystal could tell they weren't bothering to stay silent. Why would they? No one from Flint's team was anywhere near them. Justin must have assumed that Flint would try to take the most direct route into Crystal's territory, so he was taking the long way. It was a smart plan.

The team started to slow as they cut towards the center of the building. Crystal was enthralled by Justin as she watched him: there was such determination in his face that for a second, she forgot this was only a training exercise. He was a good soldier, but something about him was different today. He was more focused, more confident, and more serious than she had ever seen him before. She had never taken Justin to be a career military person—that was one of the main reasons she had decided to keep him at arm's length—but now she was starting to think she might have been wrong about that.

Justin motioned for his team to enter a room. What was he doing? They were still two corridors away from the suspected location of the flag.

She frantically clicked through the screens until she found the camera showing the room they were in. When Justin finally appeared on her screen again, he was looking up at the ceiling. He motioned again, then hoisted Henson on his shoulders. She pulled a small screwdriver from her pocket and started to remove the cover of the air vent. It was ingenious—if his plan worked, Justin's team would be able to capture Flint's flag without anyone noticing. She handed the vent cover to one of the others, then disappeared into the ceiling.

The five minutes it took for her to return were some of the longest in Crystal's life. She hadn't realized how much she wanted to beat Flint until that moment. A satisfying smile formed on Crystal's lips when Henson dropped back into the frame and gave Flint's flag to Justin.

They had reached the center of Wolf's side of the building without meeting any resistance. Desi still hadn't heard back from any of her scouts, but she tried to push that from her mind. To her relief, when she peered around the next corner, she finally spotted the first member of Wolf's team they had seen since starting the competition. Now the fun would begin. She aimed her gun around the corner and was just about to pull the trigger when Price jostled her.

"Watch where you're going, Ensign!" Desi said.

"Sorry, ma'am...it's just that half the team is missing," he said, his voice pitched low.

"Not now!" Desi hadn't heard what he said, and honestly, she didn't care. She would have to have a conversation with him about side chatter during a mission once they had won. "Hostiles around the corner."

Desi aimed around the corner again, but her target was no longer in range. She would have to move away from the wall if she was going to get a clean shot. She was about to signal her team to move forward when she saw Price raise his gun and fire it behind them.

"What the hell are you doing?" she yelled at Price.

He didn't say anything. He didn't need to—several members of Wolf's team had appeared out of thin air. Her feeling of triumph morphed to near-panic.

Grady raised his gun and fired at her. If Price hadn't grabbed her arm and pulled her to the ground, she would have been out of the game.

Hitting the hard floor brought her back to her senses. She looked over her team and for the first time realized just how many were missing. "Where the hell is everyone?"

Footsteps were coming from the other hallway—the rest of Wolf's team was on their way to join the fight. Price and the few members of her team left standing were returning Grady's fire, so Desi turned to handle the new wave of attackers on her own.

She had already taken down six of them when Price

yelled, "We have to move."

Desi didn't listen—she wasn't one to run away from a fight, not even when she was heavily outnumbered. She had opened her mouth to tell him to stand his ground when he grabbed her arm again, this time to pull her through the closest door. They were the last two members of their team still in the game.

Crystal was tracking Justin's progress back to her with the flag with all of the screens except for one. That one had been trained on Flint, but Crystal had lost track of the other team leader while she was watching Justin's team steal Flint's flag. When she found them, they were much closer to her location than she had expected. Grady needed to make his move soon.

Crystal watched the screen intently. When Tyler jostled Flint as she was about to open fire, destroying her aim, Crystal had to cover her mouth to keep her laugh from echoing around the room. She wiped her eyes and focused on Tyler instead, who kept looking over his shoulder. Did he realize that Crystal had a team following them?

Apparently, he did. He opened fire, but not at the visible opponents around the corner—he started firing at the invisible team that was following him. Several of them suddenly appeared, becoming visible.

There was no hiding now: both teams were firing openly at each other, and the sound of their gunfire was audible through the door at Crystal's back. They were close.

Crystal had just enough time to position herself behind the door before Tyler and Flint burst through it.

"I think we lost them," Tyler said, trying to catch his breath.

"I don't believe it," Flint said. She had obviously seen the flag perched in the center of the room.

"Not so fast." Crystal kicked the door closed and stepped towards them with her gun trained on Tyler. "Take one more step, and I'll kill him."

"But Crys, I'm your brother," Tyler pleaded.

"Nice try, Ensign. In here, you're just the enemy." Crystal's eyes were locked with Flint's.

"You're bluffing," Flint said matter-of-factly. "You wouldn't shoot him after what happened yesterday."

"Try me."

Flint lifted her foot. Before she could take a step, Crystal had shot Tyler square in the chest. She quickly shifted her aim to Flint, who returned the favor.

"So what do we do now?" Flint asked. "Holster our guns, take twenty paces, and then start shooting?"

"You'd like that, wouldn't you? You would probably win the draw, too," Crystal said, seeing pride wash over Flint's face. "But even if you shot me first, it wouldn't make any difference. Even if you take the flag and somehow manage to get past Grady and his team, you would still be too late."

Crystal glanced over Flint's shoulder to the wall of monitors, knowing Flint saw what she did: Justin's team was only a few rooms away from them.

"That's not possible!" Flint almost gasped. "My guards would have alerted me if your team had gotten within a hundred yards of my flag."

"Really? They would?" Crystal couldn't keep the scorn out of her voice.

A second later, Justin walked through the door holding

Flint's flag above his head, the rest of the team whooping and celebrating as they crowded into the room behind him. With a big grin on his face, Justin walked over to Crystal and placed the flag in her outstretched hand.

She faced Flint and smiled. "Sorry, Flint—looks like you've lost."

Chapter 12

Desi dreaded what she was about to do, but she had been up all night and hadn't been able to come up with a better option, so she forced her mind into calmness and headed for the mess hall. It was nearly empty when she arrived. Almost immediately, she spotted Wolf sitting at one of the tables, absorbed in her computer.

Desi hesitated. It wasn't too late to change her mind. Maybe if she just spent a little more time on the problem, she could work it out for herself. But no, she knew she had to do this. Embarrassed by her momentary lack of courage, she took a deep breath and walked over to Wolf's table.

"How did you do it?" Desi said as a way of greeting the other woman. Her tone was harsher than she had intended.

Wolf was about to take another bite of her half-eaten toast, but she paused when Desi spoke. The dark blue jam threatened to drip onto her keyboard. "Come again?"

Desi let herself fall into the chair across from Wolf. "How did you do it?" She rested her head in her hands, exhausted.

"How did I do what?" Wolf asked.

"The competition yesterday. I've been over and over it, and I still can't make sense of how you won."

Wolf set down her toast. "Then let me enlighten you: my team outperformed yours, and you lost. Any other questions?"

"I knew this was a bad idea…. Just forget it." Desi got back up. It had been a mistake to come to Wolf.

"Wait," Wolf said with a sigh. She pushed her computer to the side. "I'm sorry. What do you want to know?"

Desi nodded slightly and sat back down. "First off, the flag. I had it in a highly defensible location with guards posted at the only entrance. They didn't even realize the flag was gone until the game was over."

Crystal smiled in an almost-friendly way. "That was Anderson's idea—he developed our offensive strategy, which included using the air ducts to access the room undetected. He knew how you were likely to act, so we were able to counter everything you did."

"That's cheating," Desi said, frowning. "You used him because you know we're friends."

Wolf folded her arms. "That's not cheating," she said calmly. "We used the best intelligence on hand to formulate our plan. It just so happened that Anderson was the one who had the information we needed."

"That part makes sense, anyway," Desi said grudgingly. Part of her was proud of Justin—as far as she knew, Justin had never led a team before. She didn't give him enough credit, instead tending to think of him as the same scrawny kid he had been when they first met.

"What part doesn't make sense?" Wolf asked.

"How you managed to capture half of my team without anyone noticing. Your people were invisible. That's not something that happens every day." How had Wolf made her team invisible? That part had really been bothering her.

"On Neophia, invisibility actually is an everyday occurrence," said Wolf, her eyebrows arched. "When are you going to do a little research about this place? Honestly, if you're going to serve on this planet, you really should learn something about its people."

That wasn't something Desi wanted to hear. Still, she managed to swallow her pride and ask, "Will you help me?"

Wolf nearly choked on the juice she had just sipped. "You want my help?"

"Yes."

Wolf eyed her warily. "Where do you want to start?"

"Let's start with how you made your people invisible."

She shook her head. "I didn't make them invisible— they were born with that ability. Neophia has two races of people: the Sertex and the Aquinein. The Sertex have the ability to camouflage themselves, basically becoming invisible."

"How are you supposed to fight an invisible army?" Desi said in frustration.

"They aren't really invisible—with practice, you can train yourself to see them." Wolf squinted, as though she was looking at a Sertex over Desi's shoulder. "There's a slight blurring around the edges of their body, especially when they move. But you have to really be looking for it to notice."

Desi looked thoughtful. "Hmm....interesting." She shifted in her seat, making herself more comfortable. "So what about the Aquineins? What can they do—fly or something?"

"No, we can't fly," Wolf said with a small laugh. "But we can breathe underwater."

"Of course you can," Desi said, her tone shading to sarcastic disbelief.

Wolf held out an arm. "Aquinein skin can pull oxygen out of any liquid—we don't have to rely on our lungs the way you do." She dropped her arm and leaned towards Desi. "It's important to understand that each race has its limitations, though, and that it takes an immense amount of concentration to use these abilities. A full-blooded Aquinein who has mastered their submerged breathing ability can stay underwater for about thirty-six hours before their skin gets saturated and they drown. It's similar for a full-blooded Sertex and their camouflaging: they have maybe twenty-four hours before they no longer have the energy to remain camouflaged."

"OK... So this planet is home to these super species. Is there any way to tell who can do what?" Desi asked.

Now it was Wolf's turn to look thoughtful. "Aquineins tend to have smoother skin, while Sertex skin is rougher...but once you throw human blood into the mix, skin type gets a little unreliable. The best way to tell is eye color."

She opened her eyes wider and pointed at them. "I'm seventy-five percent Aquinein, so my eyes are a bright blue: the purer the blood, the brighter the blue. The same concept applies to Sertex, except their eyes are green. A mix of the two usually results in a teal eye color, with the dominant blood type having the stronger influence." She glanced down at her watch. "Can we continue this another time? I've got to get back to the ship yard." She started to gather up her belongings.

Desi rose to her feet as well. "Sure. And thanks for the help. I mean it."

Wolf paused to look at Desi. "If you want some help getting the most out of your Neophian soldiers, I'd be happy to tell you what you need to know. In return, you can help my team with their marksmanship. I've reviewed the tapes from yesterday, and we missed far too many shots."

Desi gave her a genuine smile. "Sounds fair."

The two women walked out of the mess hall together.

"Changing things up today?" Grady asked. Both teams were gathered in front of the firing range, and Crystal and Grady were standing off to the side. "Are we going for round two?"

"Flint came to me this morning and asked me for help, so that's what we're going to do," Crystal said.

"Help with what?"

"How to fight an invisible army."

Grady looked surprised, but in a satisfied way. "So your plan yesterday worked. She's finally starting to see that things are different here."

"Thanks to you, we are now dealing with a much kinder, humbler Flint. She even agreed to help out our team in return."

His surprise shaded to skepticism. "How could she possibly help us? We won, remember."

Crystal wagged a finger at him. "Don't get cocky, Jim," she warned him. "You missed your shot at Price and allowed him and Flint to get through to me. I'd say you're getting a little rusty."

"You're cute," he said, one eyebrow up. "Wrong but cute."

Crystal just shook her head as she observed her team. None of them had yet to acknowledge a single member of Flint's team. Even Justin and Tyler—who were roommates—were acting as if the other man didn't exist. It seemed as though the only thing Crystal and Flint had accomplished with their little feud was to pit their teams against one another. That would end today.

"Do you really think Flint's team is going to like working with us just because you two decided to play nice?" asked Grady. "I mean, we did beat them pretty badly yesterday."

She sighed. "You rubbed their faces in it, didn't you?"

"Maybe a little," Grady said with a devilish grin.

"Don't worry—Flint's team will get a chance to pay you back for that this morning." Crystal patted him on the shoulder and walked away before he had a chance to ask her another question.

"All right, everybody, gather up," Flint called.

Crystal noticed that no one from her team moved. "She said everybody," Crystal said as she took her place next to Flint. Slowly, Crystal's team made their way over to them.

"We're going to be doing things a little differently from now on: Commander Wolf and I have agreed that moving forward, we will be training together," Flint announced. Ripples of surprise went through both teams as people began to fidget and whisper.

Crystal spoke up before the whispers could get louder. "Take a good look around. We are all one team now. You need to put whatever differences you have with each other aside. If there is anything we can take away from yesterday's exercise, it's that both teams still have a lot of work to do if we want to be the best we can be." She paused to eyeball both teams. "That's true for everybody here."

Flint nodded. "Commander Wolf will be leading this morning's training. I expect you to give her your undivided attention." She stepped aside, gesturing at Crystal.

"Today, we're going to practice strategies for fighting a Sertex army," Crystal said, letting her gaze fall on each of the team members. "Every member of the Terian military is at least Sertex-dominant. Although it's safe to assume that higher rank corresponds to being more pure-blooded, all of the Terian fighters will have mastered their camouflage ability. They can stay invisible throughout an entire battle, and we need to be ready to fight that."

She paused, scanning the crowd. "Grady, Henson, Alister…can you come up here, please?"

"I don't like where this going," Grady whispered to the other two as they joined Crystal in the front of the group.

"These are three of my best Sertex soldiers," she told the teams. "They have complete control over their abilities and are nearly impossible to pick out of the background." She smiled. "All you have to do today is shoot them. Lieutenant Flint will be working with each of you to perfect your grip and accuracy. Set your guns to level 1 and let's get started."

"Do you hate me or something?" Grady muttered to her as the rest of the team was getting ready.

She playfully punched his arm. "Come on, it'll be fun. It's not like anyone is going to be able to hit you. I'll swap you guys out after a couple of rounds," she said.

Grady, Henson, and Alister took their place in front of

the shooting range and then were abruptly gone. Crystal and Flint joined the first three shooters while the rest of the team watched. Flint had them each take a couple of shots at the visible targets so she could assess their stance and aim, and then Crystal coached them on how to spot their invisible teammates.

Crystal was amazed at how well she and Flint were working together. They were turning out to have a natural give-and-take she hadn't thought was possible. If only they had started cooperating sooner—as Reed had wanted them to—they'd already have a very skilled combat team at their disposal.

After a couple of rounds, Henson and Alister had both been hit, so Crystal pulled them out and replaced them with two more of her Sertex soldiers. She was setting up the next round of shooters when she heard someone behind her say her name. She paused, shifting her attention to whatever was being said.

"I can't believe we have to take directions from a cocky self-absorbed Earthling," she heard. "Like there's anything she could teach me! Not out here, anyway. If we were back in my room, well, now…that would be another story."

Crystal whirled around and honed in on the speaker. It was a member of her own team. Mullins was his name, if she remembered correctly. His performance had always been slightly above average, but he had yet to stand out during training. She had noticed that he seemed to have a few friends, but he hadn't tried to get to know most of the team. His absence wouldn't be much of a loss.

Everyone saw her glare and stepped back, carving out a clear path to him. "You have exactly five seconds to get off my training field," she snapped.

"You're sending me home?" Mullins demanded. "For what?"

"No, I'm not sending you home—I'm kicking you off my team," she informed him, her voice hard. "I will not tolerate any hateful or discriminatory language from anyone on my team. I would make you apologize to Lieutenant Flint, but I have too much respect for her to force her to be in your presence for another minute."

"Come on, Commander, you can't be serious!" Mullins objected. "I was just messing around."

Crystal took another step towards him. "Do you really want to push me? Say one more word, and not only will you be off this team, I'll see to it that you are permanently removed from *Journey*'s roster," she said.

"You can't do that!" Mullins was sounding decidedly angry now. "Captain Reed choose me for this assignment—you don't have the authority to kick me off the ship."

She ignored his outburst. "Go pack your things, soldier. You're done." Did he really think Reed would take his side over Crystal's? The only thing he had accomplished by arguing with her was ruining his career. From the expression on his face, he was just starting to realize that.

Crystal pivoted sharply on her heel, turning her back on Mullins, and walked over to Flint and Grady.

"Who was that?" Flint asked.

"He was our medic," Grady said.

"Not anymore." Crystal looked Grady up and down. "Is there a reason I can see you?" Her voice still held a hint of anger, although not directed at him.

"Just taking a break! No harm done, I swear." Grady held up his hands as if he was surrendering.

"Do you need me to swap somebody in for you?" Crystal tried to soften her voice. Grady wasn't the one she was mad at.

"No, ma'am, I'll be good." It was strange hearing Grady address her so formally.

She gave him a tight smile, then turned to Flint. "Do you mind taking over? I have some calls to make."

"Sure, no problem," Flint said.

Crystal started to walk away, but paused when she heard Flint's voice. "That was pretty bad-ass," she was saying to Grady, clearly impressed.

"I've seen her throw people off of her team for a lot less," Grady said in response.

A satisfied calm settled over Crystal. It seemed she would be able to work with Flint after all.

"Justin! Hang on a second," Desi called out. She had been waiting outside of the locker rooms for the past hour to make sure she caught him after training. He had been avoiding her for days.

Justin kept walking. "Ensign Anderson, stop! That's an order." She hated pulling rank to get him to listen to her, but he wasn't leaving her any other option.

He stopped, but didn't turn to face her. "Yes, ma'am."

"Don't be like that."

"What do you want, Desi?" He finally turned around.

"I thought about what you said, and you're right: I haven't been acting like myself since we got here. I owe you an apology." Desi paused. When they had fought in the past, Justin had always been quick to forgive her. She had hoped that would be the case this time, but it seemed he was going to make her work for it.

She took a deep breath and continued. "I never should have attacked Wolf like that—I was being stupid and childish. I was so focused on proving myself that I lost sight of what's important, what this job is about. I'm trying to work on that." Another pause. "I even asked Wolf for help this morning."

"You asked for help?" Justin asked. "From Commander Wolf?" Desi tried not to be offended by his disbelief.

"Yes, I did," she said. "That's why both teams are training together now."

"I just assumed you two had been ordered to work together."

Desi shook her head. "No—we're working together because I realized I have a lot to learn about Neophia, and she's the best person to teach me."

Justin's expression was beginning to soften. "That couldn't have been easy."

"No, it wasn't. It sucked, actually, but what sucked the most was the way I treated you. I wish I could take back what I said. Who am I to say whether or not Wolf has feelings for you?"

"You weren't wrong." Justin's posture had relaxed. She was forgiven. He shook his head, not bothering to hide the sadness in his eyes. "She told me herself that we can never be together."

"That sounds like an answer given by her head and not her heart," Desi said.

He shrugged. "Doesn't make any difference."

"Sure it does," Desi smiled. She hated to see him looking down. "People change their minds all the time."

He perked up slightly. "So you think there's still a chance?"

"I don't know." Desi threw her arm around Justin's shoulder. "But don't give up hope— your boyish charm and classic good looks might wear her down yet."

Chapter 13

Now that she was sharing combat training responsibilities with Flint, Crystal had a lot more time to spend at the build site, which was a good thing—there was only a week left to complete construction, and she was beginning to feel overwhelmed by the sheer volume of work that still needed to be done. Only a fourth of the crew quarters were finished, there were no walls in the officers' mess hall, and several of the corridors looked like hopscotch boards. On the plus side, at least they had completed construction of the medical bay, battery room, and bridge.

She was inspecting a new electrical run when she bumped into Justin as he was coming around a corner. The momentary contact gave her goosebumps.

"Sorry," Justin said.

"No, it was my fault—I wasn't looking where I was going," she apologized.

He moved to step around her without saying anything in response.

"What are you doing on the ship?" she asked quickly.

He had been avoiding her since their last fateful conversation, and while she couldn't blame him, she missed spending time with him.

"I was helping calibrate the full-body helm control chairs."

"Right." Crystal should have known that. She had seen that item on the daily work list, but it hadn't occurred to her that Justin would be involved with the calibration process. If it had, she might have made it a higher priority to be involved, too. "How did it go?"

"Fine—we didn't have any issues." He cleared his throat. "Look, it's getting late... I should head back to the dorms."

"Do you want me to walk with you?" she asked.

Justin didn't answer right away, and Crystal could see that he was struggling to find the best answer. She was just about to let him off the hook when he said. "Sure... OK."

They walked in silence. It didn't take long for Justin to match his stride with hers, although he was careful to keep a distance between them so they wouldn't brush up against each other.

He was usually the one to begin their conversations, and she had hoped he would now, but that didn't seem likely. "What do you think of the new training methods?" she said, finally unable to handle the silence. "I know some of the guys weren't happy about training alongside Flint's team."

He kept his eyes forward as he answered. "Personally, I like it," he said. "You're both great combat leaders, and I think the teams will benefit from working with both of you. The rest of the team will come around soon. Most of them act like they're lifelong friends with Flint's team the second they leave the training grounds, anyway." Justin's stride was as even as his tone.

While Crystal was glad to hear that, she wanted to talk about something else. "And what about us? Have you given any thought to us being friends?" she asked.

Justin stopped and faced her. There was a pain in his eye she wished she hadn't seen. "It's all I've been thinking about."

"And?" She wondered if he could see the longing in her own expression.

"I don't know if I can do it," he said after a long moment. "I can't pretend that I don't have feelings for you. I know myself, and the more time we spend together, the stronger those feelings will become. I know that's my problem, not yours, but I don't think I can spend time with you outside of working hours. I'm sorry."

"I understand. We'll keep things purely professional— that way, no one gets hurt." Crystal forced a smile onto her face. As much as she missed spending time with him, she knew Justin was right. He had to protect himself, just like she did. "I guess I really should be getting back to work. You know the way to the launch from here, right?"

He nodded, no longer meeting her eyes. "Yeah."

"Good." She was looking down, too. "Well, I guess I'll see you in training."

"Goodbye, Crystal."

Crystal kept her gaze lowered for a few seconds, then watched him until he had rounded a corner and disappeared from her sight. The inside of her mouth felt sore, and there was a faint metallic taste on her tongue. She quickly blinked the moisture out of her eyes before returning to her inspections.

The bridge was dimly lit by a single row of lights, although small red lights blinked periodically around the room. Even in its idle state, the two-level bridge was impressive: the upper level held the support stations, including weapons, sonar, communication, and computer analyst stations; and the bottom level housed the helm control, engineering, and command stations. Crystal surveyed the entire bridge, letting herself feel a thrill of pride, and then seated herself at the engineering station.

The blue light from her active station shone like a beacon in the center of the large room. In a few days, this would be her permanent workstation: from here, she would be able to see everything that was happening on the ship. If a single light went out, she would know it instantly. Now, though, she merely watched as her team brought one system after another online.

Her eyes were fixed at the screen, but she couldn't stop thinking about Justin and how she had effectively cut him out of her life. As much as she had hoped there was a way for them to be friends, she understood why he couldn't agree with that. His feelings towards her clearly hadn't changed. She had done the right thing, she knew. No sense in either them of getting hurt. *Journey* was going to have 800 crew members, and no one said she had to be friends with all of them.

A familiar voice echoed through the empty room. "You're hiding, I see."

Startled, Crystal spun around in her chair. Her feet were resting on the edge of her seat with her knees pressed against her chest. She quickly lowered them to the ground in an attempt to give herself an air of authority. "What? No...I'm...uh, I'm working."

Tyler was trying hard not to laugh as he made his way across the bridge. "Of course you are. Are you thinking about Justin?"

"No," Crystal said a little too quickly.

The corners of his mouth went up again. "Thought so."

"What are you doing here?" She tried not to sound annoyed and failed.

"I actually am working." Tyler showed her the stack of disks he was carrying before he sat down at his workstation on the upper level.

"My team can find me if they need me," Crystal said, her voice low. "How's the programming going?"

"On any other ship, I'd be done by now." Tyler's hands moved effortlessly over his station. "What's with these archived databases? Do you really think we'll need all of this?"

Crystal breathed a sigh of relief. Their conversation had returned to safe waters. "You never know — I'd rather have it and not need it than need it and not have it."

He looked like he was trying not to roll his eyes. "You do know we can access these databases remotely, right? We don't have to download them onto the ship's servers."

"But that would take time, and time is something we don't always have."

Tyler shrugged. "You're the boss." He didn't say anything else, instead concentrating on his work.

Crystal refocused on her screen, faintly surprised that no one had tried to contact her — as always, there were plenty of things that needed doing. Stiner was probably intercepting all of her calls, Crystal decided. She was always getting after her to take a break.

"You know you can talk to me if you want," Tyler said, breaking the comfortable silence that had fallen between them.

"Talk to you about what?"

"Justin told me what happened between you two."

At those words, Crystal whipped her head around and glared at him.

"Don't look at me like that. He needed someone to talk to."

"That's just fantastic." Her voice was laced with anger even though the situation wasn't Tyler's fault — the story of the kiss must have made its way to every crew member by now, she knew. Still, that didn't ease the sense of betrayal she felt.

"I can tell something's bothering you," Tyler said gently. "Why won't you talk to me?"

In response, Crystal checked her watch. "In case you haven't noticed, *Journey* is set to launch in fifty-three hours, and she's still not complete," she said. "I'm sorry I don't want to talk about Justin, but I have more important things to worry about at the moment. If I can pull this off, my career is set."

"Come on, Crys, your career is already set — you're one of only two people to have graduated from the Academy in five years…and at the top of your class, I might add," Tyler pointed out. "At the age of twenty-five, you've already reached the rank of Lieutenant Commander. And how many awards have you received since you left the Academy?"

"I don't know," Crystal grumbled.

"Nine. You have nine awards for exemplary service." Tyler threw his arms up in the air for emphasis. "Not to mention that you've designed and built the most sophisticated military vessel in all of LAWON's fleet. What more could you hope to accomplish?"

"Plenty," she said curtly.

Tyler sighed. "There's more to life than work."

"Not for me."

"You can't seriously mean that?"

"I do!" The anger in Crystal's voice was replaced by a desperate sadness. She had to make him understand. "My parents were killed when I was seven, my grandparents died when I was seventeen, and you were nonexistent for most of my life. The only constant I've ever had in my life — the only thing I could ever really depend on — is the military. I've devoted everything I am to it. I can't jeopardize that."

Tyler leaned towards her. "What happened to the nerdy fourteen-year-old who would talk of nothing else but falling in love one day? The girl who spent the night of her school's formal crying to me over a video call because no one asked her to go? The girl who believed that finding someone to love was an important and noble goal?"

She pressed herself deeper into her seat and crossed her arms. "I grew up."

"And what is that supposed to mean?" Tyler asked.

"That means I've learned a couple of things about love. Like how it can be used as a weapon, how it can destroy a person and make them do things they never would otherwise. I've seen people kill in the name of love."

Tyler was shaking his head. "That's not what love is."

"Then explain it to me," Crystal said.

"Love is finding the person who completes you, the person who sees all of your flaws and wants to be with you anyway. It's looking at that person and knowing without a doubt that you're where you're supposed to be."

"And who's to say I haven't found that in the military?"

"I know deep down you don't believe that."

Crystal didn't say anything, mostly because if she did, she might let slip that he was right, at least on some level. Part of her remembered what it felt like to be that fourteen-year-old kid dreaming of finding love. That was just an idea, though, a concept. It wasn't real. "I offered him friendship," she finally muttered. "He wasn't interested."

"Can you blame him?"

"No, but it's the best I can do."

"I feel sorry for you." Tyler got to his feet. "These should finish uploading on their own." He waved at the computer and headed towards the exit.

"Tyler, wait," she called after him. "You have to understand where I'm coming from. You've had your heart broken before—you know what being in love is really like."

"You're right, I do," he said, looking down at her from the bridge door. "But I don't understand where you're coming from. I'd give anything to find love again, even if I knew it wouldn't last forever. To me, the rewards are worth the risks."

"Do you really mean that?"

"With every fiber of my being." He gave her one last look, then left the bridge.

There was so much conviction in Tyler's words that for the first time, Crystal wondered if she had made the wrong choice. After all, when she had first started seeing Ryan, life was great. Crystal had depended on him more than anyone else, which had only made his betrayal all the more painful. Could she open herself up like that again?

To Justin or anyone else? She wasn't sure.

Chapter 14

It was the first time Desi had been to the LAWON headquarters building. She had no idea why she was being summoned so close to *Journey*'s launch. Her heart was pounding as she was led into a conference room just off of the lobby. Was it possible they had found out about her medal of honor and were sending her back to Earth to be the poster girl for the military? She should have known her plan would never work—she'd only been on Neophia for a month, and now she was going to be sent home without having served a single day of active duty in the field.

Her confusion only grew when she walked into the room and saw all of *Journey*'s command team mulling around, chatting. Only Wolf was sitting alone at the table, resting her head in her hands. There were bags under her eyes that Desi didn't remember being there before. When was the last time Wolf had slept?

"What's going on? Is something wrong?" Desi asked as she sat down next to her. Wolf had been spending every spare moment helping Desi learn the basics of Neophia.

She was a patient teacher and never seemed to judge Desi when she said something stupid. They were still far from braiding each other's hair, but the tension between them had started to thaw.

"Nothing's wrong," Wolf answered. "This is just the pre-tour command briefing. It's a chance for members of the command team to meet if they haven't already, and we're told the official objectives of the tour. Don't they do anything like this on Earth?" Wolf sat up a little straighter as she talked.

Desi shook her head. "No, we usually find out the objective of the mission while we are already en-route — that is, if they tell us at all. All we usually know is the target and if our mission is to capture or destroy."

Grady's voice cut into their conversation. "Don't you two know you're supposed to be mingling with the rest of the team?" He was standing behind them with a tray of drinks.

Wolf grabbed one of them. "You, sir, deserve a medal."

"Flint?" Grady offered the tray to her.

"What are those?" The very first night she arrived on Neophia, she had had a bad experience with some kind of purple liquid she had been told was "just like coffee." After a couple of sips, she'd been so wired that she hadn't been able to fall asleep that night. Not an experience she cared to repeat.

"Kiki on the right, coffee on the left."

Desi grabbed a cup of the coffee and took a small, cautious sip. As promised, it was just coffee.

Grady went to distribute the rest of the drinks, leaving Desi and Wolf alone. Desi racked her brain for something useful to say, but couldn't think of anything. She was saved when Captain Reed entered the room with someone Desi hadn't met before. Everyone started to take their seats.

"Welcome, everyone, to the first pre-tour command briefing for *Journey*," the man who had walked in with Reed began. "I recognize some of you, but for those who don't know me, I'm Admiral Craft."

He paused and surveyed the room. "I think there's one question burning in everyone's mind that we should answer first: Commander Wolf, is *Journey* ready to set sail?"

"I feel pretty confident that she won't sink," Wolf said, eliciting a small chuckle from the others. "In all seriousness, *Journey* should make it to the Summit Meeting without any issues. Only the basic facilities will be operational for this voyage, however."

"That's good enough for me," said Reed. "Your team has pulled off an amazing feat—everyone should be very proud of the work they have done."

After pausing for the ripple of appreciative nods that went around the room, Craft resumed speaking. "The primary objectives of *Journey*'s first tour of duty are to expand LAWON's presence across the planet and increase the member nations' sense of security. When not on a specific mission, you will patrol the oceans responding to distress calls and promoting peace whenever possible."

Another pause, this time to let the mission sink in. "Your first official mission is to attend the annual LAWON Summit Meeting being held in Epislonia, the capital of Kincaron."

Reed took over. "This is the course we will be taking," he said, gesturing at the screen on the wall behind him that showed a map of their route.

Wolf spoke up. "Sir? I noticed we've altered the course from the original plan."

"Yes, it was decided it would be safer to avoid the waters immediately surrounding the mining communities," Craft said.

"So Teria has not given up control of Rexing?"

"No," Craft answered. "In fact, we believe they have increased their military presence in the colony since they first took it over four weeks ago. But that said, we do not feel they are targeting *Journey*."

"Then why alter the course?" Desi asked.

"Given that *Journey* isn't going to be at 100%, we didn't want to take any unnecessary risks," Reed said. "This new route will put us well outside the range of the Terian ships."

"Any other questions?" Craft said.

Desi looked around the table. Everyone seemed to be relaxed...everyone except Wolf.

"Good!" Craft looked pleased. "I want everyone to take the night off and then report to *Journey* tomorrow morning. We will launch at 0800 hours two days from now. Dismissed."

Crystal sat at the small kitchen table in her apartment. The apartment looked the same as it had when she moved in. Why personalize it when she was hardly there? The handful of items she had brought with her were already packed in her duffle bag. She hadn't set foot in her apartment in days—the only reason she was there now was because she was afraid that if she spent the night working at the ship yard, the rest of her team would have felt they needed to as well. Besides, she could review the schematics for the ship's fire suppression system in her apartment just as easily as she could in her office, and in her apartment, no one would notice.

The knocking at her door was a surprise given that she very rarely had visitors. She opened the door to find Grady standing there.

Before he could say anything, she held up a hand. "No!" Grady was wearing a nice pair of jeans and a white button-up shirt with a black vest. She knew exactly what he wanted.

He quickly looked her over, taking in her baggy sweatpants, well-worn Academy T-shirt, and lopsided ponytail. "Get changed. We're going out."

"I have work to do."

"No, you don't, Craft gave everyone the night off."

She impatiently shifted her weight from one foot to the other. "Why do you think I'm working here and not at the build site?"

Grady half-smiled and stepped aside to reveal who was standing behind him. "I had a feeling you might be difficult, so I brought reinforcements."

Crystal groaned when she saw Dewite and Stiner, too. All three of them brushed by her and walked into the apartment.

"At least she's not covered in motor oil. That's a start," Dewite said in greeting.

"Nice to see you, too." Crystal closed the door behind them. By the time she turned around, Grady was sprawled on a chair with one leg slung over the armrest, and Dewite was relaxing on the couch. She knew she wasn't going to be able to talk her way out of this.

"What are you waiting for?" Grady said. "Get changed."

"I really do have things I need to get done tonight," Crystal said, almost pleading.

"It's our last night off before a six-month tour," Grady said. She recognized the stubbornness in his tone. "We're going to The Ol' Briney. It's tradition."

"Weren't you banned from there?" Crystal walked into the kitchen, opened her nearly empty refrigerator, and pulled out a six-pack of beer. She had bought it over a month ago, but she had spent so little time in her apartment that it had gone untouched.

With a sigh, she grabbed one for herself before setting the rest down on the coffee table.

"No, that was The Drunken Sailor," Grady said, reaching for a beer. He tipped it in her direction before taking a sip.

"Oh, my apologies."

"Go get ready, these won't last long," Dewite said.

"I don't have anything to wear," Crystal said in a last-ditch effort.

"That's why I'm here." Stiner put down her beer and got up, motioning to Crystal to do the same.

Reluctantly, Crystal rose and let Stiner steer her towards the bedroom.

"And Monica, make sure you do something about her hair," Grady called after them.

"Bite me," Crystal yelled back. She heard Grady and Dewite erupt into giggles.

An hour later, they were seated at an old wooden table at The Ol' Briney. Under protest, Crystal had changed into a clean pair of jeans and a snug black T-shirt, and her feet were crammed into the only pair of heels she owned. Her ears felt weighted down by an oversized pair of silver earrings Stiner had lent her.

She absentmindedly ran her fingers over the names carved into the tabletop while they waited for Grady to come back with their drinks. In her mind, she was still reviewing the schematics they had dragged her away from.

She became aware that Stiner was speaking to her. "So, Crys, tell us what's going on between you and Anderson."

Crystal hesitated and was briefly saved by Grady's return. She shot him a look.

"I swear I didn't say anything," he said as he passed out the drinks.

"Even if everyone — and I do mean everyone — wasn't talking about the kiss, it's obvious that something is going on between the two of you," Dewite said.

"Nothing's going on," Crystal said curtly. "He kissed me, it was a mistake, it's done."

Grady just shook his head. "You never have been able to tell when someone has a crush on you," he said.

"Name one person who was interested in me whom I didn't know about." Crystal was sure that besides Justin and Ryan, no one had ever expressed even the slightest romantic interest in her.

"Me," Grady said smoothly. He causally leaned back in his chair and stared across the table at her.

Crystal nearly choked on her beer. The alcohol must be starting to get to her — there was no way she had heard him right. "You?"

"Yes, me." He almost looked smug.

"You never had a crush on me!" He had to be joking. Crystal was vaguely aware of Stiner and Dewite's eyes bouncing between her and Grady.

"Yeah, I did."

"When?"

"When we first met." He casually took a sip and gave her a seductive look. It was a look she had seen him use on women before...and with a fairly decent success rate. Now that it was directed at her, Crystal didn't know how to react. She was starting to wonder if she really was that obtuse. Had she misjudged her friendship with Grady all these years? Was it possible that he still wanted more from her? The idea made her uncomfortable.

"You're lying," Crystal said.

"Why do you think I was so willing to help you out when you first arrived on the *Expedition*? It wasn't because I was looking for a sidekick..." Grady let his words linger for a moment.

Crystal didn't know what to say. The combat team on the carrier hadn't been very welcoming when she had first showed up. When Grady had offered to show her the ropes, she had thought he had just taken pity on her.

"But then I got to know you," he said, "and suddenly, all of those feelings vanished." He sat up straighter in his chair and turned off all of his charm.

No more awkwardness—this was the Grady she knew. Crystal threw a handful of nuts at him.

Stiner and Dewite were chuckling. "Too bad Anderson doesn't feel the way Grady apparently did," Stiner said. "He seemed a little depressed the last few times I've seen him."

"I know... I really hate that I had to hurt him like that, but what other choice did I have?" Crystal's chin sank towards her chest.

"None—you did what you had to do," Grady said.

"That's easy for you to say," she said, sighing. "You

don't have to live with the guilt."

"Speak of the devil," Dewite said, inclining his head towards the door. Justin, Flint, and Tyler had just walked in and were looking for a place to sit.

Crystal did her best to look normal as Grady whistled and waved them over. While everyone settled into their seats, Crystal gave Justin a cautious smile.

Somewhat to her surprise, he returned it.

"How about I get us another round?" Tyler asked the group at large.

Grady held up his near-empty beer. "I always knew you were a good man, Price!"

"I'll help you," Crystal said, jumping to her feet and following Tyler to the bar. She leaned against it and looked over at their table while Tyler ordered.

"Justin's been a little more friendly around me lately," she said. "Not as much as when he first got here, but better than he's been lately."

"Oh, really?" Tyler didn't sound surprised at all.

"Did you say something to him?" She turned to face him.

He had an innocent look on his face. "I might have mentioned that trying to be friends with you was better than ignoring you."

"And he believed you?"

"It took some convincing, but after a while, he started to come around."

She eyed him with gratitude. "Thanks. It'll make this tour easier on everyone if the whole command team gets along."

He grinned. "And besides, you miss talking to him."

"I wouldn't go as far as that..." Crystal started.

Tyler just looked at her skeptically.

She rolled her eyes. "All right, fine—I miss him. A little. He's a nice guy and easy to talk to, so yeah, I miss spending time with him. As friends, though. Nothing more."

Tyler gave her an angelic smile. "I'm glad I could help. You're my little sister—it's my job to look out for you."

She couldn't resist returning his smile. "Thanks, Ty."

The drinks arrived, and he turned back to the bar to pay for them. "I was surprised to see you here tonight," Tyler said before they headed back to the group. "Would've thought you'd be holed up somewhere obsessing over work." He grabbed half of the drinks, and Crystal took the rest.

"I was until Grady showed up at my apartment to kidnap me."

They started heading back to the table. "I'm glad he did," Tyler said over his shoulder. "It's nice to see you out of uniform for a change. You work too hard, you know."

"So I've been told," Crystal said.

They managed to not spill any of the drinks as they put them on the table for everyone. Crystal took a grateful sip of her own and was about to sit back down when Grady stood up and put his arm around her shoulder.

"Price, I think you've monopolized your sister long enough. My turn."

Crystal had just enough time to put down her drink before Grady gently but firmly guided her to the dance floor.

The band had just finished setting up, so Crystal and Grady stood in the middle of the empty dance floor and waited for them to start their first song. Crystal glanced over at their table to find everyone's eyes fixed on her. Justin had a terrible poker face—he looked like he was biting the inside of his cheeks to keep from laughing.

The moment the band started playing, Grady put Crystal's arm on his shoulder and started leading her in a series of complex patterns. It had been a long time since she had last danced, and it took Crystal a few seconds to find the beat. She was pretty sure the last person she had danced with had been Grady, on a night similar to this one.

"So did you mean what you said earlier? When you said you had a crush on me?" she asked him in between spins.

"Of course I had a crush on you. You were a young, smart, crazy-dedicated new officer trying to prove yourself...I thought that was cute." He paused as she spun again. "Oh, and you were hot," he said when she was facing him again. "Hell, you still are."

Crystal shot him a look before she spun again.

"Don't worry," he said with a laugh, "I haven't had a crush to you in years. I don't tend to go for girls who can beat the shit out of me."

"That's probably a wise choice," she said, glad the music was shielding them from being overhead. "Besides, you're too old for me."

"I'm only five years older than you."

"Exactly, you're basically a senior citizen." She gave him a wide grin.

He rolled his eyes. "Would you just shut up and dance?"

Before she could answer, he picked up the pace, taking full advantage of the still-empty dance floor. She had to put all of her concentration into executing the steps. When the song ended, they were greeted with a loud round of whoops and cheers from the entire bar. Still holding hands, they took an elaborate bow.

Everyone at their table was still clapping as they reclaimed their seats. "That was impressive," Justin said.

"I honestly had no idea what I was doing." Crystal grabbed her beer and took a long sip.

"You were prefect, darling," Grady said in his most charming voice. He leaned over and planted a kiss on Crystal's cheek.

"Get off me." She playfully pushed him away as Stiner and Dewite kept laughing at their exaggerated display.

Grady sat back, but he left his arm draped protectively around the back of her chair. She wondered if he was doing that to keep Justin at bay.

The conversation flowed freely the rest of the evening as they drank, danced, and exchanged war stories. Grady regaled them with wild tales of romantic conquests, several of which ended with him having a drink thrown in his face.

Crystal found herself enthralled by everything Justin said—the alcohol had lowered her guard, and she was unable to stop herself from gravitating towards him. All of the feelings she had managed to keep at bay were fighting their way to the surface, and she wasn't sure she wanted to push them back down.

In what felt like no time at all, the band was announcing the last song of the evening. "Oh, I love this song!" Crystal said as the first notes floated through the air. "How about it, Jim?"

"Can't, I promised Monica the next dance." Grady winked at her, then grabbed Stiner's hand and headed to the dance floor.

Crystal looked around for Dewite, but he was deep in conversation with a young attractive man at the bar. Tyler was already leading Flint onto the dance floor, which didn't surprise her — they'd been flirting constantly for the past hour. That left her alone at the table with Justin, and she wasn't sure if she should ask him to dance or not. They hadn't established the rules of their new friendship, and the last thing she wanted to do was cross some kind of line and end any chance they had of becoming friends. Then again, she really did like the song...

"How about it?" she asked.

"OK." Justin drained the last of his drink, then took her hand and led her to the dance floor, directing their steps and turns across the packed danced floor to join the rest of their group. Stiner gave Crystal a thumbs-up when she saw her, and Tyler and Flint kept looking over at them and giggling. Clearly, they had all planned this.

"What's the name of this song?" Justin asked.

The song was being sung in the Neophian Common Tongue. "'Drink in the Rain,'" Crystal answered. "It's an old folk song about the Great Drought." She let the music overtake her as she danced with him.

"The ground had turned bare / there was no life in the air," she sang softly in English, translating. "Get ready — here comes my favorite part! When the skies opened wide / they all gathered outside / and they laughed, and they sang, and they drank in the rain..."

Crystal let her head fall back in anticipation as she sang the last line. The sprinkler system above the dance floor had suddenly come on. Justin stumbled over a step, hesitating. Crystal held him tighter, still moving with the music, and he joined back in.

They both laughed with reckless abandon as they kept dancing right underneath the rain. Crystal felt nothing but pure joy. Her only thoughts were of the movement of their bodies as the water fell down on them. Something stirred inside of her chest. The water was bringing her back to life, just as it had her ancestors all those years ago.

Too soon, the song ended, and everyone in the bar was gently ushered out. "That was fun," Justin said once they had stepped away from the crowd.

Crystal could still feel the music coursing through her. "Yeah, it was…we'll have to do it again sometime." She laughed and shook her wet hair out of her face.

"It's a deal."

The rest of their group joined them a few seconds later. Grady caught Crystal's eye, then glanced down at her hand. She followed his gaze to find her fingers intertwined with Justin's.

She hadn't realized she was still holding his hand, but as soon as she did, she quickly slid her fingers out from his. Justin gave no indication that he had noticed.

"Hey, Crys," Dewite called. He was standing next to a taxi holding the back door open. "Monica and I are going to split a cab. We can drop you off if you want."

"No, thanks," she called back. "My apartment isn't far from here — I'll walk."

Dewite and Stiner both waved before they got into the cab. "See you in the morning." Dewite said through the open window just before they pulled away, leaving Crystal and Justin standing with Grady.

"I'm not going to let you walk home alone," Justin said.

"I'm pretty sure I can take care of myself," she said, smiling.

He shook his head. "That's not the point. I'll walk with you."

"That might not be the best idea," Grady said. "You don't know the area that well — you'll never find your way back to the dorms. I'll come, too. Someone needs to make sure you kids behave yourselves."

"I'm not sure we're the ones you need to worry about," Crystal said, nodding towards Tyler and Flint. The two of them were standing a few feet away, deep in conversation. "Maybe we should all go together."

She walked over to Tyler and gently hit him on the back of the head. "Come on, Romeo, time to go home."

As their group of five started the short walk to Crystal's apartment, she fell into step next to Justin, but then she felt Grady tug on her arm. She slowed her step so that she was walking next to him. In response, Grady slowed his pace down even more. Now they were trailing a good five feet behind the other three.

"You better be careful," Grady said softly.

"What are you talking about?"

"With Anderson. I saw you two dancing."

"Wasn't that your idea to begin with?" Crystal asked, frustrated. After all, Justin hadn't been her first choice for a dance partner.

"That was Stiner's idea—I just went along with it."

"What do you want from me, then? I keep Justin at an arm's length, and you guys push us together. I open up to him a little, and you think I need to back off."

Grady sighed and dropped his voice even lower. "I want what I always want: for you to be happy. I don't care if that means being with Anderson or not, but you need to figure out what you want and then stick to it. Anderson's a nice guy, and he clearly has feelings for you. You can't lead him on."

Determination replaced the frustration in her voice. "Believe me, Jim, that's the last thing I want to do."

Chapter 15

Launch Bay 2 was brimming with chaos. The system Dewite had put in place for embarkment was a simple one. All supplies were to be off-loaded in Launch Bay 1, where they could be inventoried and delivered, and all crew members were to report to Launch Bay 2, where Dewite was passing out room and duty assignments. Weapons and sensitive materials were to be delivered to Launch Bay 3, where a security detail was waiting.

However, Dewite was now standing next to a crate of guns while twenty or so crew members huddled around as they tried to hear their assignments, a task that was made even more difficult by the emergency alarm echoing throughout the room. Despite the chaos, though, Crystal was enjoying the bustle of activity.

Dewite made his way over to Crystal the second he spotted her.

"What happened?" she asked. "I was only gone a half-hour."

"The alarm started going off about ten minutes ago." Dewite almost had to yell to be heard. "No one can seem to turn it off."

"I'll take care of it." She hurried over to a nearby console, her fingers flying as she entered various commands and codes. It only took her a few minutes to reset the alarm and restore some semblance of order to the room.

She signaled to Dewite. "Ah...Commander," she said, pointing across the launch bay. Several people were leaning against the unattended crate of weapons.

"You've got to be kidding me!" Dewite spun on his heel and quickly crossed the bay, shooing everyone away from the weapons.

Crystal followed behind him, still cheerful. Nothing could ruin her mood today—they were fewer than twenty-hour hours away from *Journey*'s official launch, and the ship was filling with life...even if it was an unorganized mess of life at the moment.

"If it's any consolation, I came to the right place," she said once she had reached Dewite, "although I did notice a crate of bed linens on the shuttle with me."

"Do you know where they are?" Dewite asked.

She shrugged. "Well, given that no one unloaded them, I would guess they're on their way back up to the surface."

Dewite sighed. "That's just great."

"Relax. You know the first day of a new tour is always like this."

"You're awfully calm for someone who hasn't finished building the ship yet."

"I'm working on it," she said, still unable to remove the smile from her face.

A voice rang through the air. "Commander Dewite, please report to Launch Bay 1." Both Crystal and Dewite jumped, startled.

Crystal's smile got bigger. "See? The intercom wasn't working when I left, and now it is."

Dewite snorted. "You're a real miracle worker. I need you to cover for me here while I go take care of whatever that is," he said, nodding towards the weapons crate. He tried to hand her his tablet. "And crew assignments still need to be given out."

Crystal put her hands up in the air. "No way! Like you said, I have a ship to finish building."

Tyler was weaving his way over to her. "Commander Wolf! I'm glad I found you," he said, stopping in front of her. He looked frantic. "The exhaust units keep overheating. We've tried everything we can think of, but no one can figure out what's causing the problem."

"It's fine," Crystal said in what she hoped was a reassuring tone. "I'll be there shortly."

"Great and Price can handle crew assignments," Dewite said. He held his tablet out to Tyler as the request for him to report to Launch Bay 1 rang through the overhead speakers again.

Crystal shook her head. "No, he can't—I need him to run a full diagnostic on the emergency notification system. We need to figure out what tripped that alarm."

"Sorry, Commander," Tyler said. He quickly turned and left the launch bay.

Crystal couldn't resist teasing the now-harried-looking Dewite. "Guess you're going to have to find another sucker to take over for you. Here come two now." Flint and Grady were heading towards them.

It only took them a minute to cross the bay. "I'm just here to pick up the weapons," Flint said before Dewite could say anything. She nodded towards the crate.

"It took you long enough. These were supposed to be picked up over an hour ago." Dewite said, clearly aggravated.

"I got here as soon as I could," Flint said. "It's hard to take custody of weapons around here. I'm pretty sure I had to sign away rights to my first-born."

Dewite gave a brief nod in return and quickly transferred the manifest information from his tablet to Flint's. "That leaves Grady to take care of crew assignments," Dewite said once he had finished.

Grady looked helplessly from Flint to Crystal. Crystal knew handing out the crew assignments was the last thing Grady wanted to do, but he wasn't in a position to outright refuse. Crystal racked her brain for an excuse for him.

Flint beat her to it. "He can't," she said.

"Why not?" Dewite demanded.

"I need him to inventory and assign my team's combat weapons and gear."

"And if you could just go ahead and do mine while you're at it, too, that would be great," Crystal said with a huge grin.

Grady rolled his eyes. Clearly, this wasn't the save he had been hoping for. Still, he bobbed his head in acknowledgment and left the launch bay, pulling the crate of misdelivered weapons behind him.

"I need someone to cover for me here," Dewite said as the announcement rang over the intercom for the third time.

Fortunately, that was when Crystal spotted Justin disembarking from the last shuttle. "Anderson!" She quickly waved him over. "He's a pilot—he won't have anything else to do while the rest of us finish the ship's preparations."

Dewite finally started to look somewhat relieved. As soon as Justin had reached their group, he handed Justin his tablet and left without further explanation.

Justin looked down at it, confused. "What's this?" he said to Crystal and Flint.

"The crew's room assignments," Flint said. "Good luck, buddy." She patted his shoulder and left, heading back to her own tasks.

Crystal turned to do the same. "Have fun!" she called back to Justin.

Right before she left the bay, she looked back and saw the crowd of new crew members closing in on Justin like a swarm of vultures.

By the time she finally made it to her cabin, Crystal was exhausted. She had been averaging four hours of sleep a night for the past few weeks, and it was finally catching up with her, it seemed. She had spent the last three hours reviewing every system on the ship with Tyler and Sinter, and she was certain they had done everything in their power to assure that *Journey* would have a successful launch in the morning. Now, finally, she was going to force herself to relax and get a decent night's sleep.

The cabin was spacious, with a long metal T-shaped table dividing the room into two halves. Each side had a bed built into the wall and a chest of drawers, and since this was an officer's quarters, the cabin also had a small private bathroom. Crystal felt extremely guilty that she had one of the only completed rooms on the ship—even the Captain's quarters still had unassembled furniture sitting in the corner. The finished room had been a gift from her build team.

Crystal crossed the room, heading for the duffle bag that was already sitting on the bed. As she unpacked her uniforms, she placed them carefully in the closet so they wouldn't wrinkle, but when it came to unpacking her civilian clothes, she forcibly shoved them into drawers. Her small locked box of computer chips went into one of the desk drawers. Those chips held all of the ship designs she had ever devised. Most of them would never amount to anything, she knew, but still, she liked keeping them with her.

At the bottom of her bag were four antique paperback books that had belonged to her mother. Crystal had read them so many times that she could open them at random and know exactly what was happening in the story. She placed the well-worn books on the shelf next to her bed so that she could take comfort in their pages whenever she felt lonely.

The only items remaining in the bag were three framed pictures. Carefully, she took them out one at a time. The first was from the day she had graduated from the Academy, showing her in her dress uniform sandwiched between Captain Reed and Admiral Craft. That went onto the shelf above her desk.

The next photo was of Crystal and her grandparents, taken the day they dropped her off at the Academy. They had said they were happy for her, but Crystal had known that wasn't true—after everything her parents had put them through, a career in the military was the last thing her grandparents had wanted for her. She had to give them credit, though, for never trying to persuade her to choose another profession. When they had passed away before she graduated, Crystal had found some peace in that, knowing that they would never have to worry about her the way they had worried about her parents during the war. She set that photo next to the first one.

The last picture was of Crystal and her parents outside of Marco's diner. It was the last time she had seen them alive. It seemed fitting to set the third photo next to her mother's books.

The door to the room swung open. Crystal glanced over, expecting to see Stiner, but instead, she saw Flint entering the room.

"Damn, it's hot in here! Why didn't you put any AC on this ship of yours?" Flint said as she threw her bag on the other bed.

Crystal took a deep breath before answering. If they were going to be living together, they would have to get along...and lately, Flint had been trying to be nicer. "There is a cooling system, actually—it's just that being Aquinein, I don't feel temperature changes as much. Feel free to set it for whatever you want."

Flint fumbled with the thermostat for a few seconds longer than was really necessary. Was she regretting her remark? Crystal was glad she had let it go.

"This is a nice room," Flint said. "Much bigger than anything I've ever had on Earth."

Crystal nodded. "It's bigger than the standard room size here, too. Seeing as we're going to be living on the ship for the next six months, I didn't want the crew to be cramped. Besides, the added square footage makes *Journey* seem more impressive."

"Well, I approve," Flint said with a small laugh that sounded awkward. She wandered over to Crystal's side of the room and started examining her pictures. "Are these your parents?"

"Yeah...they died during the Great War."

"I know."

"You do?"

A shade of regret passed over Flint's face. "I did some research on you when I first got here and found the video of their death. I'm sorry — I know that's a huge invasion of privacy. I just wanted to figure out how to beat you when our teams were competing."

"It's fine." Crystal shrugged. "My parent's death isn't a secret. I think everyone's seen the video."

"Have you seen it?"

"Probably more times than is healthy." Crystal took the picture of her parents off the shelf and sat down with it in her lap. Flint sat next to her. The situation vaguely reminded Crystal of late-night talks she and her roommates used to have in their dorms during their time at the Academy. If only she had a happier story to tell...

"I saw it happen live," she said in a low voice. "I was seven." She had to stop for a moment and clear her throat before continuing. Flint waited patiently.

"It happened pretty early in the morning," Crystal finally continued. "I was sitting on the floor in my grandparents' living room, eating breakfast before leaving for school. My grandma made me a couple of pieces of toast with jinko jam, a simple breakfast, she was supposed to be at work early that morning. Suddenly, the wall screen went blank, and when it came back on, there were my parents. I remember being really excited to see my mom — I hadn't seen them in person for about six months. I didn't understand what was happening..." she trailed off.

Flint was looking at her sympathetically as Crystal forced herself to go on. "My grandparents came in to see what I was yelling about… They didn't turn off the screen or make me leave the room. I'm sure they were in shock, too.

"The media was at our door within twenty minutes, and military officers arrived about an hour later. We couldn't leave the house for days. The media played up the family angle: husband and wife killed together, leaving their young daughter behind." She shook her head. "What more could a reporter ask for?"

After eighteen years, she was glad she could finally talk about her parents' deaths without completely breaking down. It almost felt like she was reciting a history lesson instead of recalling the most painful memory of her life. She still thought about it all the time, but the years had dulled the pain.

"At least some good came from it, right? I read that your parents' deaths were why you guys won the war," Flint said.

Crystal gave her a sad smile. "There really weren't any winners—both sides were hurting for resources. But yes, my parents' deaths rallied the Kincaron forces just enough to make Teria agree to peace negations. Kincaron got to set most of the terms, but Teria was allowed to form their own government without any oversight or outside influence."

"How did that happen?"

"Do you remember the soldier who gave the command for my parents to be executed?" Crystal asked.

Flint's expression hardened. "Yes. Who was he?"

The look in Crystal's eyes matched hers. "General Nathan Rank," she said, almost spitting out his name. "He led the Terian military during the war. After the war, he declared himself president of Teria and convinced the people that he was the only one who could lead them into the future. He played on their fears and their prejudice, saying that Humans were destroying Neophia and that he was the only one who could protect them from the danger coming from Earth." Crystal shook her head, still angry. "Then he set up a caste system with pure-blood Sertex at the top. Anyone unfortunate enough to have Human or Aquinein blood is at the bottom, forced to work as servants. Worst of all, they're seen as expendable."

Flint let out a long sigh. "Why don't they leave?"

"Can't," Crystal answered curtly. "Rank's outlawed emigration. The Terian military has the authority to capture or kill anyone trying to leave the country."

Flint crossed her arms and leaned back against the wall. "So the Sertex are the bad guys."

A little bit of the anger left Crystal's eyes. "It's not that simple," she said, shaking her head. "Teria is home to a little over half of the Sertex population on Neophia, and plenty of Sertex don't support Rank. Admiral Craft is a pure-blood Sertex and one of Rank's biggest opponents, for example. Just look at our own team: we have people with Sertex blood serving on this ship, and I would trust all of them with my life."

Flint looked thoughtful. "Like Grady."

Crystal nodded. "Exactly. There is no one I trust more on the planet."

"Is he a pure-blood?"

"No he's a tri-blood: about 70% Sertex, 20% Human, and 10% Aquinein."

"Is that common? Having Human blood, I mean?"

"It is for the Aquinein, yes," Crystal said. "There are very few pure-blood Aquineins left. It's less common for the Sertex, but certainly not rare. Human parentage is more common than a Aquinein/Sertex mix."

Flint looked surprised. "Why? I would have thought the Aquinein and Sertex would be more intertwined."

Crystal sat back against the wall, too. "Before the first humans arrived, the ancient Aquineins and Sertex had almost zero interaction. Neophia was a sparsely populated planet. The Aquineins liked to stay close to the shorelines, while the Sertex preferred to be inland. Tribes could go years without any sort of interaction between one another, and even when they did interact, the tribes were usually the same race: Aquineins with Aquineins and Sertex with Sertex.

"Everything changed when the humans arrived. They landed close to the Temeclian Aquinein tribe and were welcomed with open arms. They were almost seen as gods, in fact." Crystal had to shake her head at that part of the history—it still struck her as strange.

"It was the Humans who brought the Aquinein tribes together," she went on. "They were fascinated by Human technology and were eager to learn it. Not only that, they were quickly able to understand it and improve upon it. That's how they built the space ports. The Sertex, on the other hand, never wanted anything to do with the Humans."

"That's something I never understood," said Flint. "How were the Aquineins able to make such advanced improvements to our technology when they had none of their own?"

"The Aquinein brain works a little differently than Humans," Crystal explained. "Once we have an understanding of something, it's relatively easy for us to come up with ways to improve it. Our struggle is inventing technology in the first place."

Flint sounded amused. "You don't seem to have a problem coming up with new ideas. Just look at this ship."

"Exactly — look at it. Most of it I designed by improving upon standard submarine designs and technology. I didn't really come up with anything new," Crystal said.

"What about the bioskin? I've never seen anything like it."

"That was actually Captain Reed's idea," Crystal said, smiling. "I just figured out how to make it work."

"Isn't Reed Aquinein?" Flint asked.

"No, he's 100% Human, a second-generation Neophian." A sudden yawn made Crystal realize how tired she was. "It's getting pretty late — I think I'm going to turn in."

Flint nodded and stood, quietly walking to her side of the room as Crystal crawled into bed and turned off her light.

Flint was still moving around, but quietly. Crystal could ignore her easily enough. She closed her eyes and ran through her mental checklist until exhaustion overtook her.

Desi laid on her bunk, staring into the darkness. Despite her best efforts, sleep wouldn't come to her. Everything Wolf had told her was swirling around in her head. Wasn't Neophia supposed to be the better planet? They were a peaceful planet, after all. But what did "peaceful" really mean? Desi had never given it much thought before — it had always seemed like a straightforward concept. She had grown up on Earth, so she knew what war was like. She had lived it every day of her life. Wasn't peace the opposite of that? Didn't it mean that everyone was accepted and got along, that disputes were worked out calmly with everyone's best interests in mind? That's what she had always thought, but now she could see things weren't so clear-cut.

The situation in Teria angered her. She had dedicated her life to stopping injustices like the ones taking place there. It was the reason she had stayed in the service for as long as she had. She could have easily walked away after her five years of mandatory service and pursued another career, but how could she live in a world where innocent people were put in harm's way every day and not do everything in her power to stop it? And that's was exactly what was happening on Neophia, she was realizing: Rank was abusing the rights of countless people in his country, and LAWON was just standing back and watching it happen. As far as Desi was concerned, they were equally to blame.

LAWON officials knew what Rank was capable of — just look at the horrific execution of Wolf's parents. In all of her years in the military, she had never seen anything so cruel. Desi could only imagine how much they must have suffered. And to think of what Wolf had gone through growing up as the only child of national heroes. It was lot to live up to. At least that explained Wolf's excessive work ethic and need for perfection.

Desi was starting to wonder if maybe things really were better on Earth. The United State had overthrown oppressive dictators...but then again, those dictators always seemed to be replaced by new, just-as-vindictive leaders. And if you took into account the ever-increasing death toll of soldiers and civilians, was it really worth it? At what point did the costs start to outweigh the benefits?

Desi wasn't sure anymore.

Chapter 16

Flint was still asleep when Crystal crept out of their room the next morning. She spent the early hours roaming around the ship, trying to make sure everything was ready.

When she arrived on the bridge an hour before they were scheduled to launch, she wasn't surprised to find that she was the first one there. She walked slowly from station to station, making sure they were all in standby mode.

After checking every workstation and finding nothing to fix, Crystal sat down at her station in the pit. She still had forty-five minutes to wait. How could time move so slowly? Her foot unconsciously tapped out an incessant rhythm on the cold metal floor. With every passing minute, she could feel her heart beating harder.

As 0800 approached, the bridge slowly started to fill with crew. Most ignored her as they took their stations, probably because they were too busy dealing with their own nerves to give much thought to hers.

She caught Tyler's eye as he took his seat and gave him

a small, half-hearted smile. He returned it with a reassuring nod. Crystal could see the determination in his eyes. This was his first assignment — he must be aching for a chance to prove himself. At least, that's how she had felt her first day on the *Expedition*.

Justin gave her a warm smile as he made his way to the helm, and Crystal found her nerves momentarily eased. As soon as they broke eye contact, though, her anxiety resurfaced in full force.

Grady walked in next and came over to lean against her chair. "Did you manage to get any sleep last night?"

She turned to look at him. "Maybe an hour or two."

"We both know that you triple-checked everything on this ship," he said in a reassuring tone. "You have nothing to worry about."

"I hope you're right."

"Of course I am." He reached over the chair and gently tousled her hair.

"Thanks, Jim." Crystal was grateful he was there. Even if she failed miserably, she knew Grady would always be on her side.

"Stop worrying, kid, today's going to be perfect." With one last smile, he left the pit and took his place at one of the two weapons stations.

Crystal glanced down at her watch: 0755. Five more minutes. She glanced around the bridge and saw that just about everyone had arrived. They were starting to look at her expectantly. Only one of the crew was still missing…

…and she came walking in a second later. "What's everyone waiting for? Let's fire this baby up," Flint said as she sauntered onto the bridge. She wasn't showing the slightest hint of nerves as she took her place next to Grady. Crystal envied her.

"We are waiting for the Captain and Commander to arrive," Crystal said calmly.

"Well, wait no longer," came Reed's voice behind her. He entered the bridge with Dewite at his side.

"Captain on deck." Crystal said with as much authority as her nerves allowed.

Everyone rose to their feet and saluted. Reed stood at the top of the stairs leading down into the pit and returned their salutes.

"At ease," he said. "Today is a momentous day. We are standing on the bridge of the most sophisticated military vessel ever made, with the most elite crew ever assembled. I feel very fortunate to be standing here among you. We have the opportunity to accomplish great things during our time together." He gave them all an encouraging smile. "Let's not waste any more of that time talking."

The crew took their seats, and Reed stepped down into the pit and stood in front of Crystal. "Commander Wolf, will you do the honors?"

"Yes, sir," Crystal said, projecting a confidence she didn't feel.

Her heart was beating in overdrive as she took the ignition chip from Reed. She walked to the captain's station, put the chip into the computer, and—after a moment's hesitation—turned it. The bridge sprang to life.

"Sonar is showing fully operational," Stiner reported from her station.

"Communications is up and running. We are connected to LAWON's secure satellites," said Santiago from the comms station.

"I'm showing the same thing," said Tyler.

"All weapon systems are online," Flint reported.

"We have helm control," Justin called out.

"Diagnostics is showing all systems operational," Dewite reported from Crystal's station.

"Congratulations," Reed said to Crystal just before the rest of the bridge broke out in applause.

"Thank you, sir." Crystal hadn't realized she was holding her breath, but now she was breathing freely again.

"Mr. Anderson," Reed said, "Plot a course to Episolnia."

"Yes sir," Justin responded.

Crystal found that she was holding her breath again as she waited for *Journey* to pull away from the holding bay. The initial lurch was so small that Crystal was sure she was the only one who felt it. A second later, *Journey* effortlessly sliced through the water and made her way towards the open ocean.

Journey had been in open waters for two hours, and everything was going smoothly. The crew's spirits were high as they worked to ensure that *Journey*'s maiden voyage was perfect. The only one who seemed on edge was Crystal — a pit of anxious energy had been growing in her stomach ever since they had left the bay.

"Would you relax?" Dewite leaned over and whispered to Crystal.

"I'm just doing my job," she whispered back without taking her eyes off of her screen. She was in the middle of running her third full diagnostic scan.

"No, what you're doing is looking for problems, and the crew is starting to notice."

"Everyone is too wrapped up in what they're doing to

notice," she said, still looking at her workstation.

"Take a look around."

Grady caught Crystal's eye the moment she looked up. She saw his muscles tense as if he was preparing for battle. Dewite was right—he had to be picking up on her nervous energy. She smiled weakly at him and tried to relax her posture.

Crystal glanced around the rest of the bridge and saw that several members of the crew were in fact throwing her nervous glances. She had to remember that for some of them, including Tyler, this was their first assignment. They probably were thinking that if a senior officer looked nervous, there was a reason for that, and probably not a good reason.

She sighed. "All right, fine, you're right," Crystal said quietly, turning toward Dewite. "It just all seems to be going a little too smoothly, don't you think?"

"What do you mean?"

"*Journey's* completion date was pushed up nine months," Crystal said, trying to keep her voice calm. "I know my team is good, but come on. There has to be something we missed. I want to find out what that is before we wind up with any problems."

Dewite looked at her with his head tilted. "You really can't sit back and enjoy everything you've accomplished, can you?"

"Believe me, Commander, I'm trying," she said with a half-smile.

"Captain," Stiner called from the sonar station, "there are two small submersibles hovering about fifty yards ahead on our port side."

"Someone trying to get an early look at the ship?" Dewite asked.

"Unlikely—there are only a handful of small unaffiliated residential colonies around here. They probably don't even know what *Journey* is," Crystal said, making sure that her voice was so low that only Dewite could hear it. She forced her expression into calm stillness—she didn't want to betray her true emotions. What was happening now? Before, she hadn't been concerned about an external threat, knowing that their altered course had taken them well out of range of the Terian forces at the Rexing mining colony.

"Captain, they are falling in behind us," Stiner said.

"Do you think they're ready for this?" Crystal whispered to Dewite.

"Yes, I do," Dewite said.

"Santiago, get them on the line," Reed said.

The lieutenant nodded. "I have them, sir."

"Unidentified submersibles, this is Captain Johnathan Reed. You are in pursuit of a LAWON military vessel. Break off your pursuit at once, or you will be fired upon." Reed's voice was calm and steady. No one spoke as they waited for a reply.

"They're breaking off," Stiner said. The bridge crew breathed a collective sigh of relief. Crystal didn't feel relieved, although she was trying hard not to show it.

"That was way too easy," she said under her breath.

"They're coming back around." Stiner's voice cut through the bridge like a knife.

"They've fired: four torpedoes in the water," Grady called out.

"Fire intercepts," Reed said.

"No time," Flint said. "Impact in ten."

"Sound the alarm brace for collision. Wolf, tell me where they're going to hit."

Crystal's hands were flying over her screen. "The bridge, sir."

"Anderson, hard starboard." Reed commanded.

"Impact in three...two...one," Flint counted aloud.

Everyone was bracing themselves as they waited for the torpedoes to make contact. At the helm, Justin fought to turn the ship away from the incoming missiles in an attempt to limit the damage.

The instant the torpedoes hit, the ship gave a sudden jerk. Several people were thrown out of their chairs, and the bridge was plunged into darkness. A few seconds later, the emergency lighting flickered on and the critical workstations sprang back to life.

Crystal reengaged with her screen the second her workstation regained power. She wasn't overly concerned about the impact—there would be some damage, yes, but given the force of the impact, she expected it to be minimal. What was concerning her at the moment was the lack of lighting.

"Status!" Reed said.

"We've sustained minor hull damage, but the regenerative skin should repair itself in twenty-four hours," Crystal said without taking her eyes off her screen. She still hadn't found an answer to the lighting issue. Her screen refreshed again, this time with a detailed schematic of the engine rooms. That's when she saw it: the glitch she had been looking for since *Journey*'s launch.

"Shit," she muttered. Without further thought, she got up and raced out of the bridge. Behind her, she heard Reed say, "Price, tell me what the hell she found!" She toggled her earpiece so that she would continue to be able to hear what was being said on the bridge as she ran towards the engine room.

"Yes, sir," Tyler said. He took a quick look at Crystal's screen. "Looks like there is a problem in the engine room: Battery 1 is at 75 percent and is draining fast. The other three are showing no charge at all."

"Sir, the subs are coming back around," Stiner said.

"Grady, prepare to fire lasers," Reed said.

"No!" Crystal's voice rang through the bridge's speakers. "Firing the lasers will drain our remaining power supply. We would be dead in the water."

"Flint, Grady, get to the subfigthers and see if you can disable those submersibles," Reed said, quickly changing tactics. "Price, find out what we're up against."

"Yes, sir," they said in unison.

"Wolf, do you have an update for me?"

It wasn't going to be a good update—she had reached the engine room, where she found clouds of smoke engulfing the batteries. Nearby crew had just extinguished a small fire in the second battery unit.

Crystal quickly surveyed the scene. Battery 2 had become dislodged: the brackets securing it to the floor appeared to have failed, and it had toppled into batteries 3 and 4 like dominos.

"Battery 2 is completely destroyed," Crystal said aloud, knowing the bridge crew could hear her report. "We are removing it now. Once it's out of the way, we should be able to reconnect batteries 3 and 4. If we can turn the ship into the current, the water moving over the ship's skin should provide enough energy to temporarily restore full power."

On the bridge, Reed said, "It's going to be hard to maintain that position without the full force of the thrusters."

"I know, sir," came Crystal's voice over the speakers.

"I can do it," Justin called out.

Crystal's scenario worked: a few minutes later, the emergency lighting shut off as full power was restored.

Adrenaline pumped through Desi's veins. This was what she lived for. The subfighter was a small, sleek vessel with a glass dome that allowed her full view of her surroundings. She had only piloted it a few times in training, but being at the helm already felt like second nature to her. Desi didn't know what kind of improvements Wolf had made to subfighter, but whatever she had done, it was a lot easier to operate than anything Desi had piloted back on Earth.

It didn't take her long to get the attention of the enemy subs—a few close passes, and they were soon following her through the maze of rocks jutting out of the ocean floor. Grady trailed behind them, trying to get a clear shot.

"Flint, Grady." Dewite's voice rang through Desi's subfighter. "Price has identified them as drones. Feel free to take them out."

"With pleasure." Desi made a tight circle and cut between the two assailants. Grady took off after one while Desi fell in behind the other. She chased the drone along the ocean floor, firing whenever it was in range.

After three near misses, her shot finally connected with the tail of the sub. The drone lost control and crashed into a rock, exploding on impact. "One down," Desi reported. "How are you doing, Jim?"

"I haven't been able to get a clear shot," Grady said. Desi could hear the frustration in his voice.

"I'm on my way." She had gone farther away from *Journey* than she had thought, though, and it took her several minutes to find Grady. Once she did, she could see the cause of his frustration: the drone had positioned itself so that it was easily able to return every shot Grady sent its way. In addition, Grady was forced to constantly change his position to avoid being hit.

"I'll get its attention, you take it out," Desi said.

"Sounds good to me." Grady dropped back out of range while Desi cut in between them. As she had hoped, the drone honed in on her. She led it around in a large circle, easily dodging the shots it fired at her and making sure to give Grady plenty of time to position himself.

Her plan worked: Grady's next shot connected with the drone's fuel tank, and it exploded instantly.

"Nicely done," Desi said.

"You, too."

"Commander, the drones have been destroyed. We're heading home," she said.

Chapter 17

Crystal sat at the table in the ward room with the rest of *Journey*'s officers. Her emotions had run the gamut since the attack began: anger and a smug I-told-you-so had coursed through her when the drones had fired on them, only to be replaced with fear the second *Journey* lost power, when she wondered if the attackers had managed to destroy her ship only hours after it had set sail. Finally being able to bring the ship back online had brought a small amount of relief. But the strongest emotion she had felt — and the one she still felt — was failure. She placed the full blame for what happened in the engine room squarely on her shoulders.

She had finished giving a brief update on the battery situation. Now that everyone was assured that they were not in danger of losing power, they could focus on figuring out who had attacked them.

"I've managed to identify Teria as the manufactures of the drones," Tyler said. "Our records indicate that the drones were decommissioned over six years ago. Nice call on the archival databases." He glanced in Crystal's direction. The compliment did not improve her mood.

"But where did they come from?" Grady asked. "I thought our course changes meant we wouldn't go anywhere near any Teria-occupied land?"

"Rank probably assumed we would alter our course once he had control of Rexing — after all, there are only so many ways to get to the capital. He could have had those drones lying in wait for weeks without anyone knowing," Dewite said.

"Is there any chance Teria sold the subs after decommissioning them?" Reed asked, echoing Crystal's concerns. The best-case scenario was that they had been attacked by a small anti-military group, someone with no financial backing and very few resources at their disposal.

Tyler shook his head. "It's doubtful. Drone technology was developing fast back then — new models and upgrades were coming out every couple of weeks. These drones are from the beginning of that cycle. We know Teria sold some of its later models, but they were never able to find a buyer for these particular drones."

Dewite's mouth settled into a hard line. "So they were sending us a message," he said.

Crystal mind was racing, replaying the events of the attack over and over again. Something didn't feel right to her. If Teria had really wanted to send a message, why send drones that had very little chance of success? "It was a distraction," she said suddenly.

"What do you mean?" Reed asked.

"The attack was a distraction," she repeated, feeling more certain of her theory by the minute. "It was a fluke that the first strike took out our power. If the batteries had been properly secured, it never would have happened. Those drones weren't nearly powerful enough to destroy the ship under normal conditions. Rank would have known that."

Flint thoughtfully tapped her fingers on the table. "So the drones were expendable."

"Then why risk attacking at all?" Justin asked.

It was a good question—they all knew that Rank never did anything unless it directly benefitted him.

"To keep us out of the way," Crystal suggested.

"So he could do what?" Dewite asked.

"I don't know," Crystal said.

Reed touched a button on the control panel, connecting them to the bridge comms. "Santiago, I need you to review all communications that occurred in the area during the attack."

"Yes, sir. What am I looking for, sir?" Santiago's voice echoed around the room.

"Something we missed."

A heavy silence filled the room as they waited. By the time Santiago spoke again, it felt like they had been sitting there for hours instead of less than a minute.

"Captain," he said, "I've found a distress call. It's weak and only a few seconds long. They must have broadcast it while our power was down."

Crystal's sense of failure instantly doubled.

"Can you transfer it to the screen here?" Reed asked.

"Yes, sir."

A moment later, the screen at the front of the room sprang to life, showing a blurred image of a pudgy man fading in and out of focus.

"My name is Samuel Jefferies," the man was saying. "I'm the mayor of Soupionia. We are under attack by unknown forces. We are—"

The screen filled with static.

"Price," said Reed sharply.

Tyler was already tapping on the inset table screen. "Soupionia is a small residential colony with a population of around 500," he read off. "They function as an independent nation and are not a member of LAWON."

"We're still going to respond, aren't we?" Flint said. Crystal could hear a hint of anger in her voice.

"Of course we are," Dewite said calmly.

"Do you think Rank is behind whatever happened to them?" Flint posed her question to the whole room, but she was looking at Crystal.

"I do," Crystal said.

Grady was also looking at the screen readout. "But it doesn't fit his usual M.O.," he pointed out. "They have no resources Rank would find valuable, and they are nowhere near Teria. Besides, the colony's population is largely Human-Aquinein."

"Maybe he's after something else?" Justin suggested.

"Like what?" Grady asked.

"Like us." Crystal knew it was true the moment she said it. "Is there any other ship in the area that could respond?" she asked, already knowing the answer.

"No," Tyler said, "we are the only ship within a hundred miles."

Justin leaned back in his chair. "So what do we do now?"

Grady sighed. "We wait."

"For what?" Flint asked.

"The announcement," Crystal, her voice giving way to her rising frustration.

As if on cue, Santiago said, "Captain, you should see this."

"And here it is..." Grady muttered.

The main screen was filled with a young man's face, a face Crystal knew all too well even though she hadn't seen it in over three years. This attack was personal. Why else would he be delivering the message when Rank had always given his own in the past? It was the only way Rank knew that Crystal would respond.

"Citizens of Neophia, greetings from Teria," the man on the screen said with an easy confidence. His brilliant green eyes pierced into Crystal's. "The colony of Soupionia, while proud and strong, has decided that is it in their best interest to join Teria, and the people of Teria have welcomed them with open arms. To show our support for our new citizens, we have installed a military unit in the colony to insure their safety and well-being. We ask that the other nations of Neophia honor the peaceful transition that is taking place. Thank you."

The screen went blank.

"That wasn't Rank, was it?" Flint asked.

"No, that was General Ryan Young," Reed said. "The only time he's been seen in the last three years was when he was promoted to General last year—they held broadcasted ceremony for him. There's been no other intelligence about him since."

Crystal was sure Reed was watching her out of the corner of his eye as he spoke. It was widely believed that Young had been promoted in an attempt to overshadow LAWON's news about *Journey* and Crystal's own promotion, both of which had been announced a mere two days earlier.

Flint's eyebrows went up. "So it's a big deal for Young to be making this announcement," she said.

"Yes, it is," said Reed.

"It's a trap," Crystal said with a soft determination.

"They are going to use the colony as leverage to get the ship."

"What makes you say that?" Tyler asked.

"It's the only thing that make sense," Crystal answered. "Look, I know Young, and I know how he operates. More importantly, I know how Rank likes to use him."

"Have you done character profiles on the two of them?" Tyler asked.

"Not exactly."

"Then how do you know him?" Flint asked.

"We have a history."

"What kind of history?"

"We were...together..." — Crystal was careful to avoid looking at Justin as she spoke — "for a little over four years while we were at the Academy. Back then, he was known as Ryan Craft."

"As in Admiral Craft?" Tyler asked.

"Yes. Ryan is Admiral Craft's adopted son." Crystal got up and started to pace around the edges of the room. "He trained at the LAWON Military Academy, graduated second in his class."

"Behind you?"

"Yes," Crystal said simply. This was not the time to get into the finer points of her relationship with Ryan. "He defected to Teria after a month of active service. He changed his name and used his Sertex pure-blood status to secure himself a position of power in Teria's military. That first year after he defected, he was at Rank's side every time he made a public appearance. Officially, he was in charge of Rank's personal security force, but Rank liked to parade Young around to embarrass Admiral Craft and LAWON." The disdain in her voice matched the expression on everyone's faces. "Once the sting of Young's betrayal had lessened, he disappeared, only making one or two public appearances in the last three years."

"How do we take him out?" Flint asked.

Crystal stopped pacing and faced her. "We use his weaknesses against him."

"Which are?"

"He's short-tempered and proud and he hates me almost as much as he hates his father," Crystal said, almost biting off her words. "If I can get in there and push his buttons, I'm sure I can get him to make a mistake that would give the rest of you a way to free the colony. He'll be expecting me to respond, yes, but he'll never see you coming."

"It sounds risky," Dewite said, his eyes narrowed.

"It's a risk I'm willing to take," Crystal said, turning from Flint to Dewite.

"Yes, but I'm not sure I am," Reed interjected.

Crystal tried to soften her tone as she looked from Dewite to Reed. "Captain," she pleaded, "there's no other way. That message was meant for me. You know that. I have to do this. Who knows what they will do to those civilians if I don't respond?"

"If you're sure." Reed didn't look too sure himself.

She nodded, her eyes reflecting her determination. "I am."

After a brief pause, Reed nodded. "Ready your teams," he said to the room at large. "We should be at the colony in fifteen minutes. Dismissed."

The ward room was empty except for Crystal. Seeing

Ryan again had shaken her more than she wanted to admit. She had always expected to have go up against him at some point in her career, and she had thought she would be able to face him without their past affecting her — after all, their relationship had ended years ago. Now that she was about to face him, though, she wasn't sure she could keep the past at bay.

Crystal's mind drifted back to the last encounter she had had with Ryan. It was the beginning of their last year at the Academy, and it felt like Ryan had been pulling away from her for months. She had hardly heard from him over the last break, and when he did come back, he was distant and distracted. That night, he was supposed to meet her for dinner, but he never showed. She decided to track him down. What was he doing and where did he go when he disappeared?

When he left campus that day, she tailed him at a discreet distance, determined to find out where he was going. After a few miles, he stopped in front of a rundown house that had a small symbol displayed in the window. Crystal recognized it at once: it was the symbol for the Purification Movement.

"Ryan!" she called out to him. She couldn't let him go in that building.

He spun around at the sound of her voice, clearly shocked to see her standing on the other side of the street. He strode across it and faced her. "You followed me here."

"I did." She refused to apologize. Yes, following him had been a small betrayal of trust, but he hadn't left her any other option…and now she could see that he was just steps away from ruining his career and his life. "What are you doing here?"

"It doesn't involve you." There was an unfamiliar coldness in his voice that frightened her.

"Everything you do involves me. We're a team, remember? You and me against it all." She did her best to keep her voice from shaking.

He lowered his. "Please, Crys, just go back to the Academy. I'll find you when I'm done."

"Come back with me," she pleaded.

"I'm not going to do that." He started to turn away from her.

"You can't be a LAWON officer and be part of that," she said, motioning towards the house. "You can't have it both ways."

He turned back. "I knew you wouldn't understand — that's why I didn't tell you about this." He was starting to sound angry again. "Just go back to school and study some more. I know you're aching to prove how much better you are than the rest of us stupid, mediocre students. 'Look out, everyone! Here comes Crystal the Great!'" he said in a mocking tone.

Tears started to form in the corner of Crystal's eyes, but she refused to let them fall. Ryan wasn't entirely wrong — her classmates often said things like that behind her back. It got to her occasionally, but Ryan had always been the one to defend her. He understood the pressure she was under, how she felt she had to live up to her parents' reputations. She didn't know what to say now that he had turned on her, too.

Over Ryan's shoulder, she saw two men walking over to them. Each had a gun strapped to his side. "Hey, Craft, we're waiting for you. Is there a problem?" one of them called out.

Ryan turned. "No problem," he answered casually.

"Just talking to my girlfriend...you know how it is."

She didn't like the look the one on the left gave her. "I know you're irresistible, Craft, but tell her she's going to have to control herself and wait until you're done here."

"Don't worry, she's leaving," Ryan said.

Crystal glared at him. This was not her Ryan. He never would have let anyone say anything about her like that. She had to try to get through to him.

"Ryan," she said, gently taking his arm to keep him from turning away from her again, "please don't do this."

She didn't know what he was going to say, but she was shocked when he slapped her across the face without saying a word.

She released him, stumbling back. This time, she was the one who turned away.

He didn't try to stop her. Behind her, she heard Ryan laughing with the two men as she made her way down the street.

Crystal's whole face stung. Not from the slap—it hadn't been that hard—but from the cold wind blowing against her moist cheeks as she walked back to campus. She wasn't sure exactly when she had started crying.

She hoped her dorm would be empty when she returned, but she wasn't that lucky—her roommate, Maggie, was sprawled on her bed reading. "Where were you? You missed dinner," she said without looking up.

"I wasn't hungry." Crystal's voice cracked slightly as she spoke.

Maggie finally looked up, then jumped off the bed, sending her tablet tumbling to the ground. "What did he do now?"

"It's over. I don't really want to talk about it." Crystal tried to smile, but found her muscles wouldn't cooperate.

Thankfully, Maggie didn't push it, and Crystal spent the next hour pretending to read at her desk.

She wasn't surprised to hear a sudden knocking at the door. It was Ryan showing up to apologize. He had been doing that a lot lately.

"I'll get rid of him," Maggie said gently, going to the door and opening it just a crack. She positioned herself to block the visitor from seeing into the room.

"She's not here," Crystal heard her say.

As expected, she heard Ryan's voice. "You're a terrible liar, you know that?" He was calmer now — he sounded almost like his former light-hearted self.

"She doesn't want to talk to you," Maggie said stubbornly.

"Just let me in."

"No."

"Damn it, Maggie, I have to talk to her!" Now he was starting to sound frustrated.

Crystal slowly made her way to the door, knowing that Ryan wouldn't leave without talking to her. She had to face him.

"It's OK," she said, touching Maggie's arm.

Maggie gave her a hard look. "Are you sure?"

"Yeah."

"All right." Maggie stepped back from the door, allowing it to fully open. "I'll be down the hall if you need me." She gave Crystal a smile and then slipped into the hallway.

Ryan moved to enter the room, but Crystal blocked him.

"Can we talk inside?"

"No." She had to be firm — she couldn't let herself forgive him this time.

Ryan frowned. "Look, Crys, you have to believe I never meant for that to happen. I don't know what came over me. I'm just under so much pressure, you know, with my father and school. Please, you have to forgive me, I don't know what I'd do without you." His voice trembled.

Crystal wanted to pull him close, wanted to comfort him, but she couldn't. She had to be strong.

She didn't move. "I can't do this any more, Ryan. I can't forgive you this time."

"What are you saying?" His eyes were starting to look wet, but Crystal grimly clung to her resolution not to reach out to him.

"I'm saying we're over. I can't be with you anymore." Telling him that was one of the hardest things she had ever done. He was the one person she had left in the world, and now she had to let him go.

"Crys, don't do this," Ryan pleaded. "We can get past this. It's me and you against it all. I should have listened to you. I'm sorry that I didn't. I'm sorry for everything. Crystal, I love you."

She had to press her lips together and gather herself for a few seconds before responding. "You used to love me, but I'm not sure that's true anymore. You've changed, Ryan, and I don't like the person you are now."

"It was just one mistake," he begged.

She shook her head. "No. This has been going on for months, and today was the last straw. I can't keep making excuses for you. I can't keep hoping things are going to get better when they never do. I'm done."

His pleading look changed to anger almost instantly. "You know what? Fine," he snapped. "If that's how you feel, then fine—I don't need you any more. You were just holding me back, anyway." He turned and stormed off down the hall.

Crystal slowly closed the door. The sound of it shutting shattered her world. She sank to the floor and let all of her pain flow out of her eyes. She wasn't sure how long she spent there, but when she finally got up, her eyes were dry and her heart had hardened.

That was the last time she had cried.

Crystal felt a new resolve settle over her she when finally left the ward room. She was ready to face Ryan. There was nothing left in her heart for him—he was just another Terian soldier.

She was surprised to see Justin waiting for her in the corridor. "Is there something I can help you with, Ensign?"

"Are you all right?" Justin asked with more concern in his voice than Crystal thought was warranted.

"Of course I'm all right. Don't worry—if I thought I was compromised, I would pull myself off the mission."

"That's not why I was asking."

She managed to keep herself from sighing. "Then what are you concerned about? We don't have time to waste talking—we have a combat mission to prepare for."

"We're trying to be friends, right?" Justin said carefully.

She tilted her head, confused. "What does that have to do with anything?"

"Friends talk to each other when something is bothering them, and that message from Young clearly bothered you."

Crystal paused for a second. She wasn't sure what to do. She had stayed behind in the ward room to get her emotions in check, and now Justin was asking her to open up to him. That seemed counterintuitive. Then again, maybe talking about what had happened would help lighten the burden she still felt like she was carrying.

"Do you want to walk with me?" She started off down the hall before Justin could answer, knowing he would fall into step next to her.

Crystal felt herself relax as they walked. "You must think I have terrible taste in men," she said with a small laugh. "But you should know that the man we saw today is nothing like the man I used to know."

"What was he like?" Justin asked.

Should she answer that? She didn't want to hurt Justin by talking about Ryan, but at the same time, she felt like she needed to justify why she had been close to Ryan at one point—like it or not, she cared about what Justin thought of her. She shrugged.

"He was kind and supportive," she finally said. "We constantly pushed each other to improve, to be better at whatever we did. He was my protector, my rock, and my best friend—he never left my side during both of my grandparents' funerals. We did everything together. I even spent holidays with his family."

"What happened?"

They had reached Crystal's room. She leaned up against the wall, and Justin leaned next to her. She really should go inside and get ready, but she didn't want him to leave.

"It was our last year at the Academy," she said with a faint smile. "His father had started to take an active interest in my career—he was introducing me to lot of high-ranking officers, trying to find me a good placement after graduation. Ryan never said anything, but I knew that bothered him. When I started to outperform him, he really started to pull away." She paused, shaking her head. "Then he got involved with the Purification Movement. That's when I knew how much he had changed."

"The Purification Movement?" Justin looked puzzled.

"Their goal is to rid Neophia of Earth's influence and restore the planet to its natural state," Crystal said, hating to even speak their mission aloud.

"And I take it you didn't agree."

Crystal could feel her eyes narrowing. "The movement was led by a group of radicals who were known to use violence to get what they wanted," she said, her words clipped. "I tried to get him to see reason. He couldn't be involved with that group and still be a military officer."

"He didn't listen to you, did he?" Justin asked.

"No." She still felt a stab of disappointment that he hadn't.

"Did he ever hurt you?"

"Only once," she said in a small voice.

Chapter 18

"Where have you been?" Desi asked as soon as Wolf walked into their quarters. Desi had already changed into her combat gear. Normally, she would have gone straight to the combat team room to start prepping her team, but she had decided to wait for Wolf instead.

"I was talking to Justin." Wolf made her way over to her dresser and started to pull out her own gear.

"I hope you didn't break his heart again."

"Me, too."

Desi could see that Wolf was distracted. "Are you sure you know what you're doing?"

"With Justin?" Wolf snorted. "I have no idea what I'm doing." She didn't look at Desi—she was too focused on adjusting her holster.

Desi stifled a sigh. "No, that's not what I meant, but let's talk about that later. I was talking about the mission." Their plan was unlike anything she had ever carried out on Earth, where she was used to directly charging the gate and taking down the target. That method was straightforward, and she was good at it. In contrast,

Wolf's plan was more complicated, with a lot of moving pieces that needed to come together just right in order for their teams to be successful.

"I'm sure about the mission," Wolf said, finally looking up at Desi.

Desi was relieved to see that Wolf's usual confidence was back. "A lot is riding on you being able to push this guy's buttons," she warned her.

Wolf's eyebrows went up. "If you have a better idea to get the civilians out without Young noticing, I'm all for it."

"Is it so essential that we get the civilians out first? Why not confront Young head-on?" Desi asked.

"It's too risky," Wolf said, shaking her head. "If Young senses a head-on strike, he'll kill every single one of the civilians. Trust me, I know him. And I know I can get him to focus on me, giving you a clear opportunity to get the civilians out. Once everyone is safe, we take Young down." She met Desi's eyes without flinching. "Our plan is going to work."

"He could kill you."

"Maybe, but I doubt it. At least, he won't do that right away—he'll want to make sure his plan worked before he does anything drastic. If he kills me, he loses a lot of the leverage he's going to need when he tries to get his hands on *Journey*."

Desi was still skeptical. "And if you're wrong and he shoots you on sight?"

Wolf gave her a mischievous grin. "Then I guess it's a good thing you'll be there to complete the mission." She pulled a small knife from her desk drawer and slipped it into the cuff of her sleeve.

Desi chuckled in appreciation. "Knife in the sleeve—

never thought of that one," she said. "I'm more of a gun-in-the-boot kind of girl." She put her foot on the chair and briefly pulled up her pant leg. "Here — I requested one for you, too." She handed Wolf a small gun with an elastic band around the holster.

"And I have something for you. I'm not sure how things are done on Earth, but on Neophia, they like to take hostages." Wolf turned back to her desk and pulled out another knife. "This isn't a normal pocket knife: this one has a high-powered laser, a tool for picking locks, and several small blades. They are usually reserved for Special Forces, but I was able to get a couple."

"Thanks, but where would you like me to put it?" Desi had chosen the sleeveless version of the combat uniform.

Wolf handed the knife to her. "Just cut a small hole in the waistline and slip it over your hip — that way, you'll be able to reach it even if your hands are secured behind your back or in front of you."

Desi thanked her and did as suggested.

"Commander Wolf, Lieutenant Flint, please report to the bridge," a voice said through the ship's PA system.

"We must be close," Wolf said with a smile.

Desi smiled back. "Let's go find out what we're up against." She held the door open for Wolf, and together they quickly strode to the bridge.

Journey was hovering five miles away from the colony. Going any closer would put the ship at unnecessary risk since they didn't know what kind of firepower Ryan might have at his disposal. *Journey* was already operating on a limited power supply, after all — another attack could disable the ship completely. Crystal might have been willing to put her own life on the line to liberate the colony, but she wasn't willing to risk her ship and everyone on it.

Crystal and Desi stood in the pit, looking at the blueprint of the colony on the bridge's main screen. They needed to determine the best way to enter the facility.

"They've set up patrols here, here, and here," Dewite said, tapping the tablet in his hand. Red lines appeared on the main screen indicating the routes of the patrol units.

Crystal studied the screen intently before a small smile formed on her lips.

"What is it?" Desi asked.

"They're herding us," Crystal said.

"What do you mean?"

"Look at this." Crystal took the tablet from Dewite and ran her finger across it. A blue dotted line appeared on the main screen. "The patrols overlap everywhere except here. I would bet anything that the escape pod at the end of this corridor has been blown."

"Then we need to find another way in," Desi said.

"No, don't you see? It's perfect," said Crystal. "Our plan hinges on my team coming into contact with Young. All he's done is taken the fun out of it."

"So we know how we are getting in...any idea where we might find the hostages?" Desi asked.

"Let's see." Crystal hit more buttons on the tablet, and the image on the main screen shifted so that they were looking at a layout of the inside of the colony. She studied the image. What would Ryan do? At one point, she used to know exactly how he would think. Ryan had always been very strategic, she remembered. He never made a decision without considering every contingency.

"Here," She tapped the tablet again, highlighting one

of the rooms. "It's one of only a few rooms in the colony that's large enough to hold the entire population, and it only has one access point — it can easily be guarded by just a few people. It's the farthest away from our entry point, too. Since Young thinks he's laying a trap for us, I'm sure he believes we won't ever get near it."

"Works for me," Desi said after a few minutes of consideration. "Let's go prep the teams." She nodded at Crystal, and they both left the bridge for the combat team room.

Once completed, the combat team room would be one of the nicest areas on the ship, with their own locker rooms, a lounge and rec area, and a large conference room for training and prep. Given Crystal's requirement that her team do daily physical training, she had even given them their own small gym so that they wouldn't overrun the main one. Unfortunately, though, all they had at the moment was a large bare room filled with boxes and unassembled furniture.

Their teams were already there when Crystal and Flint arrived. "All right, everyone, listen up," Flint called. "We're going to start the briefing." Everyone fell silent at once.

"Soupionia is a modular colony with three main units all connected by one large atrium in the center," Crystal began. "Each of the three units holds a set of escape pods, and the main launch bay is in Unit One. There are no other exit points."

Flint took over. "We are going to take a two-pronged approach to this mission, with my team focusing on evacuating the colony's citizens."

"And my team will be the distraction," said Crystal. "I'll only need a few people for this mission." She turned, surveying the room. "Grady, Anderson, Collins, Henson, Murphy—you're with me. Henson, you just became my tech expert. Get with Price before we move out, and he'll walk you through everything you need to know." Crystal saw the looks of disappointment on the faces of the team members she hadn't selected, but no one objected. They would all get a chance to prove themselves eventually.

"All weapons are to be locked in at level 3," Flint said. "We will only be engaging with the enemy once all of the civilians are safe and secure."

Crystal nodded in agreement. "We need to target the officers first," she said. "The lower ranks are filled with mixed-blood soldiers who almost certainly have been drafted. Most of them don't want to be there, and if we can take out their leadership, they are likely to surrender." She paused to scan the room again, making eye contact with each member of her team. "It's important to keep in mind that in order for Terian soldiers to serve in the field, they have to be at least half Sertex, so be prepared—they are trained to attack while invisible."

Nods from all around.

"All right, people, we move out in five minutes," Flint said.

Crystal turned to leave, but was stopped by Alister. "Commander, what would you like us to do while you are gone?"

"Keep everyone on standby. If we run into trouble, we'll call you in for backup. Hopefully, you won't be needed."

He bobbed his head. "Yes, ma'am."

"And if you get bored somewhere in that mess is a pool

table." Crystal nodded her head towards the massive pile of shipping crates in the corner.

Chapter 19

The shuttle was crammed with Crystal's team of six and Flint's team of twenty. Justin was at the helm with Grady acting as his copilot. Crystal stood behind them, watching their progress. She tensed slightly as they made their final approach, but the patrol ship they were evading didn't alter its course.

Crystal left the cockpit to join the rest of her team. "Are you ready?" she asked Flint.

Flint grinned in reply. "Are you?"

"Of course." A slight jolt rippled through the shuttle as it made contact with the colony's hatch. Crystal surveyed her team. They looked tense but confident.

She nodded reassuringly at them, letting them know that she was confident about her plan...even though she was purposefully leading them into a trap.

"Seal secured," Grady called from the back of the ship.

"It's time," Flint said.

"Remember—no matter how bad it looks, don't make a move until we're gone," Crystal told Flint in a soft voice. "Our first priority has to be getting the civilians to safety."

"I know," Flint said with a curt nod. "Be careful."

"You, too." Crystal motioned for Grady to open the door, and she and her team quietly slipped through it.

The corridor in front of them appeared to be empty, but she knew better. She kept scanning the walls and ceiling as her team slowly progressed down the hallway. "Fourteen," she whispered to Grady.

"Fourteen what?" Justin asked.

"Sertex," Grady answered.

Even though Crystal's team had made it halfway down the corridor without even so much as a twitch from the Terian army, Crystal knew they were surrounded. They had been ever since they stepped off the shuttle. She had to get Ryan to attack before they reached the end of the hallway, or Desi wouldn't know when it was safe to move her team out. "This is taking too long," she muttered to Grady.

"Do you have a plan?"

"Don't I always?" Crystal took a few more steps before she spoke again.

"Playing hide-and-seek? Aren't we are little old for games, Ryan?" Crystal's voice rang through the corridor. "Or maybe you're hiding because you're scared. It's a legitimate fear—I always have been a better soldier than you, so I can't blame you for not wanting your whole team to watch you lose. Why don't you make this easier on everyone and give up now?"

Crystal waited a few seconds. She thought there was a chance that would get a response, but she wasn't sure. She wasn't discouraged when nothing happened, though— she still had a few tricks up her sleeve. "You've learned some patience, I'm impressed. Your father would be so proud," she said in a mocking voice.

Still nothing. "Let's test that patience, shall we?" Crystal fired at one of Young's nearly invisible Sertex soldiers. The shot hit him in the shoulder, and he fell to the ground, visible again.

"Hold your fire," Crystal said to her team as they reached for their weapons. She wanted to see if any of Ryan's team would break rank and fire at them. No one did. He must have recruited his most loyal troops to lay the trap.

"Your team didn't seem to like that," she called out. Several members of his team had flinched when her shot connected, she had noticed. She could see the Sertex soldiers' movements more clearly than she had before. At least she knew she was starting to get to them.

It wouldn't take much to break Ryan now. "You can't blame them, though, can you? It can't be easy to serve under someone who has no problem sitting back and watching his people take the fall for him." She paused to let that sink in. "You know there's a word for people like you, right? That word is 'coward.'"

Crystal could still feel the word on her lips when the attack started. Ryan had been one of the soldiers hiding in the rafters. He jumped down, dragging her to the ground with him. It took everything Crystal had not to fight back too hard as they struggled. She threw a few mis-aimed punches and one that connected with his jaw. She had to make it believable, after all. Suddenly, she felt two sets of hands grab her from behind and pull her to her feet.

Crystal glanced around at her team. Grady was the only one still struggling, with two Terian soldiers grimly hanging on to his arms. The rest of the team was standing in a small group with a Terian gun pointed at each of them. At least no one appeared to be hurt.

"Only six men? I'm insulted," Ryan sneered at her.

She snorted. "Don't be. I thought six was a bit of overkill, but this little escapade made for a nice training exercise for some of the new guys."

"Apparently, you overestimated your team."

"I don't think so—this is far from over." Crystal wanted to push a bit more. The angrier Ryan was, the easier it would be for Flint's team to get to the civilians without interference.

She smiled at him, knowing that would make him madder. "You're forgetting one key thing, Ryan: I'm better at this."

In response, he strode over to her and threw a fist at her left eye as his two soldiers held on to her arms.

She ducked in time to avoid most of the blow, but it still stung. She didn't let the pain show. "It must be easy to act tough when your opponent can't fight back. You're so brave," she said, making her voice as sweet as possible.

Crystal could see the rage growing behind Ryan's eyes and knew that she had accomplished her goal. His next punch connected with her stomach much harder than she had expected. The two men holding her loosened their grip as she sank to her knees, winded.

Ryan kicked her in the chest, sending her the rest of the way to the ground. A small gasp escaped her lips as his second kick connected with her ribcage. Crystal was sure she heard something crack.

"Not so tough now, are we?" Ryan whispered as he crouched down next to her.

Crystal managed to pull herself up to a kneeling position, one hand clutching her damaged side. Their eyes connected. The look she gave him was filled with disgust. How could this possibly be the same person she had once loved?

Ryan quickly rose to his feet, breaking the connection between them. "Get them out of my sight."

Crystal hit her head and shoulder on the wall when her captors threw her into a small room. They pushed the rest of her team in, then locked the door behind them.

She slowly pushed herself upright and looked around. There wasn't much to see—several walls had holes in them where fixtures had been stripped away, and a high-res camera had been haphazardly installed in a corner of the ceiling. The lingering smell of chemicals told her that before this room had become a prison, it had functioned as a cleaning supplies room. The disinfectant smell coupled with the pain coursing through her body was making her nauseous. Five seconds. Crystal would allow herself five seconds to feel the pain and weakness that was threatening to overtake her.

One. Crystal tried to take a deep breath, but fire erupted in her chest. Her ribs were surely cracked.

Two. She could feel her face swelling and a trail of blood running down her chin. She imagined that the others could see the skin on her face turning a bruised purple.

Three. Self-doubt washed over her. Why had she thought that she could pull off such an insane plan? Giving up was never a good option. She should have known better. She hadn't really considered what would happen if she got hurt—how was she going to lead her team now?

Four. Ryan. She hadn't felt anything when she first saw him, but now all of her old memories were flooding back.

Was it really possible that the person she had just encountered was the same man she had loved? Had that coldness and cruelty always been there, or had he become that way over the years they had been apart? Was there something more she could have done to save him? Despite everything, she found herself longing for the Ryan of her past.

Five. She pushed it all out of her mind: the pain, the doubt, the longing...all of it had to go. She had a job to do.

Crystal straightened up as much as she could and stepped away from the wall. She thought she had done a decent job keeping the pain from her face, but something must have broken through, because Justin was by her side in a second. "You're hurt."

"It's not that bad." She used the back of her hand to wipe away some of the blood she could feel coating her chin.

Now Grady was standing in front of her, too. Crystal could see the concern in his eyes, but she forced hers to show nothing except determination.

After a few seconds, Grady's smile told her that he understood. "Well, you won't win any beauty contests, but you'll live," he finally said.

"Could we move on, please?" Crystal said.

"Anything you want, Fearless Leader." Grady threw his hands up in defeat.

Crystal was grateful for the joke—she could sense the tension leaving the rest of the team now that they were convinced she wasn't down for the count.

"Henson, report," Crystal said. She had seen Henson looking at the camera as soon as the Terian soldiers had thrown them into their current prison.

"Looks like it's just a video feed—no audio," Henson

said crisply.

"Fantastic. They didn't find your microcomputer, did they?"

"Of course not." With a small smile, Henson reached under her shirt and pulled out the tiny computer. It wasn't much bigger than a postage stamp, but it was all they would need to reprogram the camera to their advantage.

"Excellent," Crystal said with an answering smile. "I think a five-minute loop should be enough."

"You got it." Henson quickly attached the chip to the camera. "All right, everyone. As you were in three...two...one..." The team rearranged themselves into the positions they'd been in when they'd first been unceremoniously tossed into the room.

Time passed slowly. Crystal tried to focus on counting the minutes to keep her mind from wandering to Ryan, but it wasn't working. He was probably loving the fact that she was still sprawled out on the ground. If only he knew it was just an act.

"Time," Henson finally said.

"All right." Crystal got back up as gracefully as she could. Pain shot through her side, but at least this time she managed to keep it from showing on her face. "Let's take inventory." In his rage, Ryan had forgotten to take Crystal's gun and communicator. Rookie mistake.

As she looked around at her team, though, it was clear she was the only one still armed. She quickly removed her weapon and handed it to Collins, who looked nervous. It was his first mission, she remembered. Was he really cut out for this? Fortunately, his confidence seemed to triple as soon as the gun was in his hand.

Rather than bend over, Crystal propped her left foot

against the wall so that she could remove the gun attached to her ankle. "From Desi?" Justin said, motioning towards the gun.

"Yeah… Remind me to thank her when this is over." Crystal glanced around at her team, trying to decide who she should give the weapon to. Murphy was holding up surprisingly well considering his lack of experience. Henson had already done a combat tour and could clearly take care of herself, and while Grady always preferred to be armed, Crystal knew he would be fine without a gun. That left one candidate.

As much as Crystal told herself he was the logical choice, she knew deep down that logic wasn't the only thing at play. "Take it," she said, and held out the gun to Justin.

"I'm not taking it from you," He put his hands up in protest.

"Don't count me out yet, Ensign—I still have a few tricks up my sleeve," she said.

"Unless one of those tricks is another gun, I'm not taking it," he said stubbornly.

The seriousness in his voice took her back a little. If Ryan was in Justin's place, he would have taken the gun without hesitating, she knew. She quickly dashed the thought from her mind. There was no point in comparing Justin to Ryan. In fact, she was pretty sure doing so would lead her down a dark and dangerous path.

"Please, Justin," she said, taking a step closer to him. She lowered her voice. "I need to know that you'll be able to defend yourself. If Young decides to target you…"

Crystal cut herself off. Ryan couldn't possibly know that Justin was important to her. If he was going to target anyone on her team to try to hurt her, in fact, he would target Grady. She had to change her line of reasoning.

"If anything were to happen to you, I..." Crystal had to stop herself again. She was having a hard time coming up with an argument that was free from emotion.

"I can protect myself you know," Justin cut in.

"I know. But just please take it." If her voice didn't betray her pleading, her eyes did.

After another hesitation, Justin accepted the gun. A thousand thoughts passed through Crystal's mind as the tips of his fingers brushed against the palm of her hand.

She breathed a small sigh of relief when she felt the weight of the weapon leave her hand. Now that she knew Justin was protected, she would have an easier time focusing on their mission.

Crystal turned back to her team. "How about we get out of here?"

"Way ahead of you," said Grady. He had already removed one of the ceiling tiles and was standing below it. "After you." He gave a familiar devilish grin.

Desi's team had reached the entrance to the module where they believed the civilians were being held. As she was about to round the next corner, however, the soft sound of approaching footsteps reached her ears. A pair of patrolmen must be heading towards them. It would have been easy to take them out—if they were on Earth, she wouldn't hesitate to do so. But, as Desi was constantly having to remind herself, they weren't on Earth, so instead she backtracked her team until they found a door that opened easily. They slipped inside and found themselves in someone's living quarters.

"Hey, Price," Desi whispered once her eyes had

adjusted to the lack of light. "Do you think you can get into the security system from here?" She had spotted a terminal in the corner—could they use it to access the module's internal systems? She would have liked to have gotten a little closer to the civilians before taking down the security camera, but the opportunity was too good to pass up.

"It's worth a shot," he whispered back.

Desi and the team waited in silence while Price seated himself at the terminal. The sound of clicking keys seemed abnormally loud as they waited for him to finish.

They were standing in someone's living room, Desi could tell—pictures of smiling children and a couple holding hands hung on the walls. Did this place resemble Wolf's childhood home? She was fairly certain Wolf had mentioned growing up in an underwater colony. She could almost envision a terrified young Wolf sitting on the floor in front of the wall screen with a forgotten plate of toast on her lap, about to watch her parents be executed.

She quickly looked back at Price, trying to distract herself. As much as Desi hated to admit it, Wolf was right: war was different here. Watching Wolf and Young had affected her more than she had thought it would. The attack was brutal, yes, but she had expected that. What she hadn't expected was how personal everything felt. Young's actions weren't about securing resources or defending his territory—there was far too much history between him and Wolf for his motivations to be that simple. He seemed to take cruel pleasure in bringing Wolf down.

Desi was grateful when Price's voice broke into her thoughts. "I'm in," he said softly.

"Can you confirm the location of the hostages?" Desi asked.

The images on the screen changed quickly as Price scrolled through the various video feeds, most of them showing empty corridors. Finally, she saw figures.

"They're here," Price said, pointing. "Right where we were heading."

"Good. Take down the feed."

He nodded, then hesitated, his fingers hovering over the keys. "Before I do, it might be helpful to locate Commander Wolf's team...make sure they're all right."

Price had been the only other member of Desi's team to witness the exchange between Wolf and Young. He hadn't taken it very well.

She gave him a quick nod. "Make it fast." It was the only comfort she could give him.

He scrolled through the feeds faster than he had before, almost too fast for her to see what was happening in each video. She squinted and leaned closer to the screen.

"There," Desi pointed at the feed showing Wolf lying on the floor of a small room. She wasn't moving, and neither was the rest of her team.

"That could be a video loop," Price said. In another feed, they saw Grady emerging from a room a few doors down.

Desi sucked in her breath. "Lock down the feed before Young sees this."

Price's fingers flew over the keys. "Done. They shouldn't realize there is a problem until they refresh their systems. That should buy us a little more time."

"Good," She clapped Price briefly on the shoulder. "Let's move out."

Desi was the first one to step into the hall. The patrol

was nowhere to be seen. She motioned for her team to join her, then silently but swiftly strode up the hallway. They still had a way to go before they reached the civilians.

Chapter 20

Crystal's team had emerged from the overhead maintenance passage just a few rooms away from where they had been held. She sent Grady out into the corridor first to make sure the way was clear. A few seconds later, he came back and nodded. They joined him in the hallway, moving towards the escape pods as originally planned. Hopefully Flint's team would meet them there.

Crystal put up a warning hand, knowing her team would stop behind her. Several yards ahead, a door was open. She signaled for her team to stay back while she went to investigate.

When she cautiously peeked around the door, she saw that several Terian soldiers were crowded around a large screen, watching some kind of sporting event. The weapons they had liberated from Crystal's team were lying on a table behind them.

She soundlessly crept back to her team. "We need to find another route," Crystal quietly told Grady.

"What is it?" he asked.

"Eight unfriendlies and our weapons." She gestured

back the way they had come. "We passed a side corridor earlier—we can use that to get around them."

Grady arched an eyebrow. "Or we could go get our weapons."

"Too risky," Crystal said, shaking her head.

"They aren't even paying attention," Grady protested. "I could easily take them by surprise and overpower them."

Crystal sighed. "We don't have time."

"You know you'd feel a lot better with your weapon back..." Grady let his words trail off, but his eyes held a challenging look.

She narrowed hers. "Fine," she finally said, "but I'm coming with you."

"No, you're not—you're hurt," Grady said.

"I've survived worse." She shifted to address the rest of the team, raising her voice just enough for them to hear her. "Change of plans, everyone—Grady and I are going to get our weapons back."

She waited for assenting nods to ripple through the group before continuing. "Anderson and Henson, cover one side of the corridor; Collins and Murphy, you've got the other. If the soldiers in there call for backup before we can take them down, you'll need to be ready."

The four of them nodded again and took their assigned spots. As soon as they were satisfied that the others were in place, Crystal and Grady headed towards the open door.

"Are you ready?" Grady asked.

She gave him a quick nod. "Let's do this before I change my mind."

Grady entered the room first, grabbing a nearby chair and throwing it at the screen. Sparks filled the room as the

Terian soldiers dove for cover. Grady seized the opportunity and charged while Crystal slipped into the room, unnoticed amidst the chaos, shut the door, and secured it. She wanted to keep the fight contained.

Two Terian soldiers had regained their composure and were fighting back, she saw. Grady was doing a good job of keeping them both at bay, but if he didn't take one of them out soon, it was obvious that they would eventually overpower him.

Crystal had almost gotten to the table holding their weapons when a shot was fired from behind her. She stumbled, and the shot missed her by centimeters. Out of the corner of her eye, she saw the shooter rushing towards the door. She flung herself at him, using his momentum to push him headfirst into the wall. He fell to the ground beneath her.

Crystal jumped back up and raced to their guns. She grabbed one and fired at one of the guys Grady was fighting. "Jim!" she yelled, and tossed her gun to him. He snatched it from midair and fired point-blank at his remaining opponent. Three down.

Crystal went to reach for another gun when someone grabbed her from behind. From the strength of the grip, she could tell that her opponent was at least twice her size. She struggled to break free, kicking at his shins and jabbing her elbows down and backwards as hard as she could.

He stumbled, but he didn't release her—instead, her opponent held on with one hand while he punched her in her already-sore ribs with the other. She screamed in agony and fell to her knees, pain clouding out her defenses.

A second later, her assailant fell down next to her,

unconscious. Through a haze of pain, Crystal realized that Grady must have seen what was happening and gotten off a solid shot at her attacker.

With a grunt of pain, she got to her feet and lurched to the table. She grabbed another gun as she scanned the room. There were only three soldiers left standing, and they had surrounded Grady: two were attempting to pin him against the wall, and the third was aiming a gun at his head.

Crystal targeted the one aiming the gun first, then fired at the soldier holding Grady's right arm. The second Grady's arm was free, he twisted away from the last soldier and shot him with the soldier's own weapon. The soldier slumped to the ground.

"Five to three," Grady said, breathing hard in the sudden stillness.

"Don't get cocky," Crystal said as she fought to catch her own breath. "Go get the others, would you?" She forced herself to breathe more deeply, willing the fiery pain in her side to subside.

Crystal still hadn't fully caught her breath when Grady returned with the rest of the team, but the pain had become more manageable. "Let's get these guys secured," she said, gesturing at the fallen Terians. "Then grab what you need—we move out in five minutes." She stepped aside as the team got to work.

A voice came from behind her. "How about we get you patched up?" Justin said. Crystal turned around to find him holding up a first-aid kit.

"OK," Crystal said reluctantly. Never in a million years would she have thought to take the time to bandage her wounds—she was already busy mapping out their next steps in her mind. Still, it was a good idea, especially while they had a few minutes to spare.

Justin started going through the first-aid kit. Crystal slowly started to unbutton her shirt, wincing as the movement made her ribs twinge again.

"Here," Justin stuttered, holding out two white tablets. "For the pain."

A deep blush had filled his cheeks. What was he expecting? It wasn't like he could bandage her ribs over her shirt—now wasn't the time for modesty. She took the offered pills, popped them in her mouth, and swallowed them both at the same time.

"Would you help me take this off?" she asked.

"Sure." He stood behind her and carefully slid the shirt down, lightly brushing his fingers along her arms. He stepped back in front of her and grabbed a roll of gauze from the kit. "Ready?" he said, giving her a tentative smile.

Crystal glanced down and saw that a large, dark bruise was covering most of her exposed skin. She stifled a sigh—that was going to take weeks to heal properly. "I'm ready."

Justin stepped closer. The last time they had been this close, he had kissed her, Crystal remembered. She started to wish he would kiss her again, but she quickly dashed the thought from her mind. It must have been the pain meds she had just swallowed.

His eyes locked with hers as he began to wrap the gauze around her ribs. Crystal didn't break contact, allowing herself to take comfort in the warmth and tenderness she found there.

"Guys," Grady broke in, "I hate to interrupt, but we should really get out of here."

Their moment of intimacy vanished. "Of course,"

Crystal said.

Justin quickly secured the bandage and stepped back. His flat expression didn't betray any of his thoughts.

Crystal felt like she had just snapped out of a trance. She wished she could have lived in that moment a little while longer. With effort, she shoved aside her thoughts and tried to refocus. "Grady, take the lead," she said, nodding at him.

She finished buttoning her shirt and followed her team out into the hall.

Desi felt excitement building inside of her. Finally, it was time to act. She had ordered the rest of her team to hang back while she went to survey the room where the hostages were being held.

Carefully, she peered around the corner. The room had three sets of double doors. Two sets were chained shut, she saw, leaving only the center set accessible. The two guards stationed at the center doors were talking casually to each other, seemingly oblivious to their surroundings. One of them was even leaning on his gun. Desi was disgusted.

Without waiting for the rest of her team, Desi rounded the corner with her gun out and ready. The first soldier hit the ground before he could even turn to face her. The second soldier reached for his communicator instead of his fallen gun.

"Not a good idea," Desi muttered under her breath. She shot him without hesitation, and he slumped to the ground next to his friend.

Desi kept her gun raised, expecting more soldiers to burst into the corridor any second. She almost opened fire on her own team when they suddenly entered the hallway.

"What's wrong?" Price asked her quietly.

"It can't be this easy." Desi scanned the halls, on edge and ready for an attack that didn't seem to be coming. She didn't understand it. The civilians were the best leverage Young had, and yet only two guards had been posted to secure the entire population? It didn't add up.

"It means Wolf's plan worked," Price said. "They don't know we're here—Young must think he neutralized the threat when he captured her team."

Desi frowned. "I can't shake the feeling we're missing something, like a bigger picture we aren't seeing." Her instincts had never let her down before, and right now they were screaming at her.

Price frowned, too. "Maybe we are missing something, but right now, there are a couple hundred people on the other side of that door hoping to be saved. What do you want to do?"

Price was right, of course—they had to free the hostages. That's what they had come here to do. She just wished the gnawing in the pit of her stomach would ease. "Send a couple of guys to secure the path to the escape pods," she said. "We won't have a lot of time before Young figures out what we're doing."

Price nodded and went to confer with the other members of the team while Desi strode to the doors, trying to exhibit a confidence she didn't feel. She pulled the doors open.

Suddenly silenced voices hung like echoes in the air, and every eye was fixed on her. The silence of the crowd was overwhelming. Desi stood transfixed in the doorway, frozen in place, until the piercing cry of a baby brought her back to her senses.

"I'm Lieutenant Desiree Flint with the United Sta—" she started to say, then stopped as looks of confusion momentarily replaced looks of fear "—with LAWON, currently stationed on *Journey*. I'm here to help. My team is standing by to escort you to the escape pods, but first I need to speak with whomever is in charge."

A voice rang out in the quiet. "I'm the mayor, and I'm in charge."

Desi searched the crowd for the voice and finally saw an older, plump man making his way across the room to her. He was walking with a limp that seemed fresh. "Can you tell me what happened?" She was careful to keep her voice calm.

"It was sudden—we had no warning," he said once he was standing in front of her. "Four subs filled with soldiers docked at our loading port and took over half the colony before anyone knew what was going on." His expression darkened. "I only had a few seconds to get a distress call out before they reached my office."

Desi gave him a respectful nod. "You did your job—you got your message out. We're here because of that distress call."

The mayor puffed his chest with pride, looking slightly more hopeful.

"Is this everyone?" she asked. "Are they holding anyone somewhere else?"

"No, this is everyone."

"Any injuries?"

"A few, but nothing serious," he answered. "In all honesty, they didn't seem very interested in us."

"What do you mean?" Alarms were going off in Desi's head. If the mayor was right and Young didn't care about the colony or its people, then why was he here?

The mayor looked as puzzled as she felt. "You're the first person we've seen since they locked us in here. It was almost as if we were an afterthought, like they just wanted us out of the way." He shrugged. "I was afraid they were going to make us an example of someone, but what do I know? I guess I've seen too many movies," he said with a relieved chuckle.

"Lieutenant Flint." Price poked his head into the room. "The hallway is secured and we are ready to begin evacuations."

"Thank you, Ensign. Can you get the first group ready to move?"

Desi stepped out of the room to let Price begin organizing the evacuation. She found a spot of relative privacy and pulled out her communicator. "Flint to *Journey*."

"Go ahead, Flint," Reed's voice came through her communicator.

"Sir, we have found the hostages and are beginning evacuations. Prepare to begin recovery of the pods in five minutes."

"And Commander Wolf's team?"

"They haven't rejoined us yet. However, we were able to locate them on the security feed before we disabled it. They appeared to be making their way to the rendezvous point."

"Good."

"Sir, have you had any communications from Young?" Desi asked.

"No, nothing yet."

"Understood. I'll keep you apprised of the evacuations." Desi slipped her communicator back into its holster, watching the first group of citizens leave the room. Her thoughts were churning. She had assumed Young would begin negotiations for the ship once he believed he had captured Wolf. Was it possible Rank didn't really want *Journey*? Was he after something else altogether?

Crystal's team moved swiftly through the hallways of Soupionia, taking down any patrols they came across. There was no point hiding now—it was only a matter of time before Ryan realized what had happened and came looking for them. The only thing that mattered now was for Flint's team to be able to get the civilians out of harm's way before that happened. It didn't take them long to reach the escape pods.

"My god!" Flint blurted out the second she spotted Crystal. "You look like shit."

"Next time, you can be the decoy," Crystal said with a smile as she joined Flint at the control console of the last escape pod.

"Are you all right?" Tyler asked. He couldn't hide the concern in his voice.

"I'm fine," Crystal said, wanting him to focus on the task at hand rather than her. "I promise, it looks a lot worse than it is. So where are we with the evacuations?"

"This is our last group, but we still need someone from *Journey* to accompany them. That is, if you—" Flint started to say.

"Don't finish that thought, Flint," Crystal said.

"It's not a bad idea," Justin said. "You need to be checked out by medical."

She snorted. "Do you really think I'm going to let

Young use me as a human punching bag and then leave just when I'm about to get the chance to return the favor?" She was sure her frustration was apparent in her voice.

She glanced at the rest of her team and saw that most of them wore expressions of concern. Grady was the only one who was avoiding making eye contact with her. He probably felt the same way the rest of them did, but at least he was smart enough to keep it to himself.

"But—" Tyler started.

She cut him off. "This is not a democracy—nobody gets a vote. This is a military mission, and I'm the senior ranking officer. I am fit enough to successfully complete this mission." She stared each of them down in turn, challenging them to contradict her. "And I have every intention of doing just that." She didn't like to throw her rank around, but if she needed to, she was more than willing to.

"All right," Grady said, giving in. He could probably tell that she was getting close to the snapping point. "But we still need someone to escort the last pod."

"Collins," Crystal said curtly.

Collins nodded and wordlessly stepped into the escape pod. Crystal closed and locked the hatch behind him, irrationally grateful to be standing on the outside of the door.

Crystal didn't turn around until Flint had launched the pod. "Phase one complete," Crystal said, once again facing her team. She gave them a determined grin.

"Time for phase two," Flint said with an equally determined grin.

Together, she and Crystal headed back into the complex, the rest of their teams falling into step behind them. It was time to liberate the colony.

Chapter 21

The first shot was too high, and, Crystal suspected, fired prematurely. The Terians had to be on edge — that was the only reasonable explanation for the mistake. Crystal's team hadn't even entered the atrium yet when the shot was fired.

She was the first one to peek around the entrance to the atrium. The large, airy space was filled with small tables and couches. Small shops lined the perimeter. She could see two other entrances across the atrium, making three in all. With so many potential places to hide, it was impossible to tell where the shot had come from, so she gestured for the team to stay behind her as she waited to see if the atrium would suddenly fill with Terian soldiers.

No soldiers appeared. It was time to take the offense, Crystal decided.

Flint stepped up next to her and surveyed the setting. "Do you want to take the right or the left?" Flint asked, nodding at the two entrances facing them. The eager grin on her face matched the one Crystal could feel on her own lips.

"The left seems as good a choice as any," Crystal said. "Let's go have some fun."

With a parting grin, Flint and her team took off towards the right entrance. Crystal's team emerged a half-second behind her, with Justin falling into step next to Crystal. His presence gave her a little extra confidence as she raised her gun and fired at random into the hallway leading away from the seemingly deserted left entrance. A soft, satisfying thud echoed back to her—her shot had connected.

Terian soldiers poured into the room from both entrances, firing wildly. Crystal barely dodged a shot as she ran to take cover behind an overturned couch. Justin joined her a second later.

She quickly popped her head above the couch to take an inventory of her team. Thankfully, they had all found cover and were returning fire. Flint's team hadn't been so lucky—one of her soldiers lay unconscious on the ground. Fortunately, two other men were able to grab his arms and drag him to cover. One examined the fallen soldier briefly, then held up his hand to signal that the man was only stunned.

Crystal breathed a sigh of relief. At least everyone was playing by the same rules.

Now that she knew the soldier would be fine, Crystal turned her attention back to the firefight taking place around her. They were greatly outnumbered, but the skill of her team far surpassed that of their enemy. Then again, more and more Terian soldiers kept pouring into the atrium.

Crystal searched every new face that entered, looking for Ryan's familiar features. He wouldn't be able to resist coming after her himself, she knew. She needed to be ready for him.

Out of the corner of her eye, Crystal saw something soaring through the air towards them. "Take cover!" she yelled to her team.

They scattered to the tables. Crystal ran to the nearest one and threw herself under it, using it as a shield. She waited there until the last of the debris had stopped pelting the tabletop. The explosion was small—she doubted it had been strong enough to kill anyone. It was probably meant to knock them out, she decided. For whatever reason, Ryan wanted them alive.

Crystal darted out from under the table with her gun raised, but she didn't see any Terians in the immediate area. She did, however, spot Justin half-buried under debris.

Panic rose in her as she rushed over to him and threw the chunks of debris aside, exposing a metal column that had collapsed. It had pinned his foot to the ground and trapped him. She tried to shift the column, but it wouldn't budge—he only winced more. "Grady, help me with this!" she called, seeing him emerge from another table.

He was at her side in a few seconds. Together, they were able to lift the column enough for Justin to pull his foot out.

Crystal sighed in relief. "Cover us a second," she said.

Grady gave a quick nod and then turned back to Justin, who was trying to lever himself to his feet. Before he could stand, though, Crystal put a hand on Justin's shoulder.

"Take a second to catch your breath," she told him. His gun was lying a short distance away. She picked it up, but she didn't give it back to him. Instead, she knelt down next to him.

"I'm fine." Justin reached for his weapon.

Crystal didn't relinquish it. "Are you sure?"

"Yes." He reached up and tucked a loose strand of hair behind her ear. The fight happening around them disappeared as his fingertips brushed against her cheek.

"This is yours." She handed him his weapon without breaking eye contact.

"Thanks," he said. He made no movement to rejoin the fight.

In her peripheral vision, Crystal saw a flash of movement over Justin's shoulder. They were surrounded, she realized. That shouldn't have been a surprise—it was the logical plan of attack, and despite everything, Crystal couldn't deny that Ryan was a good combat leader.

But that didn't mean she had to give up. "Move!" Crystal yelled, and pushed Justin away from her. She dove towards a wall as a bomb exploded right where they had just been.

The second she came out of her roll, she felt someone standing behind her. Hands reached down, grabbed a fistful of her hair, and pulled her to her feet. She didn't need to see his face to know it was Ryan.

Crystal tried every trick she could think of to break away, but as long as Ryan had control of her head, there was little she could do. What was making her even more angry was that she had taught him this hold. He was taunting her. She stopped struggling, knowing that there was no point in wasting her energy.

Ryan grabbed her arm and twisted it painfully behind her back, tossing her gun aside. In one swift movement, he brought his own gun up to her temple. The three green dots showing on the side of the gun flashed in the corner of her eye. At least he wasn't planning on killing her...not yet, anyway.

He pressed his body up against hers. "You're mine now," he whispered in her ear.

Crystal fought the urge to vomit.

"Hold your fire," Ryan yelled. The Terian soldiers stopped firing instantly, but it took Crystal's team a few seconds to realize what was happening. Every member of *Journey*'s crew pointed their weapons at Ryan.

With her body covering Ryan's, though, Crystal knew no one would take a shot at him. She saw Grady looking at her intently, searching her expression in case she had an escape plan. If only she could think of something.

"Drop your weapons," Ryan ordered. "Unless you'd like me to kill her, that is."

Nobody moved. Crystal was pretty sure he was bluffing—if he was going to kill her, he would have done it by now. Then again, if his hand was forced, he might kill her just to save face in front of his men.

Finally, Justin lowered his gun.

"That's right, lover boy," Ryan taunted him. "Put it on the ground. All of you!"

Slowly, the rest of crew followed suit. Flint was the last one to move, slowly bending down and placing her weapon on the ground. Crystal noticed that she had rested the heel of her gun on her toes.

Ryan's grip on her got even tighter. "Now that we all understand each other, let me tell you what's going to happen next," he said, his voice thick with satisfaction. "You will be escorted back to your shuttle, where you can return to your ship unharmed."

Crystal waited for the catch. There was no way he was going to let them walk out the door with no strings attached.

"That is, all of you except Commander Wolf," Ryan

continued. "She will be staying here with me so that we can have a chance to get reacquainted." He leaned over and kissed her softly on the cheek, all the while smirking in Justin's direction. Crystal's skin crawled.

"I don't think so." Flint kicked out her foot, sending her gun flying up into the air. She grabbed it midair, only to have it shot out of her hand by Ryan.

"Impressive little trick," Ryan said as he returned his gun to Crystal's temple, "but you're not the only one who can shoot."

Crystal scolded herself for not having taken advantage of Ryan's momentary distraction to free herself.

"You can't honestly expect us to walk away and leave her behind," Flint said through gritted teeth. Crystal hoped she wasn't about to lose her temper and do something unnecessarily risky.

"That's exactly what I expect to happen," Ryan said confidently.

"You'll have to kill us first."

The gun pressed harder against Crystal's temple. "As tempting as that offer is," Ryan said sweetly, "I can't have a group of dead LAWON soldiers on my hands. Bad press, you know." He slid his gun away from Crystal and pointed it straight at Flint. "On the other hand, one dead soldier might not be so bad."

"Leave, Lieutenant!" Crystal said. It would only take Ryan a second to fully energize his weapon and take out half her team with a single shot, and she refused to put them at risk, especially when she could save them. She didn't know what Ryan wanted, but it didn't really matter. This whole mess was her fault, anyway. She would be the one to pay the price.

"That's an order, Flint!"

Chapter 22

Young didn't lower his gun from Crystal's temple until his soldiers had led the rest of her team away. Once the last of them had disappeared, he pushed her towards the left entrance. "Let's go," he said roughly.

Crystal didn't fight him. There was no point—Ryan had won, at least for now. She couldn't risk making a move until she was sure the rest of her team was safe.

She noticed that only one of Ryan's men followed them out of the atrium. She guessed Ryan wasn't expecting her to put up much of a fight. He was right. Instead of struggling, Crystal focused all of her energy on memorizing every hallway they passed. If she got a chance to break free, she would need to know the quickest way out.

Ryan tugged on doors as they moved farther down the hall, pushing her inside the first one that opened. He finally released his hold on her and stood facing her, his posture rigid.

She slowly rotated her now-sore shoulder as she looked around the room. It was a small supply room with no way out. "What do you want, Ryan?"

"Spread them," Ryan said.

Crystal rolled her eyes but did as she was told. He had already taken her weapon, anyway, so there wasn't much left for him to find. "I saw you pull that Human out of the rubble," Ryan said as he ran his hand over her body. "Is he your new boyfriend?"

Crystal didn't respond.

"He can never make you happy," Ryan went on. "He's too weak. You need someone strong, someone who challenges you."

"Don't act like you still know me," Crystal said.

"Who is he, anyway?"

"What does it matter?" she snapped. "Are you going to tell me what's going on?"

"You'll find out eventually. I thought I'd try to keep things friendly, but if that's not what you want, fine by me," he said curtly. He grabbed her arms and pulled them behind her back. She felt him start to tie her hands together.

"I went to see your mom a few days before *Journey* launched," she said, hoping to distract him with something personal even though she knew that was a risky tactic. Any acknowledgement from him of his adoptive parents would been as betraying Teria. But still, bringing up the past might give her the opening she needed.

His hands paused.

"The latest round of treatments isn't working," she continued. "The doctors don't think she has much longer. You know she still has that picture of us from our formal in our fifth year on her nightstand?"

"My mother died giving birth to me 26 years ago." His

voice was robotic. From his tone, Crystal could tell he wasn't going to show any emotion towards the dying woman. He quickly finished securing her hands.

"Of course." Crystal flexed her wrists and felt some slack in the rope. Not enough to allow her to pull her hands free, but enough that she had some movement. It was a start.

Her communicator beeped and seemed to awaken Ryan from a trance—with a single angry move, he wrenched it from its holster. Whatever sympathy she may have stirred in him was gone.

"Answer it." he snarled, holding it up to her face with one hand. With his other, he pressed his gun to the back of her head.

"This is Commander Wolf," she said as calmly as she could.

"Commander, I'm glad we got you," Reed said. "I'm ordering you to return to *Journey* at once."

"Captain—" Crystal started to say.

"No arguments. Flint's team can handle the remainder of the mission without you."

"But, sir—"

Reed cut her off again. "Commander, we no longer feel that *Journey* is Rank's target. We think he might be after you."

"I'm sorry, sir, but I can't comply with your order," she finally blurted out.

"Why not?"

Ryan spoke before she could. "Because she's already been detained," he said. The gun pressed harder against her head, warning her to stay quiet.

Silence, then Reed's voice again. "Release my officer, Young."

"That's not going to happen."

"You don't have the right to hold her!" Crystal could feel Reed's anger vibrate through the small device in Ryan's hand.

"I have every right," Ryan snapped. "She has broken our laws and must face charges."

"What charges could she possibly be facing?"

"She led a raid that resulted in the kidnapping of hundreds of Terian citizens. She will be brought before a military tribunal and charged with war crimes." His voice was flat, but she could detect a sense cruel pleasure just beneath the surface.

"You have to be at war to charge a person with war crimes," Reed said just as flatly.

"Your invasion of our colony was viewed as an act of war. We don't want to engage in open warfare any more than you do, Captain, so it was decided that the best way to maintain the peace would be to charge Lieutenant Commander Wolf for her crimes against Teria. Unless you'd rather us retaliate, that is." Ryan paused, then spoke in a tone that was almost condescending. "Is LAWON attempting to start another war, perhaps? What will the good people of Neophia say when they find out?"

"Put Commander Wolf back on," Reed demanded.

"I'm not going to do that," Ryan said, pressing the gun into Crystal's head so hard that her head sank sideways towards her shoulder. "I will, however, keep you apprised of the situation once we have worked out the details. I don't expect it to take long. In the meantime, I have returned the rest of your people to their shuttle. They should be arriving back at your ship shortly."

"You won't get away with this," Reed warned him.

"I already have." Ryan ended the call and lowered his

gun.

"War crimes?" Crystal looked at him incredulously. "That's really what you're going with? No one is going to buy that."

"Let's go." Ryan pushed her out of the room and back into the hallway.

Desi's mind raced as she was forcibly escorted to the shuttle with the rest of the crew. Why had Wolf given up so easily? She had thought Wolf was stronger than that. Yes, they had been outnumbered, and yes, Young had had a gun to her head, but there had to be more Wolf could have done. Giving up was never the answer. And Wolf hadn't even given Desi a chance to try to resolve the situation.

She exchanged glances with Justin, who was also clearly trying to come up with a plan to save Wolf. Desi looked down at her boot and then back up at him, careful not to let any of the guards notice. Surely, he would understand what that meant—he was one of the few people who knew she liked to hide weapons in unusual places. He finally nodded after she had glanced at her boot for the third time.

Justin suddenly tripped and tumbled to the ground, taking three of the guards down with him. Somehow, he managed to tangle his body around and between the fallen Terian soldiers and keep them from getting back up. Two more soldiers rushed over to them, leaving Desi with seven men still standing around her.

Fortunately, none of them were able to stop her from dropping down and her pulling her weapon out of her boot. She fired at two of them before she sprang back up.

The loud thuds they made when they hit the ground caught the attention of everyone else in the hallway, and the Terians turned on their prisoners.

Thankfully, *Journey*'s crew reacted faster. Somewhere between Desi's first and second shot, Grady had managed to take a gun from one of the soldiers, and Justin had emerged from the pile of Terians with a weapon as well.

Quickly, Desi grabbed the two fallen soldiers' weapons, keeping one for herself and tossing the other to Price. Between her, Price, Justin, and Grady, it didn't take long to bring down the rest of the Terian soldiers.

"That went better than expected," Desi said as she surveyed the unconscious bodies lying around her. "Let's get them secured and help yourself to their weapons."

"So what do we do now?" Price asked as the rest of the crew did as ordered. "We were given a direct order to leave."

Desi raised her eyebrows. "The way I heard it, Commander Wolf ordered us to leave the atrium, not the colony. She really needs to be more specific when giving orders. If you aren't comfortable with that and you feel that staying would be a violation of orders, then by all means, you should go." She paused to look at their small group one by one. "But I have no intention of leaving here without every member of our team, orders or not."

"I'm staying," Justin said. No one looked surprised.

"Me, too," Price chimed in.

"I can't let you guys have all the fun without me," Grady added.

Desi nodded. "Everyone else needs to return to *Journey*, though," she pointed out. "Young needs to believe that we actually did leave if we're going to have any chance of getting Wolf back."

Nods all around, followed by determined glances.

Desi smiled. Wolf might have given up, but she wouldn't.

Chapter 23

Ryan stopped Crystal in front of a black door. In the center of the door was a silver nameplate that simply read "Mayor's Office." It was practical. They wouldn't have to get a new one every time they elected a new mayor.

"Are we waiting here for anything in particular, or did you just bring me here to show me this lovely door?" Crystal asked.

"We're waiting for confirmation," Ryan said. He tightened his grip on her arm and stood up a little straighter.

"Of what?" Crystal pressed.

"That there is no backup coming to save you."

As if on cue, a buzzing sound came from Ryan's pocket. He pulled out his communicator. "Go ahead," he said.

"Sir, the LAWON shuttle has departed and is making steady progress back to *Journey*," another voice responded.

"And you're positive the ship was not on autopilot?"

"Yes, sir — our men had disabled the autopilot."

Ryan clicked off the communicator without bothering to reply.

"So, you just have me to deal with," Crystal said, shoving aside the disappointment that she felt rising up. It would have been nice to have a little help to get her out of this mess.

"Good, because there's someone who's anxious to meet you." Ryan knocked on the door.

"Enter."

Chills ran down Crystal's back—there was something familiar about that voice even though she couldn't quite place it. Every cell in her body was screaming at her not to enter that room, but she had no choice as Ryan pushed her forward and through the door.

There were no windows in the room, and the only door was the one they had entered through. An escape would be tough to pull off, she realized, but not impossible. She would just have to time it right.

All of her potential escape plans vanished from her mind as soon as she saw the man sitting behind the elaborate desk. Her insides turned to ice. She fought to get her breathing under control as her initial chill began to transform into a white-hot rage. She had never been this angry before.

For the first time in her life, she was face-to-face with the man who was responsible for her parents' death. She had spent a lot of time thinking about what she would do if she was ever in this situation. She would stay calm and steady, she had decided. She wouldn't let her deep hatred of him tarnish her actions—she would detain him and force him to answer for his crimes in accordance with the law. If an opportunity to cause him a little pain should present itself, well...all the better. Now that she finally had the chance to confront him, though, she had to use every ounce of her self-control to keep her anger in check.

"President Rank, it is my pleasure to introduce you to Lieutenant Commander Crystal Wolf," Ryan said.

"My dear Miss Wolf. It's a shame we haven't met before this." Rank casually stood up and sauntered around the desk to face her. The sound of his voice made Crystal's stomach turn. "I would shake your hand, but…" he trailed off and glanced at her bound arms, smirking.

"Go to hell," she spat at him. Ryan raised a hand to strike her, but Rank stopped him.

"Now, now, Ryan, I'm sure she didn't mean that," he said calmly. "We all say things we regret when under stress — we must give Miss Wolf some leeway."

Crystal knew she had to get her emotions in check if she was going to have any chance of surviving this. Besides, she wouldn't be able to do anything with her hands tied behind her back. She took a deep breath and pushed her anger aside, instead focusing on her bound hands. She started to work the small knife out of the cuff of her sleeve.

"You can't use me as a bargaining chip to get *Journey*," she said, hoping to buy herself some time as she slowly, slowly, felt for the knife.

"I don't want your ship," Rank replied.

"Then why are you here?" The knife fell into the palm of her hand. Still moving slowly so as not to attract their attention, she opened the tiny blade and began to work it against the cord restraining her wrists.

"How else was I going to arrange this little meeting?" Now Rank sounded impatient.

"You did all of this to meet me?"

"Of course. You're an impressive woman, Crystal."

The insincere friendliness in his voice was grating on Crystal's nerves. She focused all of her irritation on the blade and the cord.

"What could you possibly want from me?"

He gave her a hard smile. "You are going to design a ship for me—one that's even more powerful than *Journey*—and together, we'll finally be able to put the Human invaders in their place."

Shock temporarily flooded out her rage. "You're insane!"

He dropped the pretense of a smile. "No, I'm a hero," he said, his voice tinged with anger. "The Humans have been slowly destroying Neophia ever since they set foot on our planet. They spread violence everywhere they go." His eyes narrowed. "Would the Great War have ever happened without their influence? Your parents would still be alive if it weren't for the Humans. It's time to return Neophia to its rightful owners. Teria is already leading the charge, and with the ship you are going to design for me, the rest of the planet will soon follow suit."

Rank took a step closer to Crystal, but she didn't back away. She refused to let him have any power over her. "With you by my side," he continued, "we can finally right the wrongs your ancestors committed when they welcomed the Humans. We can save Neophia together. I'd even be willing to overlook your tainted blood."

When he gently ran his fingers over her cheek, Crystal had to force herself not to flinch away. "I understand what Ryan saw in you," he murmured. "You're very beautiful, maybe even more beautiful than your mother."

"Don't talk about my mother." The knife finally broke through the cord. Her hands were free, but she kept them behind her back. She would only get one shot at this.

Rank gave her an oily smile. "I would have thought you'd be flattered. Your mother was an extraordinary woman—strong, smart, beautiful, just like you. Her only fault was choosing the wrong side. I'm giving you the chance to choose the right one."

He was playing with her, but she wasn't going to give him the satisfaction. This would end now.

"Here's what's going to happen," Crystal said, her voice was calm and even. "You are going to release me and provide me with safe passage back to my ship. You will then vacate this colony and never set foot here again."

Ryan and Rank both laughed.

"No?" She raised her eyebrows. "Then I guess we'll have to do this the hard way."

Quickly, she brought her hands in front of her and delivered two punches to Rank, one to the face and the other to the stomach. The force of the double impact brought him to his knees.

As Rank dropped to the ground, Crystal turned her attention to Ryan, sending his gun flying across the office with a well-directed kick. She attempted the same double-punch combo she had used on Rank, but although her punch to his face connected, Ryan was able to block the blow she aimed at his stomach and then go on the offensive.

Crystal and Ryan traded a furious stream of kicks and punches, each trying to gain the upper hand. Crystal had forgotten how evenly matched they were. It felt like they were back at the Academy sparring rather than facing each other in a life-or-death fight.

As the fight wore on, though, they were each becoming more aggressive. At some point, Ryan grabbed a metal lamp off the desk and swung it at her. Crystal ducked. The lamp flew out of his hand and crashed into a framed poster hanging on the wall. The glass protecting the words "With cooperation, anything is possible" shattered and fell to the ground.

Crystal took advantage of his bad aim to drop to one knee and sweep her other leg at his ankles, catching him off-balance and knocking him to the ground. He hit hard, grunting.

She darted towards the door just as the two guards posted outside of it swung it open. Their eyes widened when they saw both Rank and Ryan sprawled out on the ground, lying between broken glass and destroyed furniture.

Crystal capitalized on their the guards' momentary confusion and slipped between them, grabbing one of their guns from its holster as she went. She fired wildly over her shoulder as she raced down the hallway. If she could slow them down, she might stand a chance.

"Stop her!" Rank's voice pierced the air.

Crystal pushed herself to run even faster. Given her damaged ribs, she knew her chances of outrunning the guards were slim, but she had to try. She had just reached the end of the hallway when she felt a hand grab her and pull her backwards. She lost her balance and hit the ground hard, the stolen gun flying from her hand.

Before she could get back up, the guards each grabbed one of her arms and dragged her to back to the mayor's office. Rank was waiting for her, his face flushed.

He backhanded her across the unbruised side of her face, the ring on his finger leaving a stinging trail of cut flesh across her cheek. "Stupid!"

Slowly, Crystal turned her face back to him and looked Rank straight in the eye. She knew she wouldn't be getting out of this alive. Still, instead of crushing her, that realization only made her feel stronger. She had nothing left to lose, and she wouldn't give Rank or Ryan the satisfaction of breaking her. Her only mission now was to make their lives as difficult as possible until she drew her very last breath.

"You can't blame a girl for trying," she said.

Rank's face was devoid of any emotion as he punched her in the stomach.

Not an ounce of pain registered on Crystal's face. "Impressive. I didn't think you knew how to throw a punch," she said evenly.

"Secure her to a chair! And make sure you do a better job than Young did," Rank said to the guards, clearly biting back his anger.

They threw her into one of the metal chairs and used two sets of handcuffs to secure her wrists to the arms of the chair before they tied her ankles to the chair legs.

"Don't be too mad at Ryan—he really did more to protect you than those two buffoons did," Crystal said when the guards were finished. "Honestly, I never should have made it this far. Maybe if you had a decent training program for your soldiers, you wouldn't have to steal from LAWON." Crystal let her eyes linger on Ryan, who had been standing by, silent and glowering.

Rank towered over Crystal. The false cordialness he had adopted earlier had completely disappeared. "You will work for me, or you'll work for no one."

"And if I don't?"

"Then you'll beg me to kill you."

"I don't beg."

It was strange being alone in a room with Ryan, almost as if they had gone back in time. The casual way he leaned against the desk, the hint of amusement that always hung on the corner of his lips, the questioning arch of his eyebrow...all of that was still there. At the same time, though, so much about him had changed. She had never seen such coldness in eyes or heard such a hardness in his voice before.

Neither of them had spoken in the five minutes since Rank had left. Crystal assumed that Rank was on his way back to Teria by now. He wouldn't want to stick around in case things got messy again — that's why he had people like Ryan.

"So what's the game plan, Ryan?" Crystal said, finally breaking the silence. "How's this going to end? You know there's nothing you can do to force me to work for Rank."

"Rank really thinks that with enough persuading, you'll come around to our side." On the surface, Ryan appeared calm and in control, but underneath that, Crystal could tell he was shaken. She knew the difference between his usual confident demeanor and the air of false authority he was giving off now. He'd probably never been on the receiving end of Rank's anger before. Maybe she could use his unease to her advantage.

"By 'persuading,' you mean torture," Crystal said.

Ryan gazed at her with expressionless eyes. "Among other things. Rank's a creative and persistent man."

Crystal had heard rumors that Rank had ordered research on the effects of starvation, isolation, physical endurance, chemical dosing, and brain mapping. She guessed she would get to find out if those rumors were true. "It's never going to work."

"I know. You never did have enough sense to save

your own skin." Ryan was starting to relax now that they were talking, which was unfortunate — that was going to make it harder for Crystal to maintain the level of anger she would need to fight him. "Did you really have to hit Rank?"

"Yeah, I really did," she said.

"You only made things worse for yourself."

"Probably, but it felt good." Crystal thought she detected a hint of a smile pass his lips. Her heart beat a little faster. Was some of the old Ryan coming through? Maybe there was still a chance to save them both. "Come back with me."

"What are you talking about?"

"Come back to Kincaron with me," she repeated. "I'm sure your dad could work out some kind of amnesty deal. Your parents miss you so much. They would do anything to protect you."

His expression changed, but she couldn't read it. "You know I can never go back. Even with an amnesty arrangement, I'd never be safe. Rank would have me killed within a week."

"I could protect you." The words were out of her mouth before she really considered their implications. In order to protect him, she would have to give up her life on *Journey*. She would be tied to Ryan for the rest of her life. Ryan was right — Rank would never stop sending people to try to kill him. Crystal was surprised to find that she would willingly sacrifice everything if it meant she got her Ryan back.

"How can you protect me? You can't even protect yourself." Now he was openly laughing.

"You know that when you and I work together, no one can beat us. We could do it," she insisted. "We could leave here together, just the two of us, and disappear, go someplace where Rank would never be able to find us."

Ryan stopped laughing. "I won't betray him, Crystal. There's nothing you can say to change that."

"But you could betray your country? Your parents? Me?" She managed to keep her voice from cracking on the last word.

"You and I were over long before I joined Rank." Ryan stood up and started to walk to the door.

"Just tell me one thing," Crystal said to his retreating back.

"What?" Ryan stopped, but didn't turn to face her.

"Did you join Rank because I was doing better than you at the Academy?"

"No." Ryan left the room, turning out the lights before shutting the door behind him.

Desi gathered her small team in a room not far from where their shuttle had been docked. She wasn't thrilled about sending the shuttle back to *Journey*, but she knew they had to maintain the pretense of leaving until she figured out how they were going to save Wolf. The only thing she knew for sure was that they had passed the point of no return—whatever plan they came up with would have to end with LAWON in control of the colony.

"We need a plan, and we need it fast," Desi said. "We know we're outgunned. We also know we don't have an escape plan."

"Wolf's not going to give up without a fight," Grady said.

"It looked to me like she gave up pretty easily," Desi said before she could stop herself. Adrenaline was shooting through her, making her even less cautious about what she said.

"Didn't you see Young's thumb on the trigger setting? He was about to power up his weapon and kill us. Wolf sacrificed herself to save the team." Grady stepped directly in front of her, challenging her.

But Desi wasn't going to back down—she was in charge now. "She didn't even give us a chance to save her," she retorted.

"There was no point! It wouldn't have worked."

"You don't know that. Besides, she has a history with Young. How do you know this wasn't some elaborate ploy to be with him again?"

Grady's lips tightened as he glared at Desi. "Crystal is not a traitor!"

Justin stepped between them, forcing them both to take a step back. "We don't have time for this! We have no idea what Young's doing to Wolf. We're the only chance she has."

Grady turned his back to Desi and ran his hands through his hair. "We don't even know where Young took her," he said, sounding frustrated. "She could be on a launch headed back to Teria by now."

Price finally spoke up. "We have to assume she's still here—otherwise, we don't have a chance."

Justin nodded towards the door. "So we split up and search the colony," he said.

A familiar beep sounded. "Nobody is going anywhere yet!" Desi pulled out her communicator. "This is Flint."

"Where are you?" Reed's voice was calm and even. Desi wished she knew him better. How angry was he about what had happened?

She responded in an equally calm tone. "I'm guessing

by now you are aware that we didn't return to the ship with the rest of the crew."

"I'm aware."

"We've regrouped in a room not far from where our shuttle was docked. We're trying to come up with a plan to rescue Commander Wolf."

"Do you know where she is?"

"No. We were all in the atrium in the center of the colony when Young took her. They could be anywhere in the colony at this point." Desi thought it best not to mention that Wolf had ordered them to leave.

"Does Young know you're still there?"

"I don't believe so. We did a good job covering our tracks."

A short pause. "Well, that's something, at least," Reed said. Desi still couldn't read him.

"Sir, have you heard from Young?" she asked. "Do you have any idea what he's done with Wolf?"

"We made contact with him about thirty minutes ago. They are charging her with war crimes, though I'm sure that's just a cover story."

"A cover story for what?" Desi asked.

"At this point, we don't think Rank was ever after the ship—we believe their target was Commander Wolf."

"But what do they want with her?"

"She's the only person on the planet who can design a ship even more formidable than *Journey*," Price said. He sighed. "It makes perfect sense. They wouldn't be able to take *Journey* and pass it off as their own—there's been too much press surrounding it. To prove his superiority over LAWON, he needs a ship that's more powerful and more impressive."

"So they're going to try to force her to design ships for

them?" Desi asked. "I can't believe she would do that."

"That's what they're going to try," Reed said.

"And when she refuses?" Justin asked.

"They'll kill her," Grady said with absolute certainty. "Not right away, but eventually, they'll kill her. After Rank thinks she's suffered enough."

"Sir." they heard Santiago's voice in the background. "I have a transmission coming in from the colony."

"Flint, you and your team sit tight. I'm going to transfer you Dewite's headset," Reed said. "We might get lucky and figure out where Wolf is."

Chapter 24

Crystal counted every second she sat alone in the dark. There wasn't much else to do. She had tried to wiggle out of the handcuffs, but the only thing she succeeded in doing was rubbing off top layers of skin.

Suddenly, the lights came back on, their harshness momentarily blinding her. When she could finally see again, she saw Ryan standing in front of her with a gag in one hand.

"It's showtime," he said. Clearly, during the eight minutes and twenty-four seconds he had been gone, Ryan had gotten his emotions in check. Before, Crystal had thought she was getting through to him, but now she knew there was no hope—he radiated confidence and control and had the stance of a soldier about to carry out orders.

"You're really going to go through with this?" Crystal asked.

"Was there ever any doubt?" Ryan stepped behind her, slipped the gag between her lips, and tied the cloth behind her head. He bent to untie her ankles from the chair, then tied them together. Next, he uncuffed her arms one at a time. She wasn't surprised that he used both sets of handcuffs to secure her hands behind her back.

"You can never be too careful," he whispered in her ear, then pushed her forward out of the chair and onto the carpeted floor. As she knelt there, she looked up and realized that there was a camera mounted on the opposite wall.

Ryan adjusted the video monitor so that it pointed directly at Crystal, then stepped in front of her to face the camera. He thumbed his communicator, synching it to the video feed before making his call.

"Hello, Captain Reed," he said seconds later. He spoke with the voice of a politician, Crystal noticed. He must have picked up that ability after spending so many years at Rank's side.

"Where's Commander Wolf?" Reed said.

"She's here," Ryan said. He didn't move. Crystal knew he was waiting for the right moment to reveal her situation to her team.

"I want to talk to her."

"I'm afraid that's not possible, but I can let you see her." Ryan stepped away from the camera.

Crystal ignored the crew's shocked looks at the sight of her, instead focusing on the one unfamiliar thing on her ship: the plump man who was standing uncomfortably at the back of the bridge.

"What have you done to my office?" the unfamiliar man yelled. Dewite spun around in his chair to face him. When he turned back, Crystal noticed that Dewite's hand was up by his ear. Did Dewite have someone on his headset listening in?

"I'm sorry, Mayor Jefferies, but considering that you

chose to abandon your colony and your new country, I would think you would have realized that you abandoned your rights to your office as well," Ryan said.

"We all know that Teria has no interest in Soupionia," Reed cut in, "so why don't you tell us what you're really after?" Crystal knew Reed well enough to realize that he was stalling.

"Teria simply wants to improve the quality of life for the citizens here. It's our goal for all the citizens of our great country," Ryan said smoothly.

"Then return my officer."

"You know I can't do that. Crystal broke our laws, so she must face our penalties."

Crystal found it odd that he used her first name. Their earlier conversation must have affected him more than she had realized.

"I know you don't want to hurt her, Ryan," Reed said.

"That's not up to me. Her fate has already been decided."

"There's no way you could have held a trial already."

"Given the nature of her crimes, we felt it was imperative to put her on trial and convict her immediately," Ryan said. "Unfortunately, during the interrogation process, Wolf got a little out of control and assaulted the President."

When she heard that, Crystal couldn't keep the smile off her face. It had felt so good to punch Rank.

"You can't expect me to believe that the President participates in the interrogation of alleged criminals," Reed said.

"This is a sensitive case, and President Rank felt it was important to oversee the process to ensure it was done correctly."

"I bet he did," Reed said.

"And as I'm sure you know, the punishment for assaulting the President is death. A sentence I have been instructed to carry out immediately." Ryan's voice didn't waver. "It was nice of you to provide an audience — maybe they'll learn something from Wolf's death."

"You don't have to do this."

"I really do." Ryan stepped behind Crystal. Even though she couldn't see him, she knew he was pointing his gun at the back of her head.

"She's in the mayor's office. Hurry. It doesn't look good." Desperation rang through Dewite's voice.

"We're on it," Desi said curtly. She broke the link with Dewite and looked at her small team of four. "Anyone have any idea where the mayor's office is?"

"It's got to be towards the center of the colony. If we split up, we could cover more ground," Grady offered.

"I don't think we have that kind of time."

"I need a computer," Price muttered. He raced out of the room, the rest of the team only a step behind him. Desi hoped he had a plan — if he didn't, they might not be able to get to Wolf in time. She had to trust him.

But wait...he was running towards the escape pods, not the center of the colony.

"I'm pretty sure the mayor's office isn't that way!" Justin frantically called after him. He came to a stop.

"Probably not," Price called over his shoulder. Desi bit her lip, then nodded for the rest of them to follow Price. He cared about Wolf just as much as the rest of them did.

Ahead of them, Price reached the escape pods. As soon as Desi did, too, she saw the bank of computer screens and silently thanked Price for knowing where to go. It only took him a second to connect to the network.

His fingers danced over the keyboard. "This should make it easier to find the mayor's office." The screen displayed a layout of the colony with the most direct path to the mayor's office highlighted in blue.

"Two rights and a left," Desi said, quickly memorizing the route. "Let's move out." She took off running, knowing the rest of the team was right on her heels.

They raced through the colony's deserted hallways. As they ran, Desi noticed that Grady had fallen into step next to her, his mouth set in a hard line. Wolf's capture had affected him almost as much as it had Justin. Desi had seen glimpses of their friendship, but maybe it went deeper than she had realized. Would she act the same way if Justin had been the one who was taken?

The mayor's office was just ahead, and two men were guarding it. Finally, a target. Desi didn't hesitate to fire. As one of the guards fell, she saw the silver nameplate in the center of the door. Desi kept running without bothering to take down the other guard, kicking the door open as the second man fell to the ground. Grady's handiwork, most likely.

She had a hard time comprehending the sight that met her: Wolf was kneeling in the center of the room, bound and gagged, and Young had his gun aimed at her head.

Desi's abrupt entrance startled him as his finger hovered over the trigger. She locked eyes with him and raised her gun.

Young didn't move his away from Wolf.

Desi fired first. Young dove out of the way, firing as he fell to the side. Desi watched in horror as Wolf crumpled to the ground.

Grady ran into the room, took one look at Wolf, and hurled himself at Young. Young's gun quickly went flying out of his hand as they fought.

After landing a few powerful blows, Grady hauled Young to his feet. Price was at his side in an instant. Desi wasn't sure if he was there to help control Young or to keep Grady from breaking his arm.

Justin rushed to Wolf, his hand shaking as he pressed her wrist and searched for a pulse. "Come on, Crystal," he kept saying over and over.

"The shot barely grazed her—she'll live," Young said between ragged breaths.

Justin looked up at them and nodded. Wolf wasn't badly hurt. Gently but quickly, he removed Wolf's gag and carefully rolled her to her side to free her hands. "A little excessive, don't you think?" he said when he saw the two pairs of handcuffs.

"It was a necessary precaution," Young said through gritted teeth.

"That's my girl," Grady said, twisting Young's arm a little tighter.

Desi took five long steps over to them and dug through Young's pockets until she found the key. She tossed it to Justin.

Once Justin had removed the handcuffs from Wolf's wrists, he handed a set to Price to use on Young. Even after their prisoner was cuffed, though, Grady kept a firm grip on Young's arm.

"I need something to cut the ropes at her ankles," Justin said.

"Got it." Desi pulled out the knife Wolf had given her. It sliced through the ropes as if they were butter.

Justin carefully placed Wolf's head in his lap and

gently stroked her hair. "Come back to me, Crystal. I need you to open your eyes now."

"Stop being so dramatic, lover boy," Ryan mocked him. "She'll wake up in a few minutes without you cooing all over her. The shot was never meant to kill her—if it had been, there wouldn't be anything you could do to bring her back."

Justin glared at him. "Would someone please shut him up?" he spat out.

"Gladly." Desi picked up the discarded gag and shoved it into Young's mouth.

The only thing left to do now was wait. Desi hated waiting.

Crystal's senses started to creep back. She had been shot, she knew—the first thing to flood back into her awareness was pain. In her chest, on her face, and now there was a new burning sensation in her arm. That must have been where Ryan's shot had hit. She always forgot how much stun shots actually hurt. Why hadn't he shot her in the head? That would have made the staged execution look more believable.

She felt a gentle touch on her face. That wasn't Ryan. A soft voice broke through next. She concentrated on it, allowed it to pull her out of the fog.

"Come back to me." she heard again. It was Justin. Justin was here. He had saved her.

"Hey, there," she said as she blinked her eyes open.

"Welcome back." Justin's smile gave her strength, and she tried to sit up. "Easy," he whispered, putting an arm around her.

Crystal surveyed the room and tried to piece together

what had happened. The office door had been kicked in and a fight had obviously taken place. Given the satisfied look on his face, she assumed the victor had been Grady, an assumption proven right when she caught his eye and he gave her a huge grin.

Tyler's relief showed clearly on his face, and even Flint looked distinctly more at peace.

"You disobeyed a direct order," Crystal said to her.

She arched an eyebrow, her usual assertive expression back. "So what if I did?"

"Thank you."

"Any time." Flint's smile was genuine.

Crystal took a moment to steady herself as she got to feet. She was exhausted, but she still had a job to do. She would rest once they got back to the ship.

The camera was still on. "Sir," she said to Reed and the crew on *Journey*'s bridge, "as you can see, we captured General Young. We should have control of the colony shortly."

"Are you all right?" Reed asked.

"Yes, sir, I'm fine," Crystal said in her best reassuring voice. She knew he wouldn't believe her.

He frowned. "I'm going to send a shuttle to collect you."

She stood straighter, ignoring her various pains. "With your permission, sir, I'd like to see this through to the end." If she left before the mission was over, Ryan would have won. Not the big win he had been hoping for, no, but he would still have some power over her. More than anything, she needed to be free of him.

Reed's frown deepened. "If you're sure you're up to it."

"I am."

"I'm going to have the medical team standing by in the launch bay," he said in a tone that wasn't going to allow disagreement. "I expect you to cooperate with them."

"Understood."

"Sir," Flint interrupted, "what would you like us to do with the prisoner?" She nodded her head toward Ryan.

"There's only one thing we can do with him—we're going to have to let him go," Crystal said.

Flint stared at her. "You are aware that he just tried to kill you?, Like full on execution style."

Crystal shook her head. "He had no intention of killing me—Rank wanted him to fake my death so that he could force me to work for Teria without any interference from LAWON. Young was just a pawn in Rank's game."

"And for that, he gets to go free?" Tyler asked incredulously.

Crystal sighed. "Look, I don't like it any more than you do, but that's the way it is."

"Why?" demanded Justin. "There has to be something that we can do. We can't let him get away with this."

"Do you want to know what would happen if we arrested him?" Grady interjected. "He would be held for all of two days while a bunch of closed-door negotiations went on with Teria. Then he would be released, and probably with a formal apology to stave off any attack threats from Rank. LAWON would look like the bad guys for unlawfully detaining a high-ranking Terian military officer."

"So we just let him go? After everything he did?" Flint turned towards the camera in disbelief.

"I'm afraid so," said Reed.

"But not before he has made a public announcement revoking Teria's claim on the colony," said Crystal, turning to face Ryan. "And if you ever endanger hundreds of innocent lives again, I promise that you will live to regret it no matter what that may do to LAWON's reputation."

Reed gave them a curt nod. "Sounds like you have the situation under control. We'll see you back on *Journey*." The screen went blank.

Crystal saw a communications mouthpiece on the desk. She grabbed it and walked over to Ryan, pulling the gag out of his mouth. "I know this is connected to the colony's communications systems." she said, holding up the mouthpiece. "Tell your team to stand down and return to their shuttles."

He stared at her, his eyes flat. "Why would I do that? There are only five of you — you're outnumbered."

Crystal kept her voice as matter-of-fact as his. "Because maybe things get a little out of hand while you're leaving," she said. "Accidents happen all the time."

Grady charged his gun to level 4 and pressed it against Ryan's temple.

"You wouldn't," Ryan said. His calm demeanor was finally beginning to crack.

"Do you really want to test that hypothesis? Now, make the announcement," Crystal demanded. She toggled the mouthpiece to turn it on.

"All soldiers, return to the shuttles. Do not engage," Ryan said through gritted teeth.

Crystal gave a satisfied grunt and put the mouthpiece back on the desk as Ryan glared at her. She motioned at Flint. "Why don't you take the lead from here?" She let herself collapse into a nearby chair.

Flint gave a quick nod. "Gladly," she said, grabbing Ryan and pulling him out of the room. Tyler followed close behind, his hand on his weapon.

Grady walked over to her. "You sure you're OK?"

"Of course," Crystal said with a smile.

"I've never seen you give up command before."

"She deserves it—if it wasn't for you guys, I'd be on a one-way trip to Teria right now."

"Did they really think they could force you to work for them?" Grady asked.

"Apparently Rank thought I'd choose that option over torture and death."

Grady smiled back, then reached out to tousle her hair. "Clearly, he doesn't know you at all." His smile retreated slightly. "Don't ever scare me like that again, OK?"

Crystal gave him a mock salute. "I'll do what I can. Now, go help Flint round up the rest of the Terian soldiers."

Grady nodded and left, leaving Justin and Crystal alone.

"How about we get you down to the launch bay?" Justin asked.

Crystal let Justin help her to her feet. There were a thousand things she wanted to say to him, but she couldn't find the words. Instead, she let him keep his arm around her waist as they walked out of the office. She didn't really need him to steady her anymore, but she didn't want him to let go, either. She found comfort in his touch.

The only other person who had made her feel that way had just tried to kidnap her. She forced the thought from her mind. She wouldn't let Ryan taint another moment of her life.

Holly Ash

Chapter 25

Crystal awoke in the hospital ward early the next morning with every inch of her body aching. The adrenaline that had kept her pain at bay had finally subsided, she realized. Everything that had happened since she had first woken up and found herself in Justin's lap was a blur, but she did remember that reclaiming the colony had been simple once Ryan had ordered the Terians to stand down—not a single one of his soldiers had put up any kind of resistance. Crystal had even had the pleasure of shoving a handcuffed Ryan into the last shuttle.

The citizens had returned to the colony immediately. When Crystal, Justin, Flint, Tyler, and Grady arrived in the launch bay, Mayor Jefferies was the first person to thank them before he took the shuttle back to the colony with the rest of the Soupionians. Crystal had lost track of how many other people after that had wanted to express their gratitude to her and her team.

As promised, Captain Reed had a medical team ready to whisk Crystal away the moment she stepped into the launch bay. After an hour or so of testing and bandaging,

Dr. Emerson gave her some mild pain medication and restricted her to the med bay for the night.

Tyler had stayed to keep her company for a while, and Flint and Grady had come by to check on her after they had delivered their debriefing to Reed. At one point, Crystal was sure her hospital bed was the most popular location on the ship. It was only after several threats from Dr. Emerson that everyone had left...that is, everyone except Justin. His face was the last thing she remembered seeing before she had finally succumbed to the drugs and sank into a dreamless sleep. When the nurses woke her to check on her in the middle of the night, he had been fast asleep in the chair next to her bed.

Now that she was fully awake and clear-headed, she glanced over at the chair and was disappointed to find it empty. What was she going to do about Justin? She knew in her heart there was something between them. Forces kept pushing the two of them together, and she was tired of fighting it. She enjoyed his company, and in the short time they had known each other, she had come to need him more than she wanted to admit. But if she decided to take the next step with him, could they continue to work together so closely? Should she have him transferred to Flint's team or removed from the combat teams altogether? She didn't even know if Justin was interested in having a relationship with her. It was possible that he had changed his mind about her.

Crystal felt a small change in the ship's vibrations and knew the ship had arrived at its destination and come to a stop. She glanced at the clock on the wall across the room. They had arrived in time for the Summit Meeting despite the transit time they had lost during their little excursion at Soupionia. She wondered what their top speed had been and how the engines had performed. Having one of the battery units malfunctioning could have put extra strain on the engines. She should run a few diagnostic tests to find out, she decided. She started to get up, but the gentle tug of the IV still inserted in her hand reminded her that she hadn't been released from the med bay yet.

"Excuse me," Crystal called to a passing attendant, "is Dr. Emerson here?"

The man smiled and nodded. "She's on her way down now."

Crystal sat up straighter and did her best to look well-rested and refreshed. She had gotten good at masking her pain.

A few minutes later, her efforts paid off when Dr. Emerson walked into the room. "Good morning, Commander. I see you're feeling better," Dr. Emerson said as she came to stand by her bed.

Crystal beamed at her. "I'm feeling great. If you could remove this IV, I'll be on my way."

"Nice try," Dr. Emerson said with a smile of her own. "But you're not getting out of here until I've done a full check-up on you."

Crystal could only sigh and give in. An hour later, Dr. Emerson seemed to be satisfied that Crystal was in fact in decent shape. "I'm going to release you," she said, "but on a couple of conditions. One: you are not to perform any work for the next twenty-four hours."

"Define 'work,'" Crystal said.

Dr. Emerson ignored her. "Two: I'm going to need you to report here daily to make sure your ribs are healing properly. You will not be cleared for combat duty until I'm satisfied you aren't going to re-injure yourself." She paused, waiting until Crystal reluctantly nodded.

"Three: if I find you breaking any of my rules, I'll confine you to the med bay so I can keep an eye on you. Is that understood?"

"So I guess that means I can't attend the Summit Meeting?" Crystal asked hopefully.

Dr. Emerson only raised an eyebrow. "Unfortunately, Admiral Craft overruled me on that one—you can go. Good luck with your presentation," she said, smiling. She patted Crystal on the shoulder and then left.

Crystal wasn't sure which was worse: being confined to med bay or speaking at the Summit Meeting. Not that she had a choice. A moment later, a nurse appeared to remove her IV.

Crystal got up and went over to the chair where her combat gear sat waiting for her. Drops of dried blood dotted her shirt, and there was a small burn in the sleeve where Ryan had shot her. How had none of her visitors thought to bring her a clean change of clothes? She shook her head, laughing and sighing at the same time, and put on the stained gear.

During the long walk back to her room, she only passed a few crew members. They all looked away, either out of respect or disgust at her blood-stained clothes, she wasn't sure which. She didn't particularly care.

Unsurprisingly, her quarters were empty. Flint was probably off with her team, preparing for the Summit Meeting. Crystal wished she was with them, making last-minute preparations and strategizing, but she had agreed to obey the doctor's orders. Resigned to her fate, Crystal took a quick shower before changing into her dress uniform. The teal-and-black flag of her home country of Kincaron and the blue-and-green symbol of LAWON were dazzling against the stark white of her shirt.

She slowly pinned her medals onto her uniform. After yesterday's events, they made her feel like a fraud. Like it or not, she had played right into Ryan's hands, putting everyone at risk because she couldn't see the bigger picture. Their mission had almost failed because of her.

Crystal was about to leave to head to the Meeting when one of her pictures caught her eye and prompted her to pick it up. She settled onto her bed and took off the back of the frame. Hidden beneath the graduation photo was a candid shot of her and Ryan. She studied it carefully. It had been years since she had last looked at it. They looked so happy in each other's arms. She could almost remember what that had felt like.

She traced a finger over Ryan's face. It was the same face she had seen yesterday. Nearly every detail was the same—the only thing that had changed in the past six years was the look in his eyes: eyes that had once radiated warmth when they looked at her had been replaced with an enemy's cold, unfeeling eyes.

Crystal's hands clenched on the picture. Her mind was telling her to tear it up and move on, but something in her heart was preventing her from destroying the image. It was the last memento she had from her relationship with Ryan. Five years of love was captured in what she was holding in her hand.

She returned the picture to the frame, reattached the backing, and put it back on the shelf over her desk.

Crystal was wandering aimlessly around the luxury hotel where the Summit Meeting was being held. The organizers had informed her that her presentation had been pushed to later in the day and that she was welcome to attend the earlier sessions if she liked. She had politely declined, thinking that she might run into Justin on the hotel grounds. Instead of Justin, though, she ran into Admiral Craft as he came walking into the hotel with a large group.

Crystal stood at attention as they approached her.

"Mr. President, it is my pleasure to introduce you to *Journey's* creator, Lieutenant Commander Crystal Wolf," Craft said, gesturing to her.

"Lieutenant Commander, it is an honor to meet you. Your work with LAWON has made Kincaron very proud. I'm looking forward to hearing your speech this afternoon."

"Thank you, Mr. President," Crystal said, shaking his outstretched hand.

Craft turned to face the President. "If you wouldn't mind, I'd like to speak to Commander Wolf privately for a moment," he said.

"Of course," said the President.

Crystal stepped aside as the President and his party continued walking towards the doors leading to the main conference area. Several members of the security detail nodded at her as they passed. She nodded back, knowing that they were the few people at the event who could fully appreciate what the bruises on her face meant.

Once the President and his entourage had disappeared, Craft motioned for Crystal to follow him into a small conference room off to the side. It had been used for one of the morning sessions and was now empty.

"How are you?" Craft asked. He sat down in a nearby chair.

"I'll be fine, sir," Crystal said as she took a seat next to his.

He frowned at her bruises. "It was Ryan, wasn't it?"

"Except for this," Crystal said. She ran her finger along the cut on her cheek. "I have President Rank to thank for this one."

Craft's eyes widened. "You saw President Rank? How did you handle it?"

"I gave him a black eye."

"You didn't," Craft said with a small chuckle.

"The man tried to kidnap me," Crystal said indignantly. "He earned it."

Craft shook his head in amusement. "How's Ryan?"

Crystal wasn't sure how to answer. She couldn't tell him that Ryan was happy with his choice to join Teria — hearing that would break Craft's heart. She knew Craft was still hoping he could somehow get his son back, and she didn't want to be the one to crush that hope. "He looked healthy," she finally said. It was the safest answer she could think of.

"You know, Crystal, you can always talk to me if you need to..." Craft trailed off. He must have sensed there was a lot she was leaving out. Too bad he didn't realize it was for his benefit, not hers. "I was almost your father-in-law, after all."

"What?" Crystal asked, shocked. She had never been engaged to Ryan. They had never even talked about getting married.

"I'm sorry. I shouldn't have said anything," Craft said, his face slightly red. He started to stand up.

"Wait," she protested. "You have to tell me what you meant by that."

"Are you sure you want to know?"

Crystal paused for a second. She was fairly certain that

whatever Craft was about to tell her wouldn't change anything—there was no getting Ryan back, and for the first time in her life, she was OK with that. It was time to open her heart up to someone new. Still, she needed to hear what Craft had to say. If nothing else, maybe he could give her some of the answers she had spent years searching for. "Tell me," she said.

Craft sat back down with a sigh. "Ryan wanted to propose to you. Remember the break before you started your sixth year? You stayed at the Academy, but Ryan came home."

"I remember." Crystal tried to process Craft's words. Sixth year? That didn't make any sense. Sixth year was when Ryan had started to pull away from her. If he had been intending to propose, why would he distance himself from her?

"He brought it up at dinner during his first night home," Craft said. He sighed again. "Carolynn and I didn't think it was a good idea. It was nothing against you, of course—we both love you."

"Of course." Crystal's head was spinning. She should have let Craft walk away, after all.

Craft briefly rubbed his temples. "You were both so young. And with such promising careers ahead of you. We thought it would make more sense to wait until after you had both graduated and served your first tours before rushing into anything. That way, you would have a better idea of what your futures would be like."

"And Ryan didn't agree?"

"No. He wanted to get married right after graduation. He thought getting married before being placed on active duty would bond the two of you together even more tightly. He didn't understand how tough it would be to be newlyweds and to be completing your first assignments at the same time." Craft shook his head. "You understand, don't you?"

"Yes, I understand," Crystal said slowly. Ryan had wanted to marry her. If she had said yes, what would have changed? Would she have even said yes? She had never pictured herself as someone's wife. But why hadn't he asked her? They hadn't needed his parents' approval to get married, after all.

Craft took a deep breath before continuing. "You know that my relationship with Ryan was already strained at that point, but things really started to fall apart after that. We were fighting constantly; he was rebelling against me every chance he got. First with the Purification Movement, then defecting to Teria."

So that's how Craft had seen his son, Crystal realized: a teenager who was rebelling against his father. He probably still saw him that way—he didn't understand that Ryan truly believed in at least some of Rank's philosophies and his ideas about cleansing Neophia. Maybe it was easier for Craft to dismiss Ryan's actions as being part of a rebellious phase rather than come to terms with the man his son had become.

Craft shook his head slowly. "I should have supported him. It's the biggest regret of my life that I didn't. I could have used my connections to get the two of you stationed together. You could have made it work—you were always so strong together. Maybe if he had still had you, we wouldn't have lost him," Craft said.

Crystal didn't say anything for a long time. There wasn't really anything she could say. Would things have turned out differently if she and Ryan had stayed together? He could have still gotten involved in the

Purification Movement, engaged or not. She knew she couldn't forgive him for that. Getting married might not have made any difference. Either way it was just another thing to add to the long list of things she felt responsible for.

"I told Ryan about Carolynn," she finally said.

"That would explain the flowers and candy," Craft said, his voice uncharacteristically soft.

"What flowers and candy?"

"I got a call from Carolynn this morning. She had gotten a package. She wanted to know if I had sent it because there was no name on it. It was—"

"—midnight lilies and a box of soft caramels," Crystal finished for him. It was what Ryan had sent his mother for every birthday and holiday for as long as Crystal had known him. He had taken a huge risk sending those gifts, she knew—if Rank ever found out that Ryan had had any kind of contact with his family, he would have Ryan killed.

"Maybe there's still hope we'll get our Ryan back," Craft said wistfully.

"Maybe," Crystal said, though her heart wasn't in it.

Chapter 26

The setting sun cast orange hues over the large courtyard where the welcome reception was being held. Dinner was still an hour away, but most people had already gathered to shake hands and indulge in the open bar.

Crystal stood on the perimeter, nursing a glass of red wine. Her presentation had gone well, and she had spent the better part of the afternoon answering questions while people carefully avoided making eye contact with her. She guessed her marked face was too much of a reminder as to why they needed a ship like *Journey*.

Crystal couldn't stop watching the security detail at the dock as they checked in *Journey*'s crew. She hadn't seen Justin all day, and everyone she had asked had given her annoyingly vague answers as to his whereabouts. She had been hoping to get a few minutes alone with him before she was forced to mingle with the crowd.

Reed emerged from the knot of people and came over to her. "I think you're scaring the politicians," he said.

"The feeling's mutual," she said with a smile.

"How are you feeling?"

She wanted to be honest and answer that she was completely exhausted, but that might put her back in med bay, so instead, she said, "It's been a long couple of days."

"Why don't you take the rest of the night off? You can head back to *Journey* and rest."

She paused mid-sip. "I thought this was a mandatory event."

Reed gave her a sympathetic smile. "I think we can make an exception for you. Besides, after another round of cocktails, no one will even notice you're missing." He waved at the crowd, and Crystal saw that several people already looked unsteady on their feet.

"If you're sure it won't be an issue." Crystal wasn't sure why she was protesting—she didn't really want to be there.

A voice came from behind her, prompting her to turn. "Excuse me, ma'am, I have a message for you," said a waiter. He held out a tablet.

Crystal accepted it. Confused, she glanced at Reed before reading the message. His expression didn't give anything away.

Crystal,
I know we agreed to be friends, but I feel like something changed between us when we were on Soupionia. If I'm right, find Desi, and she'll bring you to me. If I'm wrong, then enjoy the party, and tomorrow we'll see each other as friends. I'm not trying to push you—I just know that if I didn't try one more time, I would regret it for the rest of my life. I hope to see you soon. - Justin

Crystal looked at Reed again. "Did you know about this?" she asked.

Reed smiled, but didn't say a word.

"What should I do?"

He shrugged. "I can't tell you that."

She frowned. "I wish there was an easy answer."

"Do you care about Justin?" Reed asked.

She nodded slowly. "I think I do."

Now Reed was grinning. "Then you have your answer."

"But what if it doesn't work out?"

"And what if it does?" He took a step closer to her. "Crystal, your parents risked everything to be together because they knew their love was worth it. I know they would want you to have what they did." His voice warmed. "If you think there's a chance that you can find love with Justin, then go find him."

"Thank you, sir," Crystal said.

It only took a minute for Reed to get Flint's attention. She was at their side in an instant, wearing a knowing smile on her face.

"Take me to Justin, I guess," said Crystal.

Flint's smile got even bigger. "With pleasure."

"You can take my sub," Reed offered. "It's a small two-seater." Reed handed Flint his ignition card. She took it, still grinning, and led Crystal off through the crowd.

"So where are we going?" Crystal asked once they were in the sub.

Flint arched her eyebrows. "It's a surprise."

Crystal sighed. "I hate surprises."

"Fine," Flint said, powering up the sub. "First, we're going back to *Journey* so you can change."

"Change into what?"

"Something a little more appropriate for a first date."

"Right." So that's what this was: a date. She had agreed

to go on a date with Justin.

Once they had docked, Flint led the way back to their quarters, opening the door to reveal a small box on Crystal's bed. Crystal approached it as if it contained a bomb. She would have been more confident if she had known it was a bomb, in fact — she knew how to handle a bomb.

She picked it up and removed the card that was attached to it. A handwritten message was carefully scrawled across the inside:

Can't wait to see you. - Justin

"What's in the box?" Flint asked. She was standing behind Crystal, looking over her shoulder.

Crystal rolled her eyes. "As if you don't know."

Flint threw her hands up in the air. "I don't! My job is just to get you where you need to go. Think of me as your personal chauffeur for the evening."

Crystal smiled. Flint was chauffeuring her around? That would have been unthinkable a few weeks ago.

Slowly, she pried the lid off the package. Inside was a rectangular glass box, and inside that, a strand of bright blue flowers was giving off a soft glow.

Flint murmured in admiration. "What are they?"

"They're called Beauty of the Deep," Crystal answered without taking her eyes off the flowers. "There was a grove of them just outside of the colony where I grew up. I used to sit in a viewport on the edge of our park and watch them sway in the current. Some of the strands were six or seven feet long, with flowers of every imaginable color." She lightly brushed a hand across the glass box. "It's unusual to see a strand with just one color like this."

"They look so fragile," Flint said.

Crystal smiled. "They do…but they're not. In fact,

they're almost unbreakable—they bend and stretch with even the strongest currents. The ancient Aquineins used them in place of ropes."

"Beautiful and practical."

"Exactly. Maybe that's why I've always been drawn to them."

"Was this the kind of flower Young used to give you?"

Crystal had become so used to Flint's prying questions that they no longer fazed her. "No, Ryan only ever gave flowers to his mother." She paused. "How did Justin know that these are my favorites?"

Flint shrugged. "Tyler is his roommate." She turned towards Crystal's closet. "Come on, let's get you ready."

Crystal reluctantly put the flowers aside.

"So, what do you have to wear?" Flint asked as she looked Crystal over.

"I could put on the skirt that goes with my dress uniform," Crystal offered.

"You're kidding, right?" Flint opened her own closet and pulled out a red dress. "You can borrow this," she said, tossing the dress to Crystal.

"You brought a red cocktail dress with you for a six-month tour on a submarine?" Crystal asked in amusement.

Flint gave her an exasperated look. "Just go put it on."

"Fine." Crystal went into the bathroom to change. After a few minutes, she stepped out to find Flint on her bed with a makeup bag in her lap. "What do you think?"

"You look fantastic." Flint said in an approving tone.

"I feel ridiculous," Crystal said as she glanced at herself in the mirror. She didn't usually opt for look-at-me! kind of clothing.

"Trust me, you look incredible. Now, have a seat so I

can do your makeup." Flint got up and pulled out Crystal's desk chair.

Resigned, Crystal sat down and let Flint apply concealer to hide the bruises on her face. While she worked, Flint told her a stream of stories about men she had dated, and for once, Flint didn't press Crystal for stories of her own. Crystal was happy to just listen.

Finally, Flint stepped back. "All right, I'm done," she said, sounding satisfied.

Crystal picked up the hand mirror that was sitting next to the makeup bag and looked at her reflection. The transformation was amazing: her black eye had all but disappeared, her split lip was hidden beneath light pink lipstick, and Flint had painted a flowing curve of small flowers across the cut on her left cheek.

"You do good work," Crystal exclaimed.

She could have sworn that Flint faintly blushed at the praise. "Well, we should probably go," Flint said. "Justin might try to kill me if I make him wait for you much longer."

Crystal glanced in the mirror one last time. She recognized the girl looking back at her and smiled. She hadn't seen that girl in a long time.

Crystal felt more and more nervous as the sub rose to the surface, wishing that time would slow down so that she could process all of the thoughts running through her head. She hadn't been thinking clearly when she accepted Justin's offer—the wine must have mixed with the pain meds in her system and affected her judgement. How should she act? What was the plan? This was only the second first date she had ever been on.

Flint glanced down at Crystal's furiously twisting hands. "Careful—don't break those," she said.

Crystal hadn't realized she was twisting her fingers into knots.

"You aren't nervous, are you?" Flint asked.

"Terrified," Crystal confessed.

"It's just dinner—it'll be a piece of cake compared to what you went through yesterday," Flint assured her.

That didn't make Crystal feel any better. "I'm not any good at this whole dating thing," she said. "It would be easier to singlehandedly take on the Terian army. At least then I'd know what I was getting myself into."

It sounded like Flint was trying not to chuckle. "You'll do fine—all you have to do is be yourself. He's already crazy about you. I doubt there's anything you can do to ruin things at this point." She brought the sub to a halt at the dock.

"Thanks, Desi." Crystal didn't move.

Flint gave her an encouraging smile. "Now get going, I have a party to get back to."

"You're going back to the reception?"

"I figured it couldn't hurt to shake a few hands and mingle with a few folks, especially if I want to keep up with you." She winked at Crystal.

"You have a good time with that...and thanks for everything." Crystal took one more deep breath to calm her nerves. She gave Flint a nervous smile before stepping out onto the dock. Light from the reception glittered on the smooth surface of the bay, though they were far enough away that none of the party noise reached her ears.

Justin was waiting for her on the dock, his white uniform almost glowing in the dim light. Crystal had seen countless men wear the same uniform before, but none had ever looked as good as he did in his. She felt drawn towards him.

He walked over to her and took her arm. "You look incredible," he said.

"Thanks to Desi." Crystal allowed him to lead her to a table that had been set up at the end of the dock.

He smiled. "You looked incredible before Desi got her hands on you."

"OK, now you're just sucking up," Crystal said.

"Is it working?" Justin released her arm and pulled her chair out for her.

"A little," she admitted.

"I'm glad you came." Justin took his seat across from her.

"Me, too," she said, waving a hand at the table that was weighed down with plates and candles. "I can't believe you went to all this trouble for me."

"You're worth it," Justin said.

Crystal didn't know what to say. It had been a long time since anyone had made her feel this special.

"Are you hungry?" he asked.

"Starving," she said. Justin reached over and removed the silver dome covering the plate in front of her. When she saw what dinner was, she laughed. "Hamburgers?"

"Not just any hamburgers..."

With a skeptical look, Crystal took a small bite. Her eyebrows shot up in surprise—there was only one place that had burgers like that. "These can't be from Marco's?"

Justin grinned. "No, but they're the next best thing."

"What do you mean?" Crystal said. She took another bite.

"Obviously, I couldn't get Marco here in time to

actually cook for us, so I asked him to tell local chef how to make them." Justin shrugged. "I'm not sure the chef appreciated Marco supervising every step via video call, but I think the results are worth it."

Crystal wiped her hands on her napkin. "I agree."

He picked up the bottle in the center of the table. "Champagne?" he asked.

In answer, she held out her glass. "You're just full of surprises tonight."

Justin carefully poured the champagne, stopping just before it was about to bubble over. "A toast," he said as he raised his glass to her. "To first dates."

She clinked her glass against his, their fingers briefly touching. "And second ones."

Acknowledgements

I remember getting a call from my friend Corey. I didn't know it at the time, but that call changed my life. We were in the eighth or ninth grade and she was the first of my friends to get the internet. She was calling to tell me she had found a website where people had written what I would later learn was called fan fiction about our favorite TV show. She had been so excited that she had started to write her own. I confessed I had been working on a story as well. Later that week we swapped stories where we each had introduced our own characters into the cannon, Crystal and Desi.

We spent a good part of that year passing printed copies of our stories to each other in a red ten cent grocery store folder. Looking back, the stories themselves were terrible. The characters were flat and the plot lines filled with holes, but it didn't matter. We built off of what the other had written to create a world just for us. I found my passion writing those stories with her.

While Corey and I remained close friends through high

school, we eventually stopped exchanging stories. We had become too busy with school, sports, and other normal high school things. Despite this, Crystal never completely left my mind.

I had created Crystal to be everything I thought I wasn't: smart, strong, pretty, brave. Even though I wasn't writing the fanfic I had created her for, I couldn't stop myself from inserting her into every story idea that popped into my head. She grew and changed, as did I, but some version of her was always in the back of my mind. As I got older and gained more confidence in myself, I didn't need Crystal in the same way I had as a teenager. That was when I decided to give Crystal her own story and identity. That story became The *Journey* Missions.

Corey and I have grown apart over the years, but she will always hold a special place in my heart. Without her, I wouldn't be the writer that I am today and I can't thank her enough for that.

There are so many people who have helped to make this book possible that I want to thank. First, my husband Mike, for always making sure I had the time and space I needed to write. And to agreeing to never read anything I write or if he did to never say anything about it. I love him dearly but we have very different tastes in books.

Then there is my mom, Geri, and Sue who were my very first readers. I gave them an early very underdeveloped draft that they devoured in just a few days. Their enthusiasm and praise gave me the courage I needed to keep going until the book was done. I know that I get embarrassed and try to down play it whenever you tell someone that I've written a book, but your faith in me and my writing means the world to me.

To M K Marteens, my first writer friend and critique

partner, and my other beta readers, Sara Uckelman and T J Talley. Your feedback and words of encouragement helped me to elevate the story to a level I never could have achieved on my own. To my editor Lisa Howard, thank you for making my words shine.

And finally, a huge thank you to the Cabin in the Woods writing group, especially Nay, Chief, Atty, Jen, and Joy. You all have become like family to me. You are always there whenever I need help working my way through a plot hole or just to vent about my day. Your constant and unwavering support has made me a better writer and a better person. I don't know what I would do without you all.

About the Author

Holly Ash is the author of the underwater science fiction series The Journey Missions. She has worked for the last ten years as an Environmental Engineer after receiving degrees in Environmental Science and English Literature from Central Michigan University. Holly lives in the metro Detroit area with her husband and two tiny people who constantly want her to do things for them.

Holly is also a founding member of The Cabin in the Woods Association of writers which works to help indie authors get their books seen.

Connect with Holly
facebook.com/hollyashwriter
hollyashwriter.com
Twitter: @hollyash85